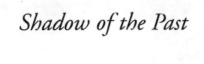

Shadow of the Past

Shadow of the Past

JUDITH CUTLER

First published in Great Britain in 2008 by
Allison & Busby Limited
13 Charlotte Mews
London W1T 4EJ
www.allisonandbusby.com

A CIP catalogue record for this book is available from
the British Library.

10 9 8 7 6 5 4 3 2 1

13-ISBN 978-0-7490-7941-3

Typeset in 11/16 pt Sabon by
Terry Shannon

Printed and bound in Great Britain by
MPG Books Ltd, Bodmin, Cornwall

Prize-winning short-story writer JUDITH CUTLER is the author of twenty-five contemporary novels, including the acclaimed Fran Harman series. Though this is only her second historical novel, her historical short stories have appeared in magazines and anthologies all over the world.

Judith has taught Creative Writing at Birmingham University and run writing courses elsewhere, including a maximum-security prison and an idyllic Greek island. She lives in the Cotswolds with her husband, fellow Allison & Busby author Edward Marston.

www.judithcutler.co.uk

*For Margi, a parson in Tobias's mould,
with great affection*

PROLOGUE

Autumn, 1811

He dragged himself out of the stream, cursing. Stream? It was a damned cascade, a torrent. In the half-light he'd taken it for a harmless gully, and, realising too late that he was mistaken, had grabbed at roots and rocks that had yielded under his hands. He had slithered and floundered in the almost liquid mud.

At last he had pulled himself clear of the raging waters and found a fallen tree to sit on, huddling his greatcoat about him, though it was so wet as to be a burden rather than a comfort. Why was one foot even colder than the other? He must have worn through the sole of his boot. But he had more miles to walk tonight. A smile approaching pleasure flitted across his face. If he folded the precious paper, it would fit inside the boot. There. All he had to do now was force his foot back in again.

He should never have taken it off. He was colder than ever, and ready to weep with the effort of cramming the frozen toes into the unyielding leather.

Darkness had fallen quite suddenly, a giant hand pinching out a candle. The day had been so cloudless he knew there must be stars, but the trees hid all but a few. If walking had been hard before, it would be cruel now.

A drop of brandy. That would help. There! The spirit burnt its way down his throat. One more swig – but a shake of his flask told him it was empty, and he slung it over his shoulder into the bushes.

Folly. He might have sold it, pawned it even, to raise a bit more of the ready. But the nobs would see him all right, wouldn't they? They wouldn't tell him to come all this way and not give him meat and drink and a fire to sit by while he dried out.

He heaved himself upright and staggered, cursing aloud again as he started to shake. Almost as if they weren't part of him, he watched his hands quiver and then dance as if at the rope's end. He couldn't have held them steady, no, not a guinea.

Best make a move. Move while he could still see. For the dark was more absolute than he'd ever known, since the Peninsula, that is, and he must get to the lights before he stumbled again. But where were the lights? Over here? Over there?

A voice moaned. It was his own!

There was someone coming towards him. Thank the Lord – it was the man he'd spoken to, wasn't it? The man who – but he must be wrong. There was no one there after all.

Maybe if he lay down a while. Just till the world stopped turning. Maybe some leaves would give him shelter. Give him warmth. He scrabbled some together.

If only his mother would tuck him up, like she used to do. Here she was, leaning over him, smiling. She rolled him on to his side, as she always used to do, and then again so he lay on his face.

Smoothed his hair.

Pressed his head.

Smoothed and pressed and smoothed and pressed and he was falling deep and easy into sleep.

CHAPTER ONE

'Stay with us for dinner, Tobias!' Mrs Hansard urged, standing with me at the open front door as the three of us watched the rain teem down. 'You will be drenched before you reach the stable, let alone the rectory. As for Titus, ask him whether he would prefer the dry of our stable or a trudge to his own, and I think we would have a plain answer.'

It was ever hard to resist Mrs Hansard's pleadings, especially when they were backed by her new husband's laughter.

'Mrs Trent will hardly expect you,' Dr Hansard said reasonably, adding, with a twinkle in his eye, 'and you would have to rub down Titus yourself, in the absence of Jem.'

My groom had been summoned back to Derbyshire to a relative's sickbed.

But Hansard was suddenly serious as a fork of lightning rent the sky, accompanied by a crack of thunder that seemed to shake the house. 'Indeed, Tobias, it is not sensible to risk your neck in this!'

A gust of wind drove rain under the handsome porch and into the house.

Mrs Hansard ended the argument by closing the door. 'We have been away such an age that we know nothing of the doings of our neighbours and it would be an act of charity to stay.' More like an impetuous child than a lady in her middle years, she leant against the door, just in case her urgings were in vain.

My dear friend Dr Edmund Hansard and his new wife Maria had returned to the village of Moreton St Jude only that day from their bridal tour of the romantic Lakes. I had come intending merely to present my compliments and to wish them well for their future, but yet another thunderstorm had blown up from nowhere, it seemed, trapping me here at Langley Park. Not that I was anything other than a most willing victim – but I was acutely conscious that I made a third in their party, at a time when they might well have preferred my room to my company. Although they were both in their middle years, they were smelt as much of April and May as if they were half their age.

I confess my protest was weak. 'But you must be at sixes and sevens—'

'We have nothing to do,' Edmund declared. 'You forget that when Maria left her employ at the Priory she was able to bring with her the poor girl being trained up as her late ladyship's abigail. She and the ever redoubtable Turner, who as you know would out-valet any valet in the kingdom, compete as to who can be the more efficient. And our new cook, Mrs Benn, is eager to prove herself in the kitchen.'

I verily believe that as a former housekeeper, Mrs Hansard would have rolled up her sleeves and taken charge of the cooking herself, had not Edmund insisted that after a lifetime devoted to others' welfare it was her turn to be waited on. I rather thought, however, that in the absence of culinary demands, Mrs Hansard would devote herself to improving Edmund's life in other ways, some of which he would not even be aware of.

'And we have two other new servants from the Priory, Tobias,' Mrs Hansard continued. 'Burns is a young man who wants desperately to be our butler, though he is of course a man of all work. And Kate, whose mother is delighted to keep her in the district – so many of the others, you know, have had to seek work far afield. Even Warwick and Leamington seem like the ends of the earth if you rely on your feet to get you there,' she added with a sigh.

'It's a sad thing when a great house has to be shut up with no master and mistress,' Dr Hansard observed.

When Lord Elham had died, the title and the estate had passed to a distant cousin, far too content with his life in Sussex to do anything more than take the revenues from the land. He wanted no improvements, no investments, no new cottages for his workers – and no new parson, though the gift of my living was in his hands. As for the Priory itself, the shutters and doors were barred; it might never be lived in again.

'But there is good news,' I told them.

'Then let us hear it in the drawing room,' Mrs Hansard declared. 'We cannot be standing all day here in the hall. Go in, gentlemen, and I will bring some wine.'

Hansard shook his head. '*Come* in, Maria, and I will *ring for* some wine.' He took her hand and kissed it, before leading her ceremoniously through the door.

Mrs Hansard blushed, though with pleasure or embarrassment I could not say.

As we sat down, I said, 'Yes, though the *Priory* is empty, at last Moreton *Hall* is likely to be occupied once more, at least according to the rumour about the village.'

'So Lady Chase has decided to return here?' Edmund asked.

'As yet it is no more than gossip.'

'So all the Priory servants sent hither and yon may be able to return to service at the Hall,' Mrs Hansard declared, clapping her hands with pleasure. She nodded at Burns, the *soi-disant* butler as he entered, bowing as remotely and soberly as if he had never hurled a cricket ball from his enormous hand or wielded the willow to the imminent danger of the church windows. He could well have given lessons in dignity.

'Some wine and refreshments, please, Burns. And please tell Cook that there will be three of us for dinner, which we will take at six.'

His eyes rounded as he registered my presence; the Burns with whom I was familiar would have remonstrated, arms akimbo, that I was surely going be as welcome as a hailstorm at haymaking. But in his new incarnation he nodded with wonderful imperturbability and bowed himself out, his silent closing of the doors coinciding with another flash of lightning and smack of thunder that might have drawn his pity and understanding.

His crows' feet aquiver with appreciation at the exquisite performance, Edmund asked, 'What brings Lady Chase back after so long an absence?'

'I know not. And know nothing of her, of course, since she left before I arrived here.'

Burns entered with wine, which he dispensed carefully, even though another flash of lightning was bright enough to make him flinch. This time, however, the thunder came several seconds later, bringing hope that the storm was at last moving away.

Edmund waited until Burns had left before he responded, 'They are an old family, originally from Somerset. His lordship was truly gentlemanlike, not at all high in the instep. Why, the first time I met him, I thought the butler must have made a mistake to show me into his study, since there was no sign of anyone in the room but a middle-aged man on his knees before the grate, trying in vain to conjure some flames. He complained of the damp kindling – you see, this isn't the first wet autumn we've had, Tobias – and he stuck out a hand. Was I to shake it or haul him to his feet? I did both, one after the other. As if we were friends – which we became and were until his sad death.' He took a reflective sip. 'That took place in London. For three long years he and her ladyship had awaited news of their son, Hugo, Viscount Wombourn, missing, presumed lost, in a skirmish before the battle of Talavera, back in '08. Chase, left without a direct heir, did all that was humanly possible to trace his son's whereabouts – I hear he even made representations to the great Arthur Wellesley himself. He advertised widely, too, in the hope of humouring his wife's unquenchable but almost certainly baseless belief that their son was alive. Then he himself is taken from us. London's bad drains,' Edmund added darkly. 'Her ladyship is a gentle but determined soul, much given to good works.' He smiled. 'My love, you will deal very well together, with your shared interest in improving the lot of the poor. You and Tobias, of course.'

Her smile stiffened – she was no doubt wandering how an aristocrat would treat a former housekeeper promoted out of her station. If Lady Chase and she had ever met, poor Maria would have been that most forgettable of women, a servant curtsying to her employer's neighbour.

Perhaps her husband did not notice, as he continued without a break, 'And I fear intervention will be made all the more necessary by this confounded rain – if ever a country needed a good harvest, ours does. But it looks as if it will be very poor again, and the price of bread will go even higher.'

'Now, let me remember,' Mrs Hansard began, rallying, 'was not young Hugo a very handsome young man who cast all the other gentlemen in the district into the shade?'

'Indeed, my love – the girls were wild about all the men in the regiment stationed near here, but they were wildest of all about him. And with good reason – dashing he might have been, but he never forgot his manners and promised well. I wonder how he would have turned out.'

'Would that be the Wombourn who was at King's several years ahead of me? He was certainly a credit to his family and I presume to his regiment,' I observed, conscious as always of my own non-military state.

Mrs Hansard gave me a searching but compassionate glance. 'There are other ways to serve your fellow men than dying for them,' she said. 'And pray recall the words of Milton. *They also serve who only stand and wait.*'

'And you, my lad, do a great deal more than wait,' Edmund concluded, in a voice that brooked no argument. 'Now, will Jem be away from us for long? A man needs his groom.' He topped up my glass.

'He assured me he would be back for the harvest, so we

look for him every day. I told him not to hurry back – his family must have first call on him in time of sickness. But he writes that his grandfather has now died and been buried and that his grandmother – a most tyrannical old lady, as tough as Derbyshire can make them – insists that he return to his post here.' My parents, for whom the whole family worked, would ensure she wanted for nothing in her solitary old age. Mama in particular regarded caring for former servants as an absolute duty, all the better performed as if it were simply a pleasure.

'And has Susan got over her pangs of youthful love for him?'

Susan, one of Mrs Hansard's protégées, was my maid of all work, and had of course become enamoured of my manly groom, though whether she appreciated his finer points I doubted. 'I cannot tell and do not like to ask. All I know is that each day she becomes less a child, more a young woman, and each week I see her strolling home from market in the company of a different swain.'

'But Mrs Trent keeps an eye on her?' Mrs Hansard asked pointedly, knowing first hand the responsibilities of housekeepers for young maids. 'The child has lost both mother and sister, after all.'

'She does indeed. And usually the very knowledge that Jem is about the premises is enough to cool a suitor's ardour. Whether he would ever return her feelings I know not – but currently he seems to stand, as I do, as a quasi-guardian. I cannot say that Mrs Trent has replaced her mother.'

Mrs Hansard opened her mouth and shut it firmly on what she had been planning to say. 'No, that is not her way,' she observed.

'But she is a good woman, and her firmness is always kind,' I said, though at times, when incidents threatened to escalate into dramas, I had to temper the wind to the shorn lamb.

'And is the girl still in deep mourning?' Dr Hansard demanded with concern.

I shook my head. 'Mrs Trent has insisted that she cast off her blacks now, and the grey she has picked out for Susan's workaday dresses is so nearly blue that it seems to flatter the child's colouring.'

'Good. In the midst of death, Tobias, we need plenty of life,' he declared.

'Some more wine, Tobias?' his wife asked. 'And then we will tell you all about our meeting with Mr and Miss Wordsworth – yes, indeed...'

Although none of us had hoped that Lady Chase would add to the gaiety of the neighbourhood, she had a gentle impact on many lives. She was still in mourning for her husband, of course. Whatever her private pain, however, her ladyship's public demeanour was unfailingly calm and polite. She attended divine service regularly, and, as Dr Hansard had predicted, swiftly assessed the needs of our poor parishioners.

My little flock had endured much hardship the previous winter, but it had not inured them to suffering, rather making them even more vulnerable, it seemed, to the illnesses I was coming to associate with poverty. Having lead my first twenty-odd years in the luxury of my family's homes, protected from the harsh realities of the world, I had been profoundly shocked when I first came to the rectory in Moreton St Jude's.

Scarce could the Holland covers have been removed, scarce the last picture hung, when I was summoned – nay, invited is a more accurate verb – to her ladyship's book room in Moreton Hall.

'The cottages on my estate are uninhabitable,' she declared. 'And I want work to begin on new ones started immediately. There must be proper drainage, a garden for vegetables. Bedrooms enough to separate boys from girls. Here they are all herded together like animals. And a school! My steward tells me you teach some youngsters but only those in the workhouse.'

I tried to correct her – I ran a school for all village children on the rare occasions I could gather them all together, but she ran on apace.

'With respect, Mr Campion, that is not good enough. There shall be reading and writing for everyone's children.'

I nodded, instantly warming to her and hoping that she would not perceive the supposed social gap between us as a hindrance to friendship. 'It is a scheme I have long wanted,' I declared. 'Alas, my hopes for sponsorship from the Elhams for a model village were tragically dashed, as I am sure you will have heard. But imagine it, Lady Chase – all the children clean, fed and not just knowing their letters but being taught appropriate skills.'

'Exactly so! Domestic skills for the girls, so they would know how best to tend their gardens and prepare nutritious meals for their families, and woodworking and agriculture for the boys. With learning comes prosperity, Parson Campion.'

In repose Lady Chase's features were mild and elegant. In animated conversation they were full of vigour, the eyes a-sparkle and the mouth mobile. Though she must have been in her forties or even fifties, she had maintained an elegant figure and a spontaneity of movement to charm the eye and the spirit. Her cap sat on soft brown locks only lightly peppered with grey. 'We must make plans now. I cannot hope that everything will be in place for this winter, but a start must be made. I prefer providing work to dispensing charity.'

I knew from village gossip that she already had a small army of women putting the house in order, and every spare man clearing undergrowth in her woodlands.

'You are clearly a lady after my own heart,' I said, 'and after the heart of the village doctor and his wife – the Hansards of Langley Park. No one could be better placed to advise you.'

'Yourself apart, Parson Campion,' she corrected me. 'Of course I recall Dr Hansard – an excellent doctor and skilled *accoucheur*, by all accounts. But a Mrs Hansard...?'

'A good, kind and charming lady,' I said. Should I reveal Mrs Hansard's past? It was not my story to tell, after all.

'Ah!' She raised a finger as if to indulge in gossip. 'Is she the housekeeper who they tell me inveigled the good man into a disastrous marriage?'

'I cannot think who told you that, ma'am,' I responded firmly. 'A housekeeper Mrs Hansard may have been, but she could never have been anything other than a lady.' I hoped and prayed that Dr Hansard had been right in his judgement, and that her ladyship would not disdain Mrs Hansard's acquaintance. Herself the daughter of an earl, her ladyship was, after all, mistress of a huge fortune of which Moreton Hall was but a small part. The Hall and the surrounding estate, along with extensive lands in the north and the West Country, had been in her late husband's family's hands since the days of the Conqueror.

But Edmund had not been mistaken in his estimation of her ladyship's character.

'When they pay their morning call,' she declared, 'I will consult them both. Unless – Mr Campion, you can tell me – would she, having face to lose, be offended if I ignored the usual formalities and invited them to sup with me directly?'

CHAPTER TWO

'Good day to you. You must be Parson Campion.' A stoutish man in his later thirties or early forties reined in his horse alongside mine. Despite the driving rain he doffed his hat, revealing pomaded mustard-coloured hair. The cut was unfashionable. For the colour to run from his locks down his forehead, revealing an unimpressive mouse, would be even more *démodé*, so he swiftly replaced his headgear.

I nodded, removing my hat too, with fewer worries about the consequences. 'And you, sir, must be Sir Marcus Bramhall.'

Neither was as prescient as it might seem. My bands, of course, and the rest of my attire marked me down for a man of the cloth. As for my interlocutor, Lady Chase had told me that her late husband's nephew had announced a visit. She had said little more. Though I was proud to consider that we were friends, she was as discreet and tactful as anyone in her position ought to be, and I knew she would prefer me to make any judgements of character for myself.

Bramhall had also brought with him, it was disapprovingly

rumoured in the village, all his family and baggage large enough to suggest a protracted visit.

The man beside me was certainly not to the country born. He might be wearing sporting clothes, but they were the sort a London tailor would conceive, and not, I regret, the very best London tailor, who would know exactly what the country demanded. No one could accuse Bramhall of being a dandy, or, at the opposite extreme, affecting the Corinthian in his dress; indeed, there was something a little too careful about him.

He nodded, but said nothing. Believing that he was my social superior, Sir Marcus should have taken the lead in any conversation, but it seemed that he was unequal to the elementary task. The task, then, fell to me.

'Are you making a long stay at Moreton Hall, sir?'

A direct question like that, a mere social counter played times without number, does not usually elicit a response I might only describe as shifty.

'Indeed, one hopes – but of course one never knows. But, yes, as long as her ladyship has need – unless she finds us—' Such conversational ineptitude, not unexpected in a lad straight from his tutor's care and lacking town bronze, came ill from a man in his prime.

I tried again. 'I trust you find her ladyship well?'

He need not know that only the day before his arrival I had spent two hours in discussion with what she was pleased to call her little committee – the Hansards and myself, in other words – on the matter of emergency housing. The local cottages were literally melting away under the incessant rain's assault on the mud bricks that constituted their walls. Every day our fears grew that the streams would break their bounds and sweep away humans and animals alike.

My horse fidgeted. Titus had never liked the rain, and today was yet another when the skies did not clear even for an hour.

'Still harking after that son of hers. You should tell her, Parson, to resign herself to the truth – to the Will of God.'

I bowed, having no such intention.

'Rattling round in that great house there. No way for a woman to live. Not even some snivelling old woman to lend her countenance. She must have some aged relative who would fit the bill.'

If I too had wondered why she had not availed herself of the company of a respectable female companion, I did not admit it to Sir Marcus. A non-committal cough was all I offered.

'Needs a bit of company. That's what I told her.'

Sir Marcus, the son of his lordship's elder sister, who had married, in the common phrase, to disoblige her family, was thus the heir presumptive. His visit might have been to cheer a lonely widow, but human nature being what it is, it might equally to have been to stake a claim in a house he reasonably believed to be his.

'Indeed, sir.' I must not be too quelling, since an important question was already on my lips. 'May I hope that you will accompany her to Divine Service next Sunday?'

He hunched further into his coat. 'Aye, they told me you were something of a Wesleyan, taking your duties uncommon seriously.' He added, 'I was trying to persuade her ladyship to refit the family chapel. It's fallen into sad neglect, sir. When did it last see a coat of paint?'

'Her ladyship has been pleased to sit alongside her villagers, in the church where Lord Chase's ancestors are buried. And yours, of course,' I corrected myself swiftly. 'Do you care to see their monuments? There are two particularly fine tombs, and an excellent brass.'

He smiled briefly, displaying teeth better than most. 'I will bring my whole family to see them. My sister, Lady Dorothea, is of a particularly historical bent, seeing romance in every fallen stone. And you, pray, Mr Campion, must share our mutton with us – why not this very night?'

'I have not paid so much as a morning visit to Lady Bramhall—' I broke off to nod and smile at young Tom Fletcher, driving some of his uncle's heavy-fleeced sheep with the aid of Nip, a dog that did its best to live up to its appellation. 'I will not answer for the consequences, Tom, if you let your dog near Titus here,' I called.

Tom called him closer to heel. Tugging his dripping forelock, he said, consciously polite, 'Good day, Parson Campion.' Casting an inquisitive glance at Sir Marcus, he added hopefully, 'Is there any more wood to chop?'

'Tom, make your bow to Sir Marcus. That's better. There's plenty of wood ready for you – but only when you've learnt the psalm I set you, young man. As if,' I added, *sotto voce*, to Sir Marcus, 'he were interested in anything other than the sweetmeats my housekeeper will find. But I keep him to his books, sir, and one day he will thank me for it.

Sir Marcus had watched the exchange with ill-concealed boredom, at last flipping the youngster a coin. So his affable reply took me by surprise. 'We will not stand on ceremony – not in the country. You will know that the Dowager Duchess keeps country hours. My dear wife is slowly prevailing on her to dine at a more fashionable time, but she is most reluctant to change. However, we have compromised on five-thirty, for the time being, that is. I will expect you then.'

'I would be delighted to accept. Thank you, Sir Marcus.' I trust my social smile covered my unease at his alluding already to her ladyship as the dowager. I hoped he did not do it within her earshot.

Our horses parted company with no backward glance. Titus was no doubt thinking of the vicarage stable and shelter from the drenching rain, and his, one of the oldest and most staid hacks from her ladyship's stable, a prompt return to its domain. His was the more fortunate – I had a deathbed to attend before we could return to the vicarage.

The cottage was little more than a hut: I have seen pigs better housed. Predictably, another was there before me, still in his great coat as the damp seeped relentlessly through the rotting thatch – my dear friend, Edmund. The little fire, recently lit, gave hardly more warmth than a candle, and certainly not enough to dry the damp bedewing the walls.

'Her ladyship sent coal and beef-tea,' he said, drawing me into a corner. 'But poor Mrs Kemp's daughter "didn't like to waste the coal",' he said in a mincing parody of the girl's thick accent, 'though goodness knows her ladyship would have sent thrice as much had she known the need! But Polly never did have much in the way of sense. Goodness knows how she'll manage without the old lady's guidance.'

I hid a smile. Dr Hansard might have carried nearly as many years as Mrs Kemp, but he never referred to himself as old, nor permitted anyone else to do so. Indeed, his marriage had brought a new spring to his step. No one would have taken him for a man who would not see fifty again.

'My dear friend, have you done all you can do for Mrs Kemp's body?' I asked gently.

'Indeed I have.' He nodded at the cadaverous face, the eyes

already closing. Together we listened to the painfully drawn breaths, each seeming to be her last until another rasp surprised us.

'In that case, Edmund, while I see what I can do for her soul, you should go home and find some dry clothes, lest you too take an inflammation of the lung,' I told him, gently mocking as I usurped his medical privilege.

Chilled to the bone and saddened by the loss of a regular and devout communicant, I would have preferred to spend the rest of the day in my own study, with my books for company. I had after all a paper to prepare for no less a body then the Royal Society. Last year they had been kind enough to approve my study of the nesting habits of the genus *Sylviidae,* and had suggested that I might care to follow it up with a similar study of another bird. Should it be genus *Strigidae?* Only last night I had seen a long-eared owl, rarer in this part of the world than its larger tawny cousin, its ears making two exclamation marks above the surprised eyes.

Yes. Owls would prove a rewarding subject. I reached for my books.

Enough of this. I must make up for any lapse in manners Sir Marcus might have detected, and, of course, meet the other newcomers. Any meetings with her ladyship were always pleasurable, whatever the circumstances. So I duly presented myself at Moreton Hall, punctual to the minute.

According to Edmund, the entrance hall had been Lord Chase's pride and joy. It was a double cube, with painted and gilded ceilings and magnificent plaster fireplaces either side of a staircase which bifurcated halfway up to very grand effect.

Family portraits from the school of Van Dyke to works by the very hand of Madame le Brun graced the walls. Greek and Roman statues occupied specially designed niches.

To my amazement, not only were both fires lit, but Sir Marcus – and what I presumed was his family – were huddled about the one on the right, their breath making little puffs of steam when anyone spoke. In none of my previous engagements at the Court, apart from a small reception for the gentry of the county, had such formality prevailed: guests always being received upstairs in the drawing room, whether the gathering was large or small. What could be the reason for such a departure from comfortable ways? I looked for Lady Chase, anxious to make my bow to her first, of course, but she was nowhere to be seen.

My host, however, was very much in evidence, wearing, to my intense embarrassment, the knee-breeches and silk stockings of fashionable evening apparel.

He waved aside my swift apology for appearing in boots, clicking his fingers quite superfluously for a footman to relieve me of my dripping greatcoat and hat.

'Welcome, my dear Mr Campion! It hasn't eased yet? No? We shall have to build an ark, shall we not? Let me introduce you to my wife, Lady Bramhall.'

I bowed low, taking in an anxious lady not yet forty, in lavender mourning which did not suit her colouring. She slid her eyes to Sir Marcus before moving her lips in something of a greeting.

'And my sister, Lady Dorothea.'

There was no agonising shyness about this creature, who would have been no more than one or two and twenty. She had indeed defied fashion so far as to wear a thick pelisse over her dark grey silk dress, and I for one would have applauded had she seen fit to swathe herself in muff, bonnet and furs, provided she still allowed her charming countenance to appear. For charming was indeed the word. Her face was heart-shaped, the sort of beauty one often associates with the more vacuous female. But hers was enlivened by a pair of speaking blue eyes, and a firm, even amused, pair of lips. Her brother's faux-yellow hair appeared on her head as magnificent corn-gold, the dazzling curls almost having a life of their own.

I thanked years of training for what I hoped was a passable bow, and a polite greeting – which was cut cruelly short.

Sir Marcus was speaking again. 'These are my sons, Adam and Charles—' he paused while the two pasty-faced lads, perhaps seventeen and fifteen, made their bows '—and my daughters Honoria and Georgiana.'

The two schoolroom misses curtsied. Both in satin, they were overdressed for such an informal occasion, but underdressed for the temperature. Mumbling incomprehensibly, they resumed their places beside a hunted-looking young woman, presumably their governess, sitting at the furthest point from the fire, which only intermittently lit her rigidly braided black hair. Even though Sir Marcus had not deigned to introduce us, I had opened my mouth to greet her, and would indeed have sat beside her.

'Nonsense, man, nonsense! Come nearer the fire!'

In a more subtle man than I deemed Sir Marcus to be, the invitation could have been embarrassing, since he indicated a place beside Lady Dorothea. I sat, trying not to shiver. I always did my best not to indulge in personal vanity, but no one wished to appear in a positive quake before a young lady of such elegance and beauty. Before we could exchange more than a formal smile, and no doubt embark on a disquisition on the inclement weather, Lambert, the butler, summoned us to dine. I might regret the haste with which it was done, but I could not regret the move to a warmer apartment. I could rely on Lady Chase to keep a properly heated dining parlour. But where was her ladyship? To ask our self-appointed host where the real hostess was would surely be a solecism. So as Lambert bowed us up the double staircase, which was guarded on either side by a dithering footman, I spoke to him.

His reply disconcerted me.

'Her ladyship indisposed?' I exclaimed. How could I have been invited to dine in such a circumstance?

'Her ladyship is not so indisposed that she cannot ask you to take tea with her in her *private* sitting room after dinner, sir.' There was a slight but unmistakable emphasis on the word. Since the whole conversation was far from the social norm, neither of us was inclined to pursue it.

Dinner was the strangest affair, served, amazingly, not in the by now familiar dining parlour but in the grand saloon. Despite the presence of the schoolroom party, it seemed the event was formal enough to discourage conversation with anyone but one's immediate neighbour. Indeed, a monstrous gilt epergne I knew had been relegated to the attic had reappeared, dominating the centre of the table. I was partnered with Lady Bramhall, with whom it was possible to exchange commonplaces for the duration of the meal without uttering or hearing one memorable phrase. Each time she spoke, she half covered her mouth. Having sunk into deepest mourning, she might never resurface.

I could hear Lady Dorothea's laughter but could not without causing offence have asked the cause or joined in. Sir Marcus, having vigorously carved a chine of mutton and a venison pasty, considered his duty as a host done until the second course appeared, when he seemed quite offended that I could no more than taste the chicken fricassee or the sweetbread tartlets. It always pained my conscience to over indulge myself when my dear flock did barely more than exist, food and dry fuel alike being so scarce.

But Lady Bramhall had initiated a subject for discussion! I agreed that the fire was giving plenty of heat; she, poor creature, wondered aloud about the extravagance of so many candles.

'But Sir Marcus is so anxious that the ceiling and the painted panels appear to advantage,' she pleaded.

'They are indeed worth seeing,' I suggested. 'They were painted by Madame Kauffman at her very best.'

My reluctance to speak down the table was not shared by Sir Marcus. 'Aye, even better than those at Attingham Park. Have you seen those, sir? Not a patch on these.'

The fellow was as full of puffery as if he had commissioned and paid for them himself.

I bowed ambiguously. My origin – in fact my family were members of the *haut ton* – was not a matter for public discussion. All I wished to be known as, all I *was* now, was a country parson.

He ignored my coldness, expounding on the artist's superiority to her contemporaries, with examples culled from who knew which country houses. If I had believed he had seen them all, I could still not acquit him of name-dropping.

Just as I was dreading a prolonged session with the port,

during which the young men learnt how to hold their liquor while their father continued centre-stage, a footman approached me, telling me quietly but audibly that I had been sent for.

Sir Marcus obviously concluded that one of my parishioners had need of me, perhaps at yet another death bed, a misapprehension I did not correct. I bowed myself out, with all courtesies to the ladies and gratitude for the evening's repast, and was escorted swiftly to her ladyship's sitting room, the least formal of all the rooms in the house, despite the silk hangings and the Grinling Gibbons fireplace.

'My dear Mr Campion, you must be chilled to the very marrow. Come in, my dear young friend.' Lady Chase extended a warm and friendly hand. In the kind firelight she appeared one of the most beautiful women I had ever seen – not for her features and figure alone, but for the sweetness of her smile.

'Pray, sit down here, Mr Campion.' She indicated the chair closest to the fire and adjacent to hers. 'I have so longed for one of our comfortable chats. Although I have been back in your parish such a short time – no more than four months, I think? – you have quite become part of my family. Now, are you still pinched with cold, or has a warm meal restored you a little?' She paused while a footman brought in more logs. 'Thank you, Jenkins – and some more candles over here, if you please.' She picked up her tambour frame as if she needed to justify her request to a man whose only function was to serve her, smiling kindly as he set a branch beside her. 'I will ring for tea when we are ready.'

As Tom Fletcher's young cousin left the room, I broke the news of Mrs Kemp's passing, receiving a sad press of the hand

and a promise of a few shillings for the funeral.

When we were alone once more, she shook her head quizzically. 'I'm afraid I cannot offer you the sort of entertainment you could expect in the salon – yes, indeed! Lady Dorothea has a pleasant little singing voice. Lady Bramhall accompanies her very well on the harp. I would have expected so foolish a creature to abandon her accomplishments on marriage, but she must have more sense than is immediately apparent. How do you find the family?' she asked, a twinkle in her eye.

'It is not how I found them but how I find you, your Ladyship, that concerns me. Are you unwell?' Truth to tell, she looked in as a perfect bloom as a widow of middle years might wish.

She pressed a slender finger to her lips. 'I am suffering from nothing more than a severe attack of ennui. Sir Marcus is almost as conscious as he ought to be of the impropriety of making a long uninvited visit, and his poor wife ran out of conversation within three hours of having stepped inside the entrance hall – where you were no doubt received this very day?'

'I was indeed, ma'am.'

'*A custom more honour'd in the breach than the observance*,' she smiled. 'Dear me, what notion does the man have of living in a house like this? Does he not realise the absolute necessity of keeping warm? Which reminds me, my dear Mr Campion, this continuing rain greatly concerns me. As we know, more than Mrs Kemp may be at risk.'

I smiled sadly.

'As our little committee agreed on Monday,' she continued, 'I have told Furnival to make sure any barns left empty – and there are all too many, after such a poor harvest – should be prepared to accommodate families driven from their homes. One can be set aside for young men, another for young women. I would dearly like to keep families with young children together, but he does not see how it can be managed. So I have suggested that the nursery wing here at the Court be opened up again. It will not accommodate many, but that is better than nothing. Poor Furnival is horrified, of course.' Her steward was ever torn between his desire to do the best for the estate and the late duke's insistence that his tenants' welfare was also his responsibility. 'But we want no more deaths.'

'You are all goodness, my Lady.'

She shook her head in irritation. 'Goodness? You know that I am merely doing my Christian duty. You will inform me of any households experiencing particular hardship, Mr Campion, just as you told me about Mrs Kemp. As I hope I will one day make clear to Furnival, I disdain the increasingly fashionable notion that you can distinguish between the deserving and the undeserving poor. In this weather poverty is even-handed, and so must we be in redressing it.' Her voice changed, taking on a curious inflexion. 'Sir Marcus tells me the roads are quagmires, so sticky and deep that they hardly permit wheels to traverse them.'

'This is their reason for protracting a visit that brings you so little pleasure?' Knowing I would be forgiven, I spoke freely.

'Indeed.' She leant forward confidentially. 'Mr Campion, Sir Marcus mentioned a court case the other day – to establish the succession, as he put it. Such a commonplace man, but capable of inflicting such great hurt.' She struggled to master her features. 'If I am to retire to the Dower House, I would rather it were to make room for someone...' She spread her hands helplessly. 'Will Lady Bramhall ever...?'

In my view Lady Bramhall was rather to be pitied than otherwise, at having to assume a duchess's mantle, and, moreover, having to replace the present Lady Chase in the villagers' affections.

I replied, more in hope than in expectation, 'Pray God that she will never have to attempt to take your place. Let us trust that one day—'

She raised an eloquent hand. 'There are dark days, Mr Campion, when even my faith fails, and I fear that Hugo will never return. But yet, as his mother, I would know if he were no longer alive. I believe I would know the instant he died. And here – here – I know he lives still!' She pressed her hand to her bosom, averting her eyes.

'Pray God you are right,' I said quietly.

She made a visible effort. 'And now, Mr Campion, tell me if Lady Dorothea has stolen your heart yet. Ah, you blush. You cannot answer me.'

'Indeed, I cannot.' For blush I fear I did.

She patted my hand. 'It is time you fell in love, my young friend. A parish needs not simply a vicar but a vicar's wife. Your good Mrs Trent, excellent housekeeper as she is, can never be a substitute for the helpmeet you need – and, dear Tobias, deserve.'

My neck, my face, my very ears now aflame, I said, 'However much an ordinary man may wish for a beautiful wife, the *clergy*man must value virtue even more.'

'And you suspect that Lady Dorothea might not be virtuous?'

'I cannot think that Sir Marcus would permit her to sink

herself so far socially...' I began with caution.

'If he knew the truth of your birth he would not regard it thus. But I tease you, Mr Campion. Let me offer you tea. I cannot think whither my manners are fled.' With a gracious smile, she reached for the bell-rope.

A card table set between us, the rest of the evening passed in a gentle game of cribbage.

At last, I was led from her presence down the back stairs, both of us laughing at the mild conspiracy into which we had been forced. But it was conspiracy of another sort that sprang to my mind – the sort that featured in Mrs Radclyffe's novels. Here in these cold, dark corridors one might imagine – if one were that way inclined – that armed men lurked in deep recesses, that abducted maidens were locked inside the rooms within. In fact, the only figure I saw was that of Furnival, the steward, running gnarled fingers through his snow-white locks. He nodded but made no attempt to pause for conversation. Then I glimpsed the weary features of that unhappy governess, whose name had never been vouchsafed me. As before I bowed, offering, I hoped, the sort of smile one might give to a child caught in mild mischief.

'Miss...?'

But, without a word, she bobbed a curtsy and scuttled back upstairs, like a church-mouse startled by a flaring candle. How could the daughters of the house ever learn their manners with such a craven exemplar? No one expected a young lady in such an ambiguous situation, neither family nor servitor, to be full of social grace, but she should at least have a modicum of poise. And why had she left a trail of damp behind her? Had she been out in this rain? The candlelight had been too weak to show if her hair or garments had been wet, but undoubtedly the corridor showed large muddy footprints.

As an excuse for being seen in the domestic quarters, I made it my business to call in on Mrs Sandys, the housekeeper, in an attempt at social ease so far denied us. Why Lady Chase had kept in her establishment such a gloomy and pinch-faced woman defeated me. She had certainly provided her with a generous-sized sitting room, and a fire the villagers must have envied. Although there was a handsome bookcase, full of enticing volumes, Mrs Sandys was engaged in sewing, her needle stabbing away at the cloth in a way I always found disconcerting. Her ladyship could make sewing calming and peaceable; Mrs Sandys' activities suggested barely suppressed violence.

'I come to thank you for your continuing generosity to my parishioners,' I said, though I knew all too well that the liberality was her mistress's.

She nodded curtly, still driving the needle through the innocent fabric.

'And now I have to ask you another favour, Mrs Sandys,' I continued. 'That young governess of the Bramhalls looks very unhappy, and I fear she may not be eating properly. Tell me, is she as...well treated...as she deserves to be?'

'Miss Southey?' Mrs Sandys sniffed.

'Indeed,' I said firmly. At least I now knew the poor creature's name. 'Does Miss Southey have a fire in her room, for instance? And hot water in the morning? Dear Mrs Sandys, consider her position, amongst strangers, serving a family that does not, in my view, value her as it ought.'

Mrs Sandys bit her lip at my rebuke. Hoping that such a

hint would be effective in improving the poor young lady's lot, I turned the conversation. I had spiritual care over the whole household, and would have the pleasure in preparing the younger ones for confirmation in the spring. Unfortunately, it was also sometimes my lot to remind a young man that he must marry his sweetheart before their baby was born.

But tonight Mrs Sandys mentioned no miscreants and I soon left her to the doubtful pleasures of her needlework.

The rain had ceased. Although there was no moon, the starlight reflecting on the puddles was enough to illumine my path home. Titus, irritated at quitting the temporary warmth and keen to return to his own cosy stable, indulged in unwontedly spirited napping. Once we had established who was in control, however, I let him pick his own way through the ruts.

I told myself I wished to review the whole strange evening, from the huddle in the hall to the charitable concerns of my patroness, and indeed the poor self-effacing Miss Southey. In truth, I wanted only to think of the beauty of Lady Dorothea. But it was only a few short months since I had been in love with another female, and one very different from this. Poor Lizzie. I had never declared my passion for her and now it was too late. Would it be an insult to her memory to love another?

Even as I thought of her, I fancied I heard her moan, as she might have done in her dying moments. Rebuking myself firmly, I nonetheless pulled Titus to a reluctant standstill, straining my ears for another sound. The copse in which I had found her dear body was scarce a mile away – on a night as still as this a sound might easily carry that far.

There was nothing. Unless—

I stood in the stirrups, peering into the ghostly darkness. I
believe I actually called out loud, 'Lizzie? Lizzie, is that you,
my love?'

The unmistakable sound of a cow lowing in a nearby byre
replied.

Shaking my head at my folly, I gave Titus his head and we
wended our way home.

'Could it be,' I stammered at last, 'that she has come back to
haunt me?'

In the warm breakfast parlour of Dr Hansard's house,
bright and cheerful with morning sunlight, a fire blazing in the
grate, the words sounded ridiculous even to my ears.

'Because you were attracted to another young woman?
What nonsense you do talk, my dear young friend,' Dr
Hansard exclaimed, his words and tone at odds with his
affectionate squeeze of my arm. His deep blue eyes fixed mine
with stern kindness. 'Did I, did my beloved Maria here,
imagine our former spouses would rise from their graves to
complain that after decent periods of mourning we would
marry again? The thought is unworthy of you, a man of the
cloth. Pray, have some more of Maria's best ham, Tobias, or
she will be the one offended.'

She clicked her tongue. 'As if Tobias could ever cause
offence. I know how much from your kitchen finds its way to
the tables of the poor – I honour you for your generosity! –
but here you must indeed eat your fill. Indeed you must, out
in all weathers as you are.' It was not only I who usurped
Edmund's role as physician.

'No more than Edmund,' I parried.

'But you do not have a wife to look after you.'

Despite her kindness, I shook my head, staring dismally at my plate.

She poured herself more chocolate, then leant forward animatedly. 'Now, if a woman might offer a word of advice on this matter of the heart, it is that you should say nothing of your former love to this new object of your affections. A lady does not like to think she is competing with the dead.'

My blush was painful. 'Nor is she. I have scarce met her.'

'She has clearly made a deep impression on you,' she laughed. 'Her blue eyes, pink lips, clear complexion and lustrous hair – she must indeed be a paragon.'

'A paragon? But true beauty lies in the soul,' I insisted, as I had to her ladyship, 'not in such outward show. Truly, Mrs Hansard, with one word you have opened my eyes to my folly. It lies not only in thinking myself unfaithful to Lizzie, but in imagining I could have fallen in love on such superficial acquaintance.' I smiled across the table at them both. 'Thank God I am blessed in my good friends. And yes, if I may, I will have another slice of this excellent ham. And that beef too.' As she heaped my plate, however, another thought occurred to me. 'But I still find it hard to believe that the first sound I heard was a cow. If it was not ghostly moaning I heard, what was it?'

'That is a question I can take more seriously,' Dr Hansard said. 'Indeed, when I go on my rounds today, I will ask everyone I see. But I think the answer is not in your ears, Tobias, but what lies between them – your over-fertile conscience and imagination.'

CHAPTER THREE

Despite my parish work and the brevity of our acquaintance, try how I might I could not keep Lady Dorothea out of my mind. Sir Marcus had promised a morning visit for the following day, but none came, nor on the day after. Though I flatter myself that no one would have noticed from my demeanour, I blush to confess how disappointed I was.

However, I was no child to be in a sulk, so I went about my Master's work with the lightest heart I could manage. One of my daily delights was to pray in our ancient church. On this occasion, however, the cold and damp almost bit into me – and I was not of a rheumatic disposition. I looked about me. The ancient stone almost bled moisture. I must remind Simon Clark, the verger, to bring in braziers on Saturday night to take the edge off the chill in preparation for the Sabbath's divine worship. It might be the only warmth my poor parishioners enjoyed that day, or indeed, any other, till the weather eased.

Chafing my hands and trying in vain to ignore a vicious chilblain, I heard voices and – God forgive me – I almost ran to the door. Even as I approached, it creaked open to admit Sir Marcus's party. It included, to my delight, Lady Dorothea, who smiled at me with every appearance of pleasure.

Our breath billowed and wreathed about us as I ushered them into the nave, ensuring that the heavy door closed behind us. If we had no form of heating, at least we could be spared the wind driving rain right through the porch. Truly, if the gale shifted but a degree to the north, I feared the rain would be transformed into snow.

Lady Dorothea, wrapped in dark furs, looked as charming as I had hoped, her golden curls peeping from a flattering hat. But I was in the House of God, and must turn my thoughts from the earthly to the spiritual. Smiling impartially at the Bramhalls, I spread my arms expansively. I had, after all, the care of a most lovely building, and felt something of the pride I fancy a mother might feel for her child.

'As you can see,' I began, 'the building itself dates back to the days before the Conquest—'

'This is the sort of organ that Mr Handel played in London,' she exclaimed, darting forward impetuously, and indeed, far more abruptly than etiquette demanded. 'And in a church as poor as this!'

But I was not offended. Indeed, much as I might have wanted to extol its more obvious wonders, such as the solid Saxon pillars and the wonderful stained glass the Almighty had somehow defended against Puritan forces, I smiled at her enthusiasm.

'It was a very generous gift from a friend of – of the family.' I did not wish to mention the missing heir's name and stopped abruptly. 'We still have a talented band of villagers who play in the gallery up there when there is no organist – or no one to operate the bellows, which is often the case.' I did not add that it was often I who had to take my place at the instrument.

No one seemed to notice either her faux pas or my indulgence.

'I told you she knew her music,' Sir Marcus declared, his voice echoing robustly in his pride. 'Did I not, Campion? As excellent a musician as you'd find.'

Perhaps regretting her impulse, she shook her head delicately but firmly. 'I may be knowledgeable but I am not at all accomplished.'

The distinction interested me. Surely it showed a fine mind. My next words came unbidden. 'But you do play?' Images of evening entertainments sprang unbidden to my mind. We might even be partners in a duet!

'I sing a little. But I do not play nearly as well as my sister-in-law,' she declared with a kind smile at Lady Bramhall.

'Lady Chase has already extolled your talents, Lady Bramhall,' I said kindly.

She blushed and fluttered her hands deprecatingly. For the first time I realised that they looked as strong and capable as mine.

'If I worked the organ bellows, you would favour us with a little music?' I asked Lady Dorothea, contriving now to ignore, as I was sure she wished to be ignored, the older lady.

'Not unless I could play without removing my hands from this muff!' she laughed.

How stupid of me. I bowed. 'Another day, perhaps?'

'Another, *warmer* day,' she agreed, with a smile.

If I had been charmed by what I imagined she was, how much more was I attracted by the real lady. With a tact surely showing an elegance of mind, she turned to the body of the church, stopping before the altar steps and pausing for several moments, head reverently lowered. I did not interrupt her prayers, and occupied myself pointing out to her brother and sister-in-law a couple of the older monuments. At last, as she raised her head and looked about her, I joined her. With an impish smile, she surrendered the comfort of her muff long enough to trace the diapered incisions on one of the older family tombs. I allowed myself to point out the squint, and the remains of what seemed to be wall-paintings, crude daubs perhaps but of interest to those who considered themselves connoisseurs. I know that when I had suggested whitewashing them, Dr Hansard showed an anger that surprised me, threatening – in jest, I trust – to box my ears if I ever mentioned the idea again, and promising to bring a friend with antiquarian interests to see them.

Having shown the party the Lady Chapel and the crypt, I returned by way of the font.

'Dr Hansard believes this pre-dates the present church, old as it is,' I murmured, fingering with reverence the huge granite basin and its heavy oak lid, its fantastical carving rising to a pinnacle like a cathedral spire. 'The cover is a fifteenth century addition,' I added.

'It must indeed inspire great solemnity, to baptise an infant using a receptacle so ancient.'

I smiled. 'Indeed, Lady Dorothea. But I fear that the recipients of the holy water do not always appreciate it – not if their cries are to be believed.'

She was gracious enough to laugh at my weak joke, and, heaven help me, all I could do was admire her beautiful white teeth.

Again it occurred to me that I was host not merely to her but to her brother and his wife, whom I was somewhat neglecting. One would be pleased, the other markedly less so. I was anxious, too, to prolong the visit. 'Might I offer you all refreshment at the rectory?' I asked.

Pulling a flashy timepiece from his pocket, Sir Marcus shook his head in a decided negative. 'I fear not, not today. We have promised to call on Sir Josiah Benton over in Leamington, but my sister would insist on seeing the church since we had to pass it.'

'Then you do me extra honour, to spend so much time here.' I opened the door for them, the ghastly squeal of the hinges reminding me to ask Simon yet again to oil them.

Lady Dorothea shivered. 'What a dreadful wail.'

Lady Bramhall caught her arm. 'Tell me, Mr Campion, do you have ghosts in your churchyard?'

Sir Marcus spun round as if the gargoyles had spoken. 'What foolishness is this?'

Quickly, to cover the moment of tension, I said, 'To the best of my knowledge, we are blessed with a quiet graveyard, all the souls at rest till the Day when we shall all be judged.' Curiosity, however, overcame me. 'Why, ladies, do you ask?'

'Foolishness, sheer foolishness,' Sir Marcus said.

To my surprise, Lady Dorothea persisted, but as if to deflect attention from her sister-in-law. 'My dresser said that she had heard noises. Moans – moans and sobs and—'

I thought of the nocturnal sounds that had so disturbed my journey. 'When did– ?'

Sir Marcus interrupted me. 'She probably heard a cow or some other creature. Now, it is far too wet to stand here talking such folly. Into the carriage, for goodness' sake, wife. And you, Dorothea. We have left these horses standing overlong already.'

It fell to me to hand in Lady Bramhall. I pressed her fingers reassuringly. 'I'm sure Sir Marcus is right. Pray, do not worry.'

It was easier to offer such advice than to take it myself, however. Following Dr Hansard's bracing words, I was perhaps more inclined to attribute the unearthly sounds to an earthly cause. I must nonetheless make inquiries myself: sometimes people would admit fears to a foolish young man like myself that they would conceal from the wise physician who could have helped them.

Simon Clark, the verger, was inclined to dismiss Lady Bramhall's fears as her husband had done, but agreed to question his fellow villagers.

'Should we do more than that, Simon?' I pulled my scarf more tightly as we huddled under the lych-gate. Despite the Hansards' bracing words, I still had a remnant of foolish anxiety. 'Should not you and I perhaps go and see if there's—'

Simon sighed as if personally affronted, his whole thin frame shaken by the effort. His wife had died earlier in the year, and though no stranger would have detected other signs of grief, this deep, racking exhalation had become habitual. 'In all this rain, Parson? When you and the good doctor are telling us all we should keep warm and dry?'

'All the more need if someone is lying out there in distress.' But I would not press him. Who could have lived after three or four days and nights of weather like this?

He clearly saw that I was weakening. 'Poor Mrs Kemp, God rest her soul,' he continued. 'About her funeral—'

'What about it, Simon?'

He sighed again. 'It'll be right hard, burying her, that is. The ground's so wet the grave'll likely flood. She can't lie where she is any longer, poor lady. What are your wishes?'

I knew my place. 'What do you usually do in circumstances like this?'

'Line the grave with planks so the sides don't fall in. Takes a lot longer, that's your problem.' He looked expressively at the sky.

'Then you must start straight away. Secure a couple of stout men to help you, Simon, so that no time is lost.' I wondered why he had needed to raise the problem, one he must have dealt with times without number. But his confidence had gone into the grave he'd dug for his wife. 'Now, remember, Simon, there must be braziers in the church on Saturday night.'

'What about other nights too? Those old pictures Dr Hansard's so taken with – they'll be peeling off the wall if we're not careful.'

I nodded. Perhaps as Hansard always insisted, we had a duty not just to our own generations but to others in the future. 'Could you undertake to keep them lit all the time?'

'I may have to if the brook bursts its banks, as they say 'tis like to do. Because that'd take out all Marsh Bottom, and where would the poor folk live then but here?'

'You know Lady Chase is expecting to accommodate people rendered homeless in her barns and even the Hall?'

'No one would want the Marsh Bottom type in their byre, let alone their barn. And as for the Hall, I reckon his lordship's death must have turned her head. Isn't natural, folk like that living same as decent gentry. Old vicar, he always used to say people should be put in the workhouse, but they say the ground floor's under three inches of water already.'

'The church it is, then,' I said mildly, worrying all the same about the fabric of a building, the heart of my first cure of souls, I loved dearly. 'And most important, Simon! – whoever asks for alms, none shall be turned away. Lady Chase will provide whatever I cannot.'

'As long as she's the Duchess,' he hissed, 'not the Dowager Duchess. That there Sir Marcus won't be so free with his brass. You mark my words. He'll be too busy spending it on himself.'

'Come, man – where is your Christian charity?'

He hawked and spat. 'Christian is as Christian does. You can tell a man like that. Just by looking at him. And,' he conceded, 'by talking to his servants. Anyway, braziers I suppose you shall have. I'll get on to it now...'

Lady Chase's open-handedness to the village was matched only by the anxiety of her steward, Furnival, who could not have been more careful if it had been his own money he was trying to save. In her personal life, too, her ladyship was generous, overcoming her reluctance to pass her time with Sir Marcus, and regularly joining his family for dinner – though mercifully without the freezing preamble in the hall. I too was frequently invited, and was delighted if my parish duties permitted me to accept.

Lady Bramhall would play the harp, and Lady Dorothea sometimes sang to my all too inadequate accompaniment. Much as I would have loved to prove her wrong, Lady Dorothea was accurate in her estimation of her talent. She knew much about the works she sang, and was a mine of biographical information about their composers. Nor was there any doubt that she loved her music. Her voice, however, was very uneven: her head and chest notes alike were sound, but there was very little in between. If only she had had the benefit of the sort of master who had taught my sisters.

'But you, Mr Campion,' she was pleased to say, 'are a wonderful accompanist, knowing when to play *pianissimo* to support my voice and when to play *fortissimo* to drown my weaknesses. I would sing with you every evening of my life.' Realising the implications of what she had said, she covered her mouth with her hand, retired to the sofa nearest the nursery party and understandably refused to converse with me alone for the rest of the evening – not, of course, that I would have said anything to put her to the blush.

At a click of Sir Marcus's fingers the governess slid silently on to the piano stool, flexing and chafing her fingers either with nervousness or to restore the feeling after sitting so long in the circle further from the fire. If my word to Mrs Sandys had improved her comfort in the house, I had done nothing to ameliorate her life with the family. By now at least I knew her name to be Anne Southey; I judged her to be in her mid-twenties. The modest black gown she wore was not kind to her colouring or complexion, and her eyes, which I suspected were her best features, were always kept demurely lowered. Politeness rather than personal interest made me offer to turn her pages, a suggestion she accepted without any prevarication that might draw attention to her.

I expected the humdrum music so often provided simply as an accompaniment to vacuous chatter; instead I found myself listening to music by that vehement German, Herr Beethoven. By disregarding all the *fortissimo* and other markings to show the composer's passionate intention, Miss Southey turned the music into social nothingness. But I never doubted for one moment that – had she dared – she could have unleashed every scrap of the music's power.

At the end of the sonata, I earnestly wished to speak to the musician, but she turned swiftly away, returning, under cover of the shouts of the schoolroom party demanding a game of speculation, to the shadows whence she had come.

Lady Dorothea joined in with a will, a tiny glance at me suggesting that she might not find me an unwelcome addition to the group. At first I was too conscious of her presence to play well, and perhaps she felt a similar constraint. However, as the game progressed, so she relaxed, her laughter ringing out like the clearest bell as she lost heavily or recouped her losses. Her eyes, blue as the silk of her gown, flashed; her teeth gleamed like the pearls round her long, slender neck; and I caught myself in a selfish prayer that the weather might stay so vile even longer, constraining her to stay at the Hall, if not in perpetuity, at least for a further week.

A deathbed and the need to baptise an ailing babe prevented my returning to the Hall for several days. By this time, Lady Dorothea had possibly put her embarrassing slip of the tongue from her mind, consenting readily to join me at the fortepiano for a duet. We played two or three pieces only, before retiring to listen to Lady Bramhall.

Lady Dorothea made no reference to her own performance, which in truth, was, as before, competent rather than excellent. My own was inexcusably bad, attributable perhaps to her proximity to me. I need not add that I would rather have sat beside her and played duets badly than played a great cathedral organ well.

When Miss Southey was summoned to the piano, I felt obliged to offer to turn her pages – she was playing Mozart, this time. I almost exclaimed aloud at the sight of her arms. They were empurpled with bruises. Had she suffered some terrible accident? Before I could speak, she said, 'I believe Lady Chase wishes to speak to you – no doubt about further provision for the poor.'

Thus dismissed, and with such venomous resentment, I did indeed retreat to her ladyship's side, if not to converse – we were both too well mannered to insult the musician in that way – but to wonder about the manner of my dismissal. I had always assumed her to be a victim of the family, suppressing all her emotions. Now I had seen another side, which disconcerted me.

Miss Southey herself remained at the instrument. Lady Dorothea made no remark as she unobtrusively – and to my silent applause – obliged the musician as a page-turner. Since the fortepiano never rose above a delicate murmur, I assume the composer's instructions were disregarded in this case, also. At the end the two young ladies exchanged a few inaudible words. The short conversation over, Lady Dorothea looked in my direction and offered a hesitant smile, which I returned, much, I suspect, to Lady Chase's private amusement. But she did nothing so crass as to make the least remark. Lady Dorothea returned to her sister-in-law's side, and soon the tea-tray arrived.

Under cover of passing the cups, I spoke to her in a low voice, 'It is good of you to be kind to poor Miss Southey. I fear hers is not an easy life, and she needs the friendship of...of someone like you.'

She said lightly, 'I cannot imagine any governess having a pleasant existence, poor thing. Miss Southey is a notable musician, is she not?'

Honouring her for turning my clumsy compliment, I agreed, but we were unable to pursue our conversation. Just as I prepared to sit beside her, a footman tiptoed over to me. I was needed at another deathbed.

CHAPTER FOUR

At long last the rain stopped. To my eyes it was a sudden event. My parishioners, however, nodded and sucked their teeth and said they'd seen how it would be, all along.

'They are able to predict the weather?' Lady Dorothea asked, round-eyed but also amused.

We were in the church porch after matins. Most of my flock, including Lady Chase and her nephew and his wife, had long since gone home, but Miss Southey and her charges were dawdling round the graveyard. They and Lady Dorothea were no doubt determined to enjoy a bracing walk in the brief burst of sunshine.

'Their livelihoods – indeed, their lives – depend so much upon the weather that they are certainly skilled in reading the signs. Much as you or I can read music, which would perplex them.'

'So your church musicians played all by ear?'

'They may have had some knowledge of notation. At Christmastide they reform their band and will come with the carol-singers to the Hall to serenade you. You will have mummers, too,' I added, hoping that she would still be present to enjoy them.

She might have read my mind. 'There is talk of our returning to London. But only talk, and once my brother is settled anywhere, it is hard to move him.'

I could not argue, more than conscious of her ladyship's feelings about the situation. 'There is nothing like a country Christmas,' I declared, 'when all the villagers are gathered together to celebrate, regardless of rank. Lady Chase is said to be more than generous – she does not limit her hospitality to her tenants, but opens her doors to all.'

'You used the same phrase in your sermon,' she observed.

'Then I was speaking of the Almighty.'

'And urging us to follow His example.' She nibbled an elegantly gloved finger, as if unsure whether to put her next question. At last she responded to my encouraging smile. 'What made you take up religion, Mr Campion?'

Take up? She made it sound like an interesting hobby. I bit my lip.

'Was it the typical last refuge of the youngest son?' she continued blithely. 'Would not the army or the law have suited you better?'

'The army, never.' Now was not the time to tell her how my cowardice had once paralysed me. 'And I have no interest in the law. But do not misinterpret what I am saying. The Church was an active choice. A calling. It was not a matter of what suited me. It was a matter of what suited my Master.'

'Your Master would not have thought you suited to a more fashionable parish?'

'It did not appear so. I can only respond to His Will, Lady Dorothea. Did we not say together this morning, using the prayer His Son taught us – *Thy Will be done?*'

'Of course. But they are only words, are they not?'

'Not in my experience.'

She glanced over her shoulder. 'I see my nieces and poor Miss Southey are waiting. Will you excuse me, Mr Campion?'

Suddenly the day did not seem so bright. I returned to my church, and repeated the solemn prayer.

During the next few days the pale winter sun did its feeble best to dry the sodden land. To my amazement, if not that of my parishioners, we had been spared serious life-threatening floods, though many suffered the inconvenience of having water in their sculleries and kitchens. Most sufferers had phlegmatically endured their lot, moving their sticks of furniture to the upper storeys and relying on their employers for soup and bread.

The Marsh Bottom hovels had indeed collapsed, but by then their inhabitants were safe in one of the Chase estate barns; they did no more harm than let their urchins of children chase a few chickens foolhardy enough to venture within. Lady Chase's sour-faced steward, Furnival, was under instructions to build some modern new cottages for them – on higher ground. In the village there was considerable grumbling, since it was felt that ne'er-do-wells should not benefit from their total lack of thrift. In fact, since the families were actually in the employ of another landlord, the plans came to naught, until Lady Chase cut the Gordian knot and insisted the menfolk would be employed as labourers on her own land. Eventually they would be rehoused in cottages left vacant as the most loyal employees were promoted to her new model site, still currently no more than the plans on much folded paper, to be realised when the ground became dry enough to lay foundations. All this was, as one may imagine, the product of long discussions in her ladyship's unofficial little committee, comprising herself, the Hansards and myself, which met privately in her ladyship's sitting room.

To my chagrin, although she regularly asked intelligent questions about our progress, Lady Dorothea never evinced any desire to participate. I ascribed that to a ladylike reluctance to appear unbecomingly forward. Similarly, although I was sure Sir Marcus must have resented the spending of every single groat that might have formed part of his inheritance, he and his wife seemed as uninterested in these plans as Miss Southey's charges were in whatever she was trying to teach them. The boys had returned to Winchester, where I hoped they were benefiting from their education rather more than Lady Honoria and Miss Georgiana, who were far more interested in tittering at secrets than in any mature conversation.

Today I encountered the young ladies on a country walk. As I first heard distant voices, I had hoped, with a leaping heart, that Lady Dorothea was of their company – she often was, though I have not embarrassed myself by recording the trivial details of conversations quite meaningless unless one's heart was involved.

This time I was disappointed.

To celebrate the pallid sun I had permitted myself a half-holiday and strolled through my favourite tract of woodland, spongy and waterlogged though the paths might be. I might even have been whistling or singing a favourite hymn: there is nothing like the glory of the Almighty's handiwork to make the heart glad. Back from the woodland echoed – giggles.

Ceasing my noise immediately I waited until the young ladies came into sight, ready to smile and doff my hat. But they appeared not. I could hear the murmur of Miss Southey's serious voice, followed by more giggles and veritable screams of laughter – in boys they would have been jeers.

I would find out the cause.

I strode towards the source of the sound, at last breaking into a run. I could see no cause for the cruel hilarity, just three young women whose boots were covered with mud and whose skirts and petticoats were six inches deep in the stuff. For once I looked Miss Southey full in the face. There was no doubting the pain I saw there. I must ask dear Lady Chase to discover its cause. And Lady Dorothea could – nay, *should* – befriend her. A sudden and quite inexplicable wave of anger gushed over me, choking any words in my throat.

A lesser woman would have raised her eyes heavenwards in an attempt to solicit my sympathy; Miss Southey permitted no change in her countenance whatsoever as she said politely, 'Good afternoon, Mr Campion.'

'Lady Honoria; Miss Georgiana; Miss Southey,' I said, doffing my hat. 'Such an excellent day for a walk.'

'It is indeed,' Miss Southey agreed, attempting with a sharp glance to quell the giggles that punctuated each utterance. 'Are you a student of nature?' Miss Southey prompted me.

'Indeed I am. Some months ago I wrote a paper for the Royal Society on the warbler family. It was, I am pleased to say, so favourably received that I am tempted to embark on another.'

'On the same subject?' She seemed to be interested.

There was no doubt that the young ladies were not, but it

was she with whom I was conversing, so I pressed on. 'This time it will be on *genus Picidae*.'

'Woodpeckers,' she explained to her charges. 'We have already heard the drumming of the great spotted woodpecker, have we not, girls? And we also saw—? The bird that laughs, Honoria?' She explained with scarce subdued asperity, 'The green woodpecker, Honoria.'

The very idea of a green woodpecker seemed to destroy the last vestiges of self-control in either girl, and, as much out of pity for their governess as with irritation at their behaviour, I made my farewells and left them.

I hoped to see no more of them that day.

I had not, however, walked more than three or four hundred yards when the quiet was shattered once more – this time by true screams. Surely they betokened genuine terror! Abandoning all thoughts of woodpeckers, green or otherwise, I ran as fast as I could to the source of the growing hysteria.

Although the swollen streams had generally subsided, here, upstream of a little bridge, the waters threatened to burst their banks and had formed in fact a veritable pond. For some reason Miss Southey was flailing around in it, up to her waist in water. Had she fallen? Or been pushed? Surely she could not have waded in voluntarily? Yet only the lower half of her person was wet, which suggested the latter. Then I saw a possible explanation – a bonnet, the sad rusty black bonnet I had last seen on poor Miss Southey's head, was floating in the middle of the stream. Even such an outrage could surely not have been, however, the reason for such apparent terror, in not just Miss Southey but in the young ladies.

'Miss Southey! What in heaven's name—?'

She could do no more than point at the bridge, her arms shaking and her face distorted with panic.

And then I could see why the stream had formed a pond and why the ladies were in such a quake. The bridge was partially blocked by a man's body.

I spoke sharply to the girls. 'Silence! Run for help!'

They screamed on. Bending, I scooped a handful of the icy water and dashed it in Honoria's face. 'Do as I tell you – this instant! And take your sister too.' The latter wasted no time waiting for my unchivalrous cure but turned on her heel and sped back towards the Court. I was afraid I would have to slap her sister's face to achieve the same end, but at last, seeing that I intended to leave her to attend to her soaked and shaking mentor, she abandoned her histrionic display and followed her sister.

Holding my hand out, I reached for Miss Southey's icy hand and pulled her towards me, gently but firmly. 'Avert your gaze, dear lady, from that hideous sight, and watch where you place your feet. Should you miss your step, the water is swift enough to carry you downstream,' I added.

At last she comprehended what such movement would entail – the unwilling embrace of the drowned creature by the bridge. She nodded, her mouth still frozen into a silent scream. Gradually I brought her back to dry land.

As soon as she was safe, I stripped off her pelisse, replacing it with my greatcoat and wrapping my scarf about her thin neck. But what should I do next? If my first thought was for the living, the second must be to prevent the corpse being swept further downstream. I could no more rely on it staying where it was than I could expect an explanation from her charges to be sufficiently coherent to send assistance to us.

But it seemed that the arrival of two sobbing girls without their governess occasioned sufficient alarm for several outdoor servants to come running towards us, shouting Miss Southey's name.

Consigning her to the care of two of them, I sent the third for Dr Hansard, suggesting he bring his fishing gear and a change of clothes, and a fourth to the rectory, with a message for my groom Jem to bring me dry clothes and boots. My first care must have been for the ladies' welfare, but now I was shaking uncontrollably from the cold. If I was to be of any use to Dr Hansard, I must avoid becoming one of his patients. I added blankets and brandy to the list – all who were to be involved in retrieving that man colder than us all would need something to warm them as the bright day slid swiftly into chill evening.

Lit by several lanterns, with not even a handkerchief over his mouth, Dr Hansard bent over the waterlogged and stinking corpse now lying on the bridge that had impeded its progress. 'My suspicion would be that this poor man was caught in the rain, and, losing his way, fell into the torrent. On the other hand, you will note some decay of his flesh. Surely that must have occurred before immersion.' He cocked his head in doubt. 'I will ask my colleague Dr Toone to assist me when I examine him.'

Jem nodded approvingly. 'He seems to be able to read the dead like others read books or maps.'

Hansard smiled. Some villagers regarded Toone's ability with suspicion, others with downright hostility. Jem, however, with an enthusiasm I was quite unable to share, regularly observed the two doctors' post-mortem examination of those patients whom Hansard's skills had been unable to save.

Jem peered more closely at the ravaged visage. 'I'd say he's a stranger to the area,' he observed.

He earned a smile. I could only look puzzled. 'And for confirmation look at his boots, worn right down,' Hansard told me. 'Now,' he continued, straightening, 'let us have this fellow carried to my cellar so that I may have a closer look at him.' He turned to the waiting men. 'Could you take that gate off its hinges so we may lay him on it?'

Jem was still peering at the body. 'Do you have any hope of identifying him? There may be a grieving family waiting for him to return, hoping for the best, but fearing the worst.'

'How can Hansard identify…that?' I pointed to the ghastly facial remains.

'I do not say I can, but as Jem says I must make the attempt. For one thing, I have that unusual hair to go on.'

I nodded. The man's hair was more than ordinarily dark and coarse, slightly kinked. 'It is unusual, is it not?'

'Indeed, the only time I have seen any like this it was on the – mercifully living – head of a black servant of a Bristol friend of mine. Servant! I should say slave – but I know you share my views on the iniquitous Trade. Now, what else can the dead man say?'

'He was not a wealthy man,' Jem said. 'It is not just his boots that have worn through – the coat is threadbare.'

Hansard nodded. 'Turn back the collar – yes, where it is not so worn it tells us the cloth was good.'

'So it was the garment of a gentleman,' Jem agreed. 'But old-fashioned, at that.'

'Indeed it is so dirty, so out at elbows, that I suspect it was discarded years ago and came at least second hand into this man's wardrobe.' He straightened and looked at me. 'You look disappointed.'

'I know not whether to be disappointed or relieved. Lady Chase still awaits the return of her son, you will recall, and the hope must be that any stranger arriving unannounced in the village might be that young man.'

'Well, Viscount Wombourn was dark, as I recall. Take a twig and push back what remains of his lips.'

Revolted but intrigued, I did as I was told. The teeth I revealed were surprisingly strong and even.

'Many a rich man would envy them,' Jem said. 'They're well nigh perfect.'

Dr Hansard sighed. 'I recall young Wombourn falling off his horse at the last hunt before he joined the army. He broke no bones, but chipped a front tooth, not badly enough to turn the tooth black, but enough for me to tell you that this is not he.'

'Thank God,' I said fervently.

'Amen. So I can please her ladyship and irritate that pipsqueak Sir Marcus,' he said, with a grim smile. 'A court case to oust her ladyship from the Court and remove her to the Dower House, indeed! What does your Lady Dorothea think of the idea?'

'She is not *my* Lady Dorothea and we have not discussed the matter.'

Jem shot a reproving glance at me. As usual, he was right. Edmund was an old friend and I should not have been so curt. 'In fact,' I added by way of an apology, 'she is always so closely chaperoned it is impossible to exchange more than commonplaces – should she want to.'

'Well, I fear that if he means to embark on what will no

doubt prove a drainingly expensive court case, he will need his sister to make a profitable match, with a very interesting settlement – from what my London friends tell me he has precious little in his own coffers. More than this poor man, perhaps,' he conceded, returning to his task. 'Perhaps he sat down to rest and the cold finished him and then the waters rose and carried him off.'

'The cold?' I was unexpectedly relieved. 'No human had a hand in this?'

'I can see no obvious injury, but that is not to say there was none.'

'I was thinking,' I confessed, 'of the moan that so upset me – the one I feared was a ghostly rebuke. In fact,' I mused, 'Lady Bramhall asked me on one occasion if the churchyard was haunted – perhaps she heard the same sound.'

He peered at me over his spectacles. 'So another heard it?'

I hung my head. 'Indeed. I would have instituted a search, there and then, but for the weather.' The blame must be mine, not Simon's.

'Ten to one you would have found no more than a corpse and had half the village down with the influenza,' Hansard said mildly, but I felt Jem's reproachful eyes upon me. 'When did Lady Bramhall mention the haunting?'

'One day at the church. And Sir Marcus certainly did not like such talk.'

He mocked me gently. 'And since then your attachment to Lady Dorothea drove it out of your head?'

'Temporarily. But the floods and my poor flock... Truly, Edmund, I have had other things to think of than the product of what I believed was my fevered imagination.'

'It may be that that groan was the product of a dying man,

Toby – have you thought of that?' Jem asked bluntly.

I nodded.

Hansard intervened kindly. 'The rain was torrential, like the monsoons I experienced in India. It is most unlikely he would have been found alive.'

'But why should he moan so loudly?' I asked.

'I suspect that your memory has amplified the sound. Enough of speculation. Now, what evidence do we have here?' Then he bent again to look at the boots. To my horror, he eased one off. I turned lest I see a sight I could not bear.

'See! The poor man had stuffed this paper into it to keep out the cold and wet,' Hansard said, prising open the folds. But the paper was sodden, and he desisted. He passed it to me. 'No, don't drop it, man! Take care of it, if you please. That is so far our only clue as to where he came from and when he set out. The date, man, and the place the journal was printed!' He raised his eyes heavenwards in exasperation.

Holding it at arm's length, I wrapped the soaking wad in my handkerchief. 'Now what do we do?'

'I'll go down to the Court to chivvy a couple of barrowloads of ice out of old Furnival,' Jem declared, implementing what was becoming quite a well-rehearsed system. 'I know he'll say the icehouse is getting low, but the poorer quality stuff that the cook would turn her nose up at will do to preserve our new friend.'

'Excellent. I would certainly rather continue my examination at table height. Neither my knees nor my back will tolerate this position for long. Dear me, my winter rheumatism already!' Wiping his hands on the greensward, he pushed himself upright. 'We will meet back at Langley Park, Jem.'

* * *

Unlike Jem, I could not bear to act as my friend's acolyte as he performed his examination of the poor stranger. Mrs Hansard, apprised of her husband's latest occupation, offered me wine, but I felt honour bound to refuse it. Moreton Hall must by now be abuzz with rumour, and Lady Chase ought to receive the news from me in person.

Mrs Hansard nodded. 'And so she shall. But not until you have drunk some of my special punch. Heavens, Tobias, you have been chilled to the bone, and even now your hands are like ice. When you are warm, I will accompany you to the Court. Her ladyship, not knowing whether to hope or despair, may want a little female companionship that a poor honey like Lady Bramhall cannot supply.'

'Miss Southey, too, may need attention,' I added.

'I already have some of Edmund's best composing drops for the poor girl,' she said.

Possibly not entirely to my surprise, Mrs Hansard had even insisted that we were provided with hot bricks for our short journey in their gig down to the Court. George, their groom, knew better than to remark on it, but I was shamefully relieved when she told him that she feared she was starting a putrid throat and that Dr Hansard had warned her against taking cold.

Though it must have been the hour when her ladyship and the rest of the family were dressing for dinner, we were shown directly up to Lady Chase's boudoir. She appeared a few moments later, saying something over her shoulder to her no doubt anxious abigail.

She was pale, and far from composed. 'I have been expecting you this hour. The body in the stream—?'

'Was not that of your son, your Ladyship. Dr Hansard is

certain of that. The front tooth was not chipped.'

'Of course. Dr Hansard attended him after his hunting accident. Thank God!'

'Amen.' I should have told her that the situation she was in was neither better nor worse than before, but she had swung from agony of mind to blessed relief in a heart beat.

Mrs Hansard produced some drops from her reticule. 'My husband thought you might need these, your Ladyship.'

Lady Chase shook her head emphatically. 'I do not need physicking – though, pray, thank Dr Hansard for his kind thoughts. Where is he, by the way, that you, however welcome, are his representative?'

'He is examining the poor man's body. He has sent for a learned colleague, Dr Toone, to assist him. In the meantime, he relies on Tobias's groom Jem. As you know, Jem is a most unusual young man, and very capable.'

'Of course. One wonders what might have become of him had he been a gentleman.'

Bowing, I said firmly, 'There is no greater gentleman in nature than Jem.'

'Forgive me. I expressed myself ill. I should have said, had he been *born* a gentleman, with all the advantages of education that that would have brought.'

'Indeed you are right. He took to reading and writing like a duck to water, your Ladyship – it is my constant regret that he did not have the benefit of my masters at Eton,' I added. 'But I must turn to the next object of Dr Hansard's care, poor Miss Southey. She has had a most terrible experience.'

'And may well be in need of Dr Hansard's excellent drops,' her ladyship said with her charming smile, ringing for a maid to conduct us into the servants' quarters.

It seemed that my request to Mrs Sandys to improve Miss Southey's lot had fallen on deaf ears. She was still housed in the nursery wing, the coldest part of the house, rather than in what I hoped were the warmer quarters of the upper servants.

'The poor girl should not be in accommodation as paltry as this,' Mrs Hansard exclaimed, huddling more deeply into her pelisse as we trod the uncarpeted and unheated corridors. 'If Miss Southey is unwell, Tobias, it will be as much as a result of her treatment here as of her afternoon's soaking.'

I nodded, trying to stop my teeth chattering. 'The social placing of the governess was ever problematic, of course.'

Mrs Hansard nodded. 'She is neither flesh nor fowl, and often ends up as being less than a good red herring. Yet in some households valuing education she may be treated even better than the housekeeper, with a servant of her own.'

'Alas, it does not need this afternoon's evidence to show that the Bramhalls do not value poor Miss Southey.'

'And, Tobias, that Lady Chase herself did not value her own governess, if she kept her up here. And yet now she is the most generous and considerate of people.'

'Clearly I will have to speak to Lady Chase.'

The little maid tapped at the schoolroom door – at least Miss Southey was allowed that much dignity. She knocked again, more loudly. At last, she turned back to us, puzzlement writ large over her face. 'Mrs Hansard, ma'am, Mr Campion, sir – there is no reply.'

'We will go in anyway,' Mrs Hansard declared, with as much authority as if her chatelaine held keys not for Langley Park but for this very house.

'But—'

Mrs Hansard ignored the poor child's protest and almost strode into the room, which was deserted. Miss Southey's bedchamber lay the far side. The door was open and we could see that the room was empty.

CHAPTER FIVE

'Do you think,' I ventured quietly to Mrs Hansard, 'that Miss Southey might have sought comfort of one I have encouraged to befriend her? Lady Dorothea?'

I did not quite believe that my friend was hopeful, but she told the servant to ask Lady Dorothea to spare a few moments of her time. We were ushered back into the warmer world the other side of the green baize door.

We waited many minutes in the library.

'Young ladies of quality lead very busy lives,' Mrs Hansard observed at last, with a satirical smile unsurprising in one who had worked – hard – for her living. But her face softened as she saw me biting my lip. 'Forgive me, Tobias. It may be she has already started to dress for dinner and it would not be fitting for her to receive us *en déshabille.*'

'Of course not,' I agreed, my voice falsely bright. I did not dare voice my hope that at this very moment Lady Dorothea might be offering comfortable words and warm clothes to the poor governess. I had a suspicion that Mrs Hansard would not oblige me with credence.

The ormolu clock ticked another three minutes, then the door was flung open and Lady Dorothea veritably flew into the room.

'I have just this minute returned from Leamington,' she declared, casting aside her pelisse and unfastening her bonnet. Seeing that the ribbon was becoming unaccountably tangled, Mrs Hansard stepped forward to assist her. 'Thank you – you are very kind. But what is this I hear? Pray, Mrs Hansard, Mr Campion – explain.' She sank to a seat, and indicated that we might sit.

My narrative was brief, omitting the most horrible details. It was interrupted with quick gasps, and stifled protestations. To my chagrin, I must have emerged as somewhat of a hero, and Lady Dorothea's eyes anxiously darted from Mrs Hansard's face to mine.

'You are safe and sound, Mr Campion?' she asked at last.

Did my heart beat more strongly at her interest? This was not the moment for such a thought. 'Thank you, yes. Your nieces I cannot speak for,' I said, with forbearance, 'but undoubtedly Miss Southey was profoundly shaken. I dared to hope that, since she was not in her room, she had turned to you or Lady Chase for succour. Or Lady Bramhall, of course,' I added though the tone of my voice might have indicated that that was an unlikely option.

'If I had known – if I had been here – of course I would have sought her out. But as you can see, my mother and I were delayed on the road – a trifling problem with one of the wheels – and now I am late for dinner. Pray believe that when Miss Southey returns I will do all in my power to comfort her. But for now…you know my brother's views on punctuality.' With an agitated glance at the clock, she rose.

We did the same. Our farewells were necessarily brief. But I had never before known that her brother was worried by time.

Mrs Sandys, standing stolidly on the threshold of her parlour, denied any knowledge of Miss Southey's whereabouts.

'If she's left, that's the family's business, not mine,' she said in chilly tones, stepping back and trying to close the door on us.

I placed a foot between it and the frame. 'Did I not ask you to show particular kindness to her? Come, Mrs Sandys, you must care what has befallen a fellow human being.'

'I can't care if those who pay the lady tell me not to,' she objected. 'Such a shouting and argumentation those fires and that hot water caused. You'd have thought Sir Marcus was paying for it all himself.'

'And did you not appeal to Lady Chase?'

'Go over the head of one who may be owner of the Court any day now?' Her expression told me I was a fool.

Mrs Hansard now stepped forward. 'So when did Miss Southey leave, and how?'

'As to that, you'll have to ask Sir Marcus – and it's more than my job's worth to disturb him while he's dining – as you should know of all people should know, Mrs Hansard, having been in service yourself,' she added insultingly. 'As for Lady Chase, tonight she dines with Sir Marcus, so that cock won't fight either.'

'In that case, *when* it is convenient,' I said, with great irony, 'you may inform them that they may expect questioning by a Justice of the Peace tomorrow morning.' I was sure that Dr Hansard would take a similar view of the situation to mine –

and even if he did not, he was such a loyal friend that to save my face he would pretend to. Meanwhile my anger was such that I said with as much hauteur as I could conjure, 'Pray send for Mrs Hansard's gig, Mrs Sandys.'

As soon as I had handed Mrs Hansard into her gig, I begged her pardon and begged for five minutes' indulgence while I spoke to the stable-lads.

Apart from one, however, a lad with fewer than half his wits whom the Chases had employed out of kindness to his father, there were no outdoor servants around. Poor slack-mouthed Alfie could no more have told me his name than flown to the moon, so there was no point in asking him if he had seen Miss Southey depart. Mindful that Mrs Hansard was waiting, I merely slipped a penny into his hand and patted his shoulder before turning on my heel and returning to the gig.

'Until Toone arrives there is no more that we can do,' Dr Hansard said, sounding as much relieved as exhausted. He had changed for dinner, which his estimable cook had contrived to delay. The three of us were sipping sherry before a welcoming fire. 'Not, I suspect, that there is more. Try as I might I can find no sign of injury. His bones appear to be intact. I can see no bruises or contusions – though they might be on flesh already consumed. My conclusion, Tobias, is that he died of natural causes. And you two – what success have you had? Mrs Hansard was too busy selecting a gown to respond to my questions.' He cast a teasing smile in her direction: she had chosen a fashionable gown in pale blue, with a dark-blue overdress suited to her still-dark hair. Her lace cap, in accordance with Edmund's preference, was minuscule.

So often did we tarry over supper, my good friends pressing me to stay the night, they had been kind enough to designate a bedchamber as mine. I kept not only a nightshirt there, but also spare clothes for both day and evening. Thus I too was respectably dressed. As for Jem, who also kept spare attire in his own particular room, he insisted that he was happier dining with George and Turner, Hansard's admirable valet. Without doubt young Burns would have been horrified to learn that during Edmund's bachelor days, both Turner and Jem had eaten with us as the equals we believed them to be.

'We broke the news to Lady Chase without incident,' I said, adding with a smile, 'as I am perfectly sure Mrs Hansard will have told you.'

'She heard it with a very distressing joy.' Mrs Hansard shook her head sadly. 'She does not see, alas, that the death of one man who is not her son means that her son is any more alive. As for Mrs Sandys, however – nay, I will ask Tobias to recount that part of our adventure lest I am betrayed into very unladylike sentiments.'

'The woman is a toadying fool,' I said dismissively. 'Unfortunately she has nailed her colours to the Bramhalls' mast, not her ladyship's. In doing so she has forgotten her manners and her duty to a suffering human being. In short, she neither knows nor cares what has happened to poor Miss Southey.'

'Tobias, I do not think that you noticed the poor girl's trunk was still in her bedchamber,' Mrs Hansard said quietly. 'In my experience, it could mean that she has been dismissed hugger-mugger, her things only being sent on when she has notified her old employers of an address to send them to.'

Edmund frowned. 'Or that she has quit her post herself, my

dear, with similar haste. It is very unfortunate. I would have liked to question her.'

'As to that,' I began, casting a conspiratorial glance at Mrs Hansard, 'I think you will be able to speak to Sir Marcus tomorrow. We – er – I, that is – left a message to that effect with Mrs Sandys.'

To my amazement, he looked less than pleased. But at last his face softened. 'Normally I prefer to make such visits without prior warning, Tobias. But what is done cannot be undone, and it will be interesting to see what effect your words have had. But I fear it would be better if I made my morning call alone. We do not want this to smack of conspiracy, my friend.'

I hung my head in shame all the deeper for the gentleness of his rebuke.

Mrs Hansard rose swiftly. 'Poor Cook will be in agonies of distress if those fowl cook one minute longer. Gentlemen, shall we dine?'

While Dr Hansard, with all the weight of his office on his shoulders, set out for Moreton Hall, promising to report what transpired when we gathered for luncheon, I returned to the parsonage, with Jem riding beside me. He kept clearing his throat as if it pained him. I had irritated one friend, and now it seemed that I must irritate another.

'Jem, you are ailing, are you not?'

''Tis nothing, Toby – just a tickle.'

'A tickle – or a putrid throat? Be honest, man. You have been stifling coughs ever since we set out. I am persuaded that a mustard footbath is the only thing for you. That, and a hot infusion. No, do not attempt to stable the horses – you taught me how to rub down an animal to your satisfaction years ago, and I fancy I have not forgotten.'

'You wouldn't dare forget.' He tried to laugh, but broke off, clutching his throat.

'I want your word that, by the time I have finished with Titus and Ben here, you will be in your chamber, a blanket about your shoulders and your feet already soaking.' I spoke with mock-seriousness, but for all that I was very worried. Jem was never ill, always a tower of strength when everyone else was succumbing to the influenza or even to the smallpox.

The horses thoroughly dealt with, I ran inside, to be greeted by Susan's anxious face. She was carrying a kettle of hot water she was clearly reluctant to surrender to me.

'He would not want you to take any infection,' I said gently as I took it. Privately, I suspected that Jem was a man who would prefer not, as he would put it, to be fussed over. Besides, it was hardly proper for a handsome young man in his nightshirt to be closeted with a young maid who once fancied herself in love with him – even though his having his feet in a bowl of mustard and hot water might prove a deterrent to passion.

'But you are the parson, and must keep well for all the villagers.'

'I must indeed. Now, Susan, I cannot think that Jem will want to eat much today, but I know that for a fever Dr Hansard swears by lemon and barley water. Would you be kind enough to prepare some? And I will ensure that he drinks every last drop.'

It took every ounce of my persuasive power to convince Jem that he must not only remain indoors, but should take to his bed. Undoubtedly he was feverish; the pain in his throat, he admitted, was spreading down to his chest. He conceded that Susan's potion might well be of assistance, and watched in grudging silence as I set and lit a brisk fire.

'Do not deny you have the head-ache,' I said, standing back to admire my handiwork. 'I am persuaded that it would do you a great deal of good to lie down, and permit me to bathe your temples with vinegar or some of Mrs Hansard's excellent lavender water.'

'You are joking me,' he growled.

'I am indeed.' I waved my coal-blackened hands at him. 'But I have the most selfish reasons for wishing for your speedy return to health, Jem. Clearly Miss Southey must be found, and although Dr Hansard may invoke the force of the law, I would not be surprised if you and I were involved somehow.'

He grinned. 'Then I'd best endure all the hot plasters and poultices Dr Hansard can wish on me.'

When I looked in on him a few minutes later, he was in an uneasy sleep, and fought off the coverlet I tried to pull over him.

Anxious not to alarm Susan, but concerned for my friend's health, I wrote a note to Dr Hansard, explaining that I would be unable to join him and his wife at one, as we had arranged, and begging that he would send George down with whatever medicine he judged helpful in such a case. I sent the gardener's lad off, with a sixpence for his pains, telling him to run all the way.

I was so confident of Edmund's response that I suggested to Mrs Trent that she might need to lay extra covers for luncheon, and I was not disappointed. Within the hour,

Edmund's gig bowled up, Mrs Hansard clutching a basket on her knees as Edmund himself handled the ribbons. While the former went to find Mrs Trent in her kingdom, Edmund set off apace for Jem's room.

Edmund was so long with Jem that both his wife and I feared the very worst, though neither cared to admit it to the other. At last, however, he came into my sitting room, smiling broadly and smelling strongly of lavender water.

'One of Dr Toone's ideas,' he said, not quite apologetically, wafting his hands before us. 'As you know, I believe very strongly in ridding the hands of noxious smells after treating patients living or dead. Dr Toone goes further, not only scrubbing his hands and fingernails, as I do, but also dousing them in lavender water. Is it efficacious? I know not.'

'It is very pleasing to our nostrils at least,' Mrs Hansard said with a smile.

Before another word could be said, Mrs Trent summoned us to the dining room, where she had laid out an admirable repast, the greater part, I was sure, conjured from her own supplies: she had her pride to consider, after all, despite Mrs Hansard's generous gifts.

Whether or not the girl was pleased with our decision, we dismissed Susan, saying that we would serve ourselves.

'Firstly let me say that I have told Jem all I am going to tell you, Tobias – the man was restless enough at having to submit to my examination and I thought it would provide a diversion. Secondly, Maria has heard some of it—'

'Chiefly in the form of smothered oaths and imprecations,' she said, a twinkle in her eye.

'If by my ill-chosen words I have harmed your enquiries—'

'Let that pass, Tobias,' he said kindly. He paused, while I helped him to beef and pickle, waving a hand to signal enough.

Mrs Hansard took one of the dainty sandwiches. 'Edmund, why do you not explain exactly what transpired? You could not have a more attentive audience, I promise you.'

'But how am I to eat this excellent repast if I am talking?' he asked impishly.

'Slowly,' Mrs Hansard said with flat finality. 'Poor Tobias deserves to hear it all, and I to hear the sections you omitted as we drove down.'

'Very well.' He laid down his knife and fork. 'Sir Marcus – on his own – received me in the library. He was very much on his dignity when I was announced, saying that he did not need to justify his actions towards his employees to anyone. Without saying a single word, I let him bluster on until he had no more to say. At length, standing before the fireplace looking extremely foolish, he stopped. I told him that while he did not necessarily need to justify his treatment of Miss Southey, however despicable that might be, I held him responsible for either permitting or indeed encouraging one who was certain to be called as a witness at the Coroner's Inquest to leave the district. It was not only irresponsible but possibly constituted contempt of court.'

'Does it?' I asked, round-eyed.

'I neither know nor care. At very least, I told him, he must provide me with details of her destination.' He stopped to load his beef with mustard.

'And could he – did he – oblige?'

Mouth full, he shook his head.

'Apparently,' Mrs Hansard responded in her husband's stead, 'he claimed to know nothing at all of her whereabouts.

In other words, he now implied that Miss Southey had left of her own free will and gone he knew not whither.'

'So why did he not say as much at the start of your conversation?'

'Perhaps because he is a foolish man who likes to exercise what little power he imagines he has – or one day might have,' Edmund replied, dabbing his mouth with one of the snowy napkins that were Mrs Trent's pride and joy. 'Who would not wish to leave the place where she made such a dreadful discovery?'

'Not to mention the ill-treatment meted out to her by the young ladies who should have respected her?' I put in. 'You have seen their veiled insolence in public, my dear friends. As I told you yesterday, you would have been shocked by their all too open rudeness when they believed that they were unobserved. In fact, the more I think of it the more I am inclined to believe that they may actually have torn Miss Southey's bonnet from her and thrown it into the water, forcing her to attempt its rescue.'

'I wondered if that was the case,' Maria sighed. 'My sex is supposed to be a civilising influence, but I have seen young ladies, gently born and well brought up, behaving in a way that I believe boys of a similar age would find excessive.'

I said nothing, having experienced bullying at Eton – from Toone, no less, though he at least seemed to have forgotten all about it.

'You have not seen boys in the herd, my dear,' Edmund observed cryptically. 'But I should certainly question the young ladies—'

'Separately,' Mrs Hansard declared.

'Very well. And possibly with you, my dear, or Edmund in

attendance. I was permitted to do no more than take their pulses and check for feverish symptoms this morning. Their mama fears for their lives after yesterday's events,' he explained, in a simpering voice. 'I tell you roundly, however, that they were a good deal less afflicted than poor Jem. In fact, they were in the very bloom of health. Had I been prepared to dispense with my fee, I should have told them as much. As it was, I shall bill them steeply for my fine words.'

With other patients needing his attention, Dr Hansard soon declared that he must quit the table. Though his wife was prepared to walk home – even stating that she preferred to do so – he cut short all arguments by declaring, in the most forceful tones, that he insisted on conveying her. She might say her farewells to Mrs Trent while he cast one more eye on poor Jem, and then they would depart.

Both embarrassed by his vehemence, neither of us spoke aloud our suspicion – that he might be afraid for her safety.

'It is always better to overreact in a case like this than to underreact,' Hansard declared a few minutes later, as he handed Mrs Hansard into the gig. 'But now I conjecture that tomorrow poor Jem will find there are not enough handkerchiefs in the world to tackle his streaming nose. Yes, a humble cold is what ails him. You will have the devil of a job to make him keep to his room, Tobias.'

'I have the very thing,' I said, smiling.

And I had.

In the midst of the previous day's activities, I had forgotten to remove the fragments of paper from my pocket. Now I took them to Jem's room, where, already weary of all the fuss he had attracted, he was preparing to don his breeches. I stemmed his rebellion by asking humbly for his help. With a sigh, he shrugged on his dressing gown and slippers.

Together we carefully separated the damp pieces of paper, and set them to dry on the hearth on a cloth I had begged from Mrs Trent. Then I fetched a card table and we tried to piece them together, but it was a fiddly business, like the jigsaw puzzles that afflicted my youth. And now, Jem's cold – for such indeed it was   had started to break in good earnest, and his sneezes threatened to blow them all into the fire. It was with little reluctance that I bade him a fond farewell and stepped over to the church, where I implored the Almighty to have mercy on all that suffered. At least, knowing I could leave all in His divine hands, I set out once again to show the Hansards what little Jem and I had found.

'All I can report is failure, Edmund,' I confessed, tipping the newspaper fragments on to his desk. 'We have toiled over these fragments of paper almost all the afternoon, until poor Jem's head began to split and my patience wore thin. Alas, the top of the newspaper has been torn off. All we have is half a sheet of advertisements.' I picked up a couple of pieces and tossed them down again.

'Advertisements for what?' He was as alert as if he hadn't done a hard day's work.

'The usual: haberdashers, horses, hats.'

'Look more closely, man. And turn each fragment over carefully as you read it. If only the light were better!' He summoned a servant and asked for more working candles. 'If there is anything to find, Tobias, I resolve to find it before we sup.'

In the event, I am pleased to report that it was I who made

the find. One of the advertisements was for a missing person. *Dark hair…tall…military bearing…*Such a description would fit Hugo, Viscount Wombourn. It might be that the man who had died in the woods had news of the missing heir. If only we could find the rest of it. But we searched in vain.

Although we had handled no more than paper, Dr Hansard insisted once more on the hand-scrubbing routine before we retired to change for dinner. Our toilet at last completed, we sat down to an excellent meal. Dr Hansard having spent much time in India, he was inclined to ask for dishes that were strange to an English palate. Tonight's was a curry soup. This was followed by a raised pie, and a selection of vegetables from her ladyship's succession houses. Then came a ragout of chicken and a pig's cheek. Neither of us men had a taste for sweet things, a whim Mrs Hansard always reflected in her choice of dishes.

As long as Burns and Kate, their maidservant, were in the room, we kept our talk general, but once they had left the Stilton for us, we could discuss what to do next. Mrs Hansard never withdrew when there were just the three of us, Hansard always indulging her with champagne while we drank port.

'How do we break the news to her ladyship?' I asked bluntly.

Mrs Hansard regarded us over the brim of her glass with amused eyes. 'In private?'

'Indeed, the further from the pricked ears of Sir Marcus as possible,' I agreed with a laugh. More seriously I added, 'I am happy to speak to her – but should not you, Edmund, as her medical adviser be present?'

'If the two of us approach together, she may draw the wrong conclusion altogether. We have more news for her, but not *bad* news. Merely the information that someone was making his way to the Court with an advertisement for her son in his shoe.'

'Will she not make the obvious deduction? That someone knows the whereabouts of her son? That he is alive?'

'Did they never teach you logic at that university of yours?' Thus Dr Hansard, an Oxford man, dismissed Cambridge. 'You make the same mistake as her ladyship. That may be the *obvious* deduction, but it is not a *deduction* at all. All we can deduce is that someone was sufficiently motivated by the advertisement to wend his way hither. With no masthead to the paper we do not even know whence he came!'

'As her steward, Furnival will surely know where – and moreover when – the advertisements were placed.'

'True. Now, my enquiries about the village have failed to produce anyone who admits to having seen the poor man about the neighbourhood. Tomorrow, before we tell her ladyship about the newspaper or interview the young ladies, I suggest we cast our eyes once around the stream in which you found the poor man and see...if he dropped anything.'

'You mean, whether the foxes and other marauding animals that were tearing his flesh dropped anything,' Mrs Hansard suggested unflinchingly.

'Exactly so. But we will not tell her ladyship that. I hope that Toone will be here about noon. His sharp eyes may observe things that I have failed to notice.'

'So may I suggest a council of war here at one? You gentlemen need your food and I need to hear the latest information. *Then* you may call on her ladyship.'

Hansard smiled tenderly at his wife, and reached across the

table to take her hand. 'Take my advice, Tobias – find yourself a woman as good as mine.'

His tone of voice, his smile, showed how much he appreciated her. She could never have been pretty, but age had added a beauty that no little miss would ever achieve. Age, and her love for my dear friend.

Though they would have denied it, it was clear that a third person would be de trop in their parlour this evening. I must make my excuses and leave them alone, with, lest I embarrass them, an unshakeable excuse.

'I doubt if I could, Edmund,' I laughed, knowing that when he laughed he secretly agreed with me. 'But now I must take my leave. While you hold the health of the village in your hands, I must care for a very important patient – our good friend Jem.'

CHAPTER SIX

As soon as the light was good enough, we met the following morning in the meadow, through which a now quiet stream coursed unchallenged, slipping gently under the unencumbered bridge.

Dr Hansard greeted me with an upraised eyebrow. 'No Jem?'

I shook my head. 'I refused point-blank to let him come.'

'He is no better, then?' His voice was serious.

'His throat and chest no longer trouble him, but he is still feverish – and your predictions about handkerchiefs have been fulfilled. His nose veritably glows, poor man. He will be able to read in bed without a candle.'

Edmund smiled reassuringly. 'That means he is on the way to recovery. I must ask Maria to send him some of that Indian soup we had at dinner the other night – he'll be able to taste it and I believe it will clear his head. Now, you know Luke, my gardener.'

'Parson Campion, sir.' Luke knuckled his forehead. He had brought a wheelbarrow containing a couple of rakes, a shovel and a riddle.

'And this is Joshua, Luke's nephew.' A sturdy ten-year-old made his bow. Thereafter, mindful of his company, he was obedient and largely silent.

At first the implements remained in their barrow. All four of us, walked slowly and solemnly backwards and forwards along the banks of the stream, searching for something – anything – which might be unusual in such a place. Not even the lad's eagle eyes found anything.

'Very well,' Dr Hansard said resignedly, 'we must try harder. A rake, Luke. Lightly, at first, as if you were combing the grass, not fiercely, as if to scarify it.' He threw the spare rake to me, promising to take over as I tired.

As we raked an area clear, the lad gathered up and riddled any loose earth and checked thoroughly for anything untoward. We had laboured in vain for the best part of an hour, Edmund bearing a hand as he had promised each time we paused for refreshment. Though the day was chilly, we soon needed to strip to our waistcoats and take long draughts of ale. Luke's face became more and more set as, no doubt, he thought of the tasks clamouring for his attention in the Hansards' garden. But at last the lad called out.

We hurried over. Joshua held in his palm a tiny leather bag, no more than two inches by three. His uncle took it. The drawstring was broken.

'Something gave that a damned good yank, sir,' Luke said, holding the end.

'Indeed. But let us see what is inside – go on, man, open it.'

All our heads bent intently over his hands, as he worked at the stiff leather. Either one of us would have seized it from him, but I at least knew I could not match the strength of his fingers and their horny nails.

''Tis gold! Look, a gentleman's ring.' Luke held it in his palm, looking from face to face.

Hansard took it carefully, holding it with the tips of his fingers at arm's length, as if it might bite him. He peered at it one way and another. At last, clicking his tongue in irritation, he passed it to me. 'Your eyes are younger than mine, Tobias. Why, when the Lord makes our eyesight worsen with age, does He not compensate by giving us longer arms?'

'Making them grow in proportion as we get older? We might end up dragging them apelike as we walk.' I laughed, taking the ring, warm from his hand. 'Let me see. A gentleman's signet ring, with a fantastical design both inside and out. But the gold is so worn I can hardly make out the initials myself. Perhaps an *S*, perhaps a *W*? We need an eyeglass, Dr Hansard.'

'It's being old and worn may tell us something in itself,' he said. 'My guess is that it is a family ring, an heirloom, if you like.'

'You remember Viscount Wombourn's broken tooth – would you not remember a ring like this?' I prompted sharply.

'If he'd worn it regularly. But it's not the sort of thing you'd wear every day, is it?' He pressed his fingers to his forehead, as if to help him recall something. He removed them, leaving muddy marks, and shook his head. 'Her ladyship has to see this, Mr Campion.'

'And she will when we visit her later. We may uncover other information, as may Toone. The fuller the picture we can paint the better.'

He shook his head doubtfully. 'I must take some drops to help her to bear all these shocks.'

'Do you not think you should save the drops until she has

to deal with the worst blow of all, lest she become inured to them?'

He looked at me from under his grizzled eyebrows. 'I sometimes think you would have made a good doctor, Mr Campion.'

I was about to make a riposte to the effect that he would have made a good parson, but Luke called out again. This time he had found a battered brandy flask.

Dr Hansard sniffed. 'Cheap spirits. So the poor man takes one last swig and throws it away. See – it is dented on one face, as if he threw it thus and it landed on a stone. Or someone trod on it,' he added, screwing his face and stretching his arm to see better. 'Devil take these wretched eyes of mine.'

When we walked into Langley Park, there was no sign of Mrs Hansard. Burns, as if by magic, materialised into the hall to relieve us of our coats and hats, and to relay the news that Dr Toone had arrived and was in the cellar. This we understood as a euphemism for *looking at the corpse*.

By unspoken consent, not even pausing to make ourselves presentable, we made our way straight to the head the cellar stairs. Before we could descend, we heard voices, two voices – Toone's Eton drawl and a light, feminine one. Standing beside Dr Toone in the scullery, her sleeves rolled above her arms, was none other than Mrs Hansard. He was drying his hands, she scrubbing hers. Surely she could not have been attending him as he examined the cadaver. Every feeling was offended. And yet she was wearing a voluminous apron to match his – surely this could not be.

Even Edmund looked disconcerted.

Toone turned towards us, his hand, smelling strongly of lavender water, outstretched. Edmund shook it firmly, before it was offered to me. Mrs Hansard, meanwhile, extended her fingertips to her husband, who responded by sniffing them and nodding. Only then did she tip away the bowl of water and tip the bottle of sweet-smelling liquid on to them.

'Shall we go into the parlour, gentlemen?' she asked, as calmly as if she had just come in from gathering eggs.

'The man did not drown, but suffocated,' Toone declared.

'And your evidence?' I demanded. Toone had treated me brutally at Eton and though he had now become an eminent physician, whom Hansard considered his superior, I could never be easy with him. At least Hansard and I were now as neat and sweet-smelling as our visitor, though beside his modish attire our clothes marked us out as country cousins.

'It was my learned colleague who should answer that.' He made a graceful gesture towards our hostess, and sank his Madeira in one gulp.

'Surely – a lady such as yourself – pray, Mrs Hansard—'

'Dear Tobias, we women are far more accustomed to death in all its forms than you gentlemen. You merely kill the pheasants or rabbits we eat, and, moreover, stand at a distance to do it.' She mimed using a gun. 'It is we who skin them and draw them. It is we who deal with their maggots when the meat cellar is not cold enough. So one poor sad corpse holds no terrors for me, nor should it, given Edmund's interest in the secrets of the dead.'

Edmund made a valiant effort to smile naturally. 'And what was it you found, my dear?'

'Earth inhaled deep into his nostrils,' Toone answered on

her behalf, accepting with a careless nod another glass of Madeira. 'No water in the lungs.' I did not enquire how he had discovered that. 'He was dead by the time the water swept him away.'

'Did he simply fall and inhale the mud, or was he held face-down?' I asked, trying for once not to betray a lack of logic. I did not want to be ridiculed, however kindly, in front of Toone. 'And if the latter, why did he not struggle?'

Maria nodded swiftly, as if it were a question that had troubled her for some time.

For answer Dr Hansard produced the battered flask. 'I think he drank himself into a stupor and fell asleep. I thought he might simply have died of exposure to the elements, but you think otherwise?' He asked not his friend but his wife.

She gave a charming shrug. 'I merely noticed the mud. You and Dr Toone are the ones to make *deductions*.' She shot a mischievous smile at me.

'We found something else as we searched the meadow,' I said, reaching into my pocket for the leather pouch.

'I'll fetch a magnifying glass,' Edmund said, suiting the deed to the word.

Even with the glass, however, we could discern no more than the *S* and *W* I had detected earlier.

'*W* for Wombourn?' Mrs Hansard suggested.

'That is what we must ask her ladyship.'

'After luncheon,' she declared. 'Dr Toone insists he must journey back home immediately. However, I am equally insistent that he will not do so until he has taken refreshment.' She hooked her hand into his proffered arm. 'This way, please, Dr Toone.'

* * *

We had been correct in our estimation of Lady Chase's character. Sitting bolt upright, she demanded to know every detail of our discoveries.

'And you believe that this poor soul had come here in response to the advertisement? I wonder why he did not simply present himself to my bank in London.'

'Madam,' Dr Hansard said gravely, 'we cannot tell. The poor fellow may have made the journey to break bad news in person. Or it may be simple coincidence. However, you may be able to clarify it a little.' He dug in his fob pocket and produced the little pouch.

She gave no sign of recognition.

'Let me show you this, then,' he said, his tone full of warning. He tipped the ring on to her open palm.

All colour drained from her face, even from her the lips.

In a second Dr Hansard had seated himself beside her, smelling salts to hand.

She waved him away, in a little show of irritation. 'The ring was my late husband's. Having some foolish – we then thought – premonition that he would die before Hugo returned from the war, Chase pressed it on to his finger at the moment of departure. Nothing would have separated Hugo from that ring. Unless he was dead,' she conceded bleakly.

'There is another interpretation, my Lady – a much more positive one,' Dr Hansard declared. 'Imagine he was unable to reach you and sent his envoy on ahead with proof of identity! Alas,' he added in more sober tones, 'we cannot know which is correct.'

'*Dum spiro, spero,*' I suggested.

But for long moments she stared into the middle-distance, unaware, I would have sworn, of our presence. Dr Hansard stepped across to the decanter, pouring half a glass of wine, which he placed gently in her ladyship's hand. Almost visibly coming to her self, she agreed to take a sip. Then, something like gaiety returning to her eyes, she insisted that we join her too. 'Provided that we drink a toast, gentleman: to Hugo – no longer Viscount Wombourn but now Lord Chase.'

'To Lord Chase,' we responded.

The glasses set aside, we discussed our next moves.

'Will you make enquiries,' Lady Chase began, 'about the poor man who died so close to warmth and shelter? I will bear all his funeral expenses, Tobias, it goes without saying. When Furnival returns from Warwick I will ask him in which journals he placed advertisements.' She rang. A maidservant appeared as promptly, as magically, as they did at my parents' houses. 'The moment Mr Furnival enters the house, send him up here. The very instant, do you understand?'

The girl bobbed a reply and scuttled off.

'Pray, your Ladyship, do not make demands so particular,' Edmund begged her. 'Normality – that is the key.'

She made a moue, half-irritated, half-apologetic. 'Soon we can determine what to do next. Oh, what it is to be a woman, and unable to help you in your search for the truth.' She beat her fists on her lap in frustration.

I began to understand why Mrs Hansard should have joined Toone in his examination of the corpse.

'And worse, my Lady, to be unable to confide in a soul,' Dr Hansard added with quiet authority. 'No. I pray you, not a word to anyone. Anyone at all except us – and my dear wife, of course.'

'But—'

'Your Ladyship, if someone killed this man, it could have been because he did not want you to receive the information he carried. It is not inconceivable... Madam, the last thing I want is to put you in danger.'

'Danger? Nonsense, Dr Hansard. From whom could I possibly be in danger? From revolutionary villagers? We are not in France.'

'And I thank God for it. I was thinking of danger rather closer to home, Lady Chase.'

She stared, regally. Rarely have I seen her regard someone *de haut en bas* but that, for an instant, was what she did now. As Edmund met her eye, unflinching, she dropped her pose, however, and burst out laughing. 'My dear friend, the only fear I have from Sir Marcus and his family, still clinging on like bedbugs despite the clemency of the weather which clearly permits travel, is being *bored* to death. I know our young friend here has a *tendresse* for Sir Marcus's pretty sister, but in truth, she lacks conversation, and has this much courage in love.' She snapped her fingers. 'Discouraged by my idiotish nephew from casting her eyes in the direction of the only eligible man in the neighbourhood, indeed. Oh, poor Tobias, did you not know? I am so sorry. He means her to make a good match – a profitable one, in other words.'

I stared at the carpet, my face, even my ears aflame.

'Come, Tobias, you may have the demeanour of the humblest clergyman, but I know that your family is one of the most noble in the country.' She watched me intently. 'Poverty was not thrust upon you: you chose to embrace it. Why?'

Why on earth had she chosen this moment to make such an enquiry? Fearing she would not approve my opinion of the origins of old families, I cast around for an explanation that would convince her without sounding sanctimonious. This was not a room in which one repeated what Our Lord said about rich men and the eyes of needles. At last I smiled, at her and at Dr Hansard equally. *'Noblesse oblige,'* I said.

I was spared the need to elucidate by a knock at the door. It was Furnival, still dressed for travel. He gave the half-bow her ladyship preferred from her household.

'Dear Furnival, I wonder if you would be so kind as to tell me in which journals you placed advertisements asking for tidings of my son, Lord Chase.'

'Advertisements, my Lady?' Furnival repeated, as if the sudden warmth of the parlour fire had melted his wits.

But there was no warmth in her ladyship's voice. 'Advertisements, Furnival. For news of my son.'

He shook his head as if doubting what he heard. 'I have tried all the provincial periodicals once or twice, without success. But of late I have confined myself to the *Morning Post* and the *Times*. I believe the last one in the latter would have been inserted in early October. But I assure you, my Lady, that there have been no responses, none at all.'

'Of course there have not. I merely wished to enquire. And the advertisements will continue at regular intervals?'

'I fear it is no more than throwing good money after bad, madam.'

There was no doubting her fury. 'You wish to desist in our efforts to find Lord Chase? Good God, man, how can that be a waste of money? Spend all this and you do not spend half enough.' In her rage, her ladyship strode to her writing desk and produced a purse, which she flung down. It shot off the polished surface and landed at Furnival's feet.

No one moved.

Even though his position as a most loved and trusted retainer had surely given him the right to mention his misgivings, I was shocked that he had questioned her orders. I was even more shocked, truth to tell, by a side to her ladyship I had never seen before. He bent painfully slowly, scrabbled on the floor with his poor swollen fingers, and straightened with what dignity he could.

'Thank you, Furnival.' It was not an expression of gratitude. It was the coldest dismissal. Lady Chase waited till he had quitted the room before saying, 'October. London. So can we *deduce*, Dr Hansard, that that is where the poor dead man came from?'

'We can make an intelligent guess that it was, Lady Chase, but that is all.'

'If we make it our premise,' I rushed in, 'then I will set out myself in the morning.'

Her ladyship flung up her hands. 'And now I will have to demand my purse back from Furnival,' she said ruefully. 'Or humbly ask him to supply me with guineas.'

'It would be good to return to friendly terms with such a loyal servant,' I began.

'Not so friendly that you tell him the reason why,' Hansard put in. 'No, Tobias. No, your Ladyship. All this is too hasty. Tobias cannot dash off anywhere without knowing whither he is dashing. We must put local enquiries in train before he makes a grand assault on the capital. There is, after all, another enquiry to make – what has happened to the young woman who found the corpse? Where is Miss Southey, and why did she disappear so swiftly?'

The person who should be able to answer that was of course, Sir Marcus, deny it as he might. By chance, we encountered him with his wife on the main staircase. However, before we could raise the matter, he pressed on us an invitation for dinner, overriding whatever Edmund was trying to say.

'Nay, I insist, gentlemen – my wife and I will not take no for an answer, will we, my dear?'

'But—' I objected weakly. How could we cross-question a man in a social situation? In any case, I could scarce forbear to glance at my watch – surely it was almost five o'clock already.

'You will recall we now keep town hours, gentlemen.' His bow was an uneasy mixture of the arrogant and the ingratiating. 'No, I will accept no excuses. Lady Chase herself has promised to honour us with her company at seven. Dr Hansard, what do you say?'

Whether or not Edmund felt similar inhibitions, he responded with a civil bow. 'My wife and I would be pleased to accept your invitation,' he said clearly, with what I saw as a challenge in his eye. Lady Chase treated Mrs Hansard as an intimate friend, but the presence of a *mere* doctor's wife might not be as welcome to this upstart.

'Excellent,' Sir Marcus declared, not missing a beat. 'A new batch of music arrived this very morning, Mr Campion. I trust you will not disappoint my sister?'

I already had done that, of course, with my chosen mode of life, but let that pass. In any case, Lady Chase's words about Lady Dorothea still ringing in my ears, I felt positively queasy. Nonetheless, forbidding myself even a glance at Dr Hansard, I declared I should be charmed indeed. 'Will Lady Bramhall be pleased to play on her harp?' I pursued.

A curtsy and a blush were my reward. Indeed, despite the

length of our acquaintance, she was still more of a simpering miss than a matron in her behaviour. No wonder her daughters were so lacking in savoir-faire with such a model before them. And with such a domineering father, no wonder they were bullies. I could always treat them as if they were subjects of scientific inquiry. Perhaps if I did so, I would after all look forward to our conversations this evening.

CHAPTER SEVEN

I returned to the rectory to change for dinner, thanking goodness, for once, that the Bramhalls had persuaded Lady Chase to adopt London hours for dining. As I hurried past the churchyard, I saw Simon Clark still at work tidying some graves, although it was nearly dark. He deserved my courtesy as much as the Bramhalls did, so I stopped to greet him.

Simon seemed pleased to be interrupted. He leant on his scythe, contemplating the mound he'd just neatened, though the grass hardly grew at this time of year.

I complimented him on his endeavours. 'You have another grave to prepare now, of course, Simon. That poor lost soul. Lady Chase has undertaken to bear his funeral expenses.'

'That man Dr Hansard cut open?'

How on earth did he know that?

He spat. 'It's not right, Parson, that it isn't, opening a man's insides. With Mrs Hansard under the same roof, too.'

Little did he know how closely I shared his feelings, but I said bracingly, 'Dr Hansard and Dr Toone merely wish to learn more about the poor man's death, and they believe that is the best way.'

He straightened and looked at me sideways. 'Learning more, indeed. He's dead, that's what he is, and that's all you can say.'

I was sure there was much more to say. However, it was not an argument I wanted, but progress in my enquiries. 'What we really must discover now is his identity.'

He narrowed his sad eyes. 'Seems he's mighty important, with all this fuss.'

'My friend, if your son were lying in a strange churchyard, would you not wish to know? Until we know his name, we cannot can trace his family. They will never know what fate befell him, never be able to mourn him.'

''Tis no worse than losing a lad to they press gangs for godamany years,' he argued. 'And what the head doesn't know the heart can't grieve over.'

'And while there's life there's hope,' I agreed ironically. Seeing no response, I continued, 'But Simon, you can't want an unnamed gravestone in the area you tend so diligently. Let us make an effort to lay this man to rest with all due dignity – and dignity, to my mind, involves a name.'

Jem received the prospect of curry soup with pleasure, having, he said, often enjoyed it at Langley Park. He had kept to his room, he assured me, toasting himself before the fire which even now glowed brightly.

'I did venture out to your study, Toby,' he confessed, 'while young Susan stripped the bed and made it anew. I brought these back with me.' He patted a pile of books on his fireside table. But he somewhat negated his good report by succumbing to a bout of sneezing. He waved me away with the hand he was not employing with his handkerchief, and I did not argue.

Changing with some haste, I set off as briskly as I could. It was already dark, and the gig's puny lamps did little beyond warn other travellers that I was on the road. However, not many folk stirred abroad at that time of night, and though I made my way unhindered to the main gates of the Hall, Old Mother Powell was just about to close them. Since Mrs Trent had charged me to deliver a fine cake, I hopped down.

Nothing ever seemed to give the old lady more pleasure than to dose me with her cowslip wine, which she reckoned was a powerful preventative of all ills from gout to the ear ache. My theory was that, having drunk enough of the innocent-seeming but potent brew, one cared not what ills might afflict one.

'No Master Jem?' she demanded.

I explained that he was unwell. In her mind a common cold became inflammation of the lungs, and the sounding of the death knell.

'To be sure, you must take him a bottle of my blackcurrant wine,' she said.

'Blackcurrant?' I repeated stupidly.

'Ah, you were thinking of my cowslip wine. Cowslip is a wonderful preserver of health, Parson, but if you've succumbed to an ailment, then it's my blackcurrant wine you need. Come along in and I'll find you a bottle. He's a good young man, Jem,' she said, bustling ahead of me, 'always ready with a smile and a jest. Cheers Mr Powell up something proper when he's in his dismals.' Mr Powell was so old that he was in truth little more than Lady Chase's pensioner, his wife carrying out all the duties she could and other estate workers undertaking anything she was unable to tackle.

Before I knew it I was inside her kitchen, a glass in my hand. I raised it to Mr Powell, who, slumped in a Windsor chair, responded with a sad smile. At last, his wife produced a nip for him, too, though this was a different colour – rosehip gin, she said. She'd heard it might cure his joint pains, and even if it failed in that regard it would warm his old heart.

'It is not I who am unwell,' I protested, 'and indeed, I am expected any moment at the Hall.'

'Just a sip will set you up nicely. There's bad things happening up there, they tell me. Poor Miss Southey.'

I sat on the stool she had polished with her apron and raised the liquid to my lips. Never had the call of duty been so sweet. 'What was it that occurred at the Hall that resulted in her dismissal?'

'With no roundaboutation, the story is that she set her cap at you, Parson,' came her unflinching reply.

'Come, Mrs Powell, you know that the young lady never lifted a flirtatious finger in her life.'

She regarded me steadily, her eyes bright despite the mesh of wrinkles surrounding them. 'Nor, I'd stake my life on it, did you compromise the poor girl's reputation.'

I gasped. 'I–I—'

'Of course you didn't,' she said comfortably. 'Indeed, the talk downstairs is that you are sweet on Lady Dorothea, though I always say—' She stopped abruptly.

'Say what, Mrs Powell? You know that nothing will go beyond these four walls.'

She looked at me appraisingly.

'Come, we are old friends, are we not?'

She swallowed hard. 'Indeed, sir. Which is why I always said you had too much sense.'

Now it was my turn to blush. 'Lady Dorothea is a very talented and attractive young lady.'

'Yes, indeed. But as I have always said to them as match-made, sir,' she added firmly, 'you want someone like Mrs Hansard, and that's the truth. Pretty faces won't make a clergyman's wife, and no more will fingers clever on the fortepiano. A young Mrs Hansard,' she concluded with a nod.

'And will you look out for such a one for me?' I asked gaily. The cowslip wine must have been even stronger than I remembered. I set the glass aside firmly, though it was still three-quarters full. A gleam in Mr Powell's eye told me it would not go undrunk.

'With all my heart.'

It was clearly time to bring the talk back to more conventional lines. 'So, Mrs Powell, what really made them dismiss Miss Southey?'

'And without a reference they did, God help the poor young lady. At least that's one thing that's said, though 'tis also put about that she left of her own accord. It was all done behind closed doors, sir, you know how it is, and ask how I might I can't find the truth. Those young minxes might have had something to do with it. Always trying to find fault, just because she was trying to cure *their* faults. It was they that told Sir Marcus about the fires lit to give her comfort in her room, and next thing Mrs Sandys knew was that fires were forbidden and she threatened with I don't know what if she disobeyed. And her having to support her old parents, too.'

I nodded slowly. Perhaps that explained Mrs Sandys' hostility to me.

'Sir Marcus said Miss Southey was invited to the drawing room every evening and had no need of a fire. And then he would have her play to them all. It was almost as if...'

'Go on, please.'

''Tis said it was almost as if they were goading her, like boys teasing a stray dog. But she never snarled, never gave any cause to dismiss her. And suddenly, there she was, gone.'

'Someone must have seen her depart?'

'Not according to what they say. And neither did I, Mr Campion. I may be slower than I was, but I've still got my eyes and ears, thank the Lord. And I swear to you I saw neither hide nor hair of her passing through my gates.'

I did not even raise an eyebrow to question her. If she said it was so, it was so.

'Which makes me think she must have been in such disgrace as to be sent out through the servants' gate – oh, yes, did you not hear? Seems Sir Marcus has taken it on himself to open the old lodge gates, to keep working folk away from the gentry.'

'Has he indeed?' What had Lady Chase made of that? 'Thank you for telling me all this, Mrs Powell. It makes my task easier.'

She stood up, smoothing down her spotless apron. 'Task?' she repeated shrewdly. 'Mr Campion, you aren't ever going after her? Now, that would set tongues a-wagging.' She shook her head disapprovingly.

'Did anyone mention a loving home? Even distant relatives

with whom Miss Southey might seek sanctuary? No? Well, tell me this, Mrs Powell, how may a young woman, alone, unattended, with little money, and, I hazard, no references, find her way in the world?'

'Indeed, I know not, Mr Campion. 'Tis a sad fix to be in. But take care not to make her difficult situation worse.' She stared at the fire for a moment before continuing. 'If you ask questions, Mr Campion, people may remark upon it. But if an old gossip like me asks where Miss might be travelling, it's only to be expected, isn't it? And I've got plenty of people passing this way every day. Trust me, I shall keep my ears open.'

I grinned like the schoolboy she treated me as. 'I'm sure you will and I thank you for it.'

She patted my hand – it might just as well have been my head. 'We see alike, Mr Campion. Now, tell Jem to dose himself on that blackcurrant wine, regular as clockwork, and pray send my very best compliments to Mrs Trent on that fine cake…'

My late arrival at the Hall went unremarked since the Hansards were even later, if only by a minute. While not exactly saying that I had accompanied Hansard to his patient's sickbed, I let it be assumed that that was the case. Edmund and Maria rose handsomely to the occasion, as if they guessed that I had been doing something I would rather not disclose. As always in dress they were truly the gentleman and lady: his evening wear was at least the equal of Sir Marcus's, and she looked rather better than Lady Bramhall, possibly because she held herself like a queen.

We were received, as before, in the bitter damp cold of the

entrance hall, and for what was to be no more than a family gathering, too. However, the moment our outer garments were respectfully borne away, Lady Chase descended the stairs and in person requested the pleasure of all the company in her salon. Sir Marcus was inclined to bluster, but she quelled him with the merest lift of her eyebrow and within moments we were ensconced in the warm and gracious room.

To the surprise, no doubt, of her family, but not of her three guests, she had provided her best champagne, occasioning an ill-stifled exclamation at the expense from Sir Marcus. The girls were provided with ratafia. If we conspirators minutely lifted our glasses in a secret toast, no one remarked on it – except for Lady Dorothea, tonight in the most vivid pink, the button holes picked out in gold, who appeared to assume that I was honouring her. With hardly a blush, she curtsied deeply, and then raised her glass quite particularly to me. Perhaps rumours of my family's rank had at last reached her brother, and he now wished her, in the common phrase, to set her cap at me. How should I respond?

Would I – should I—? I knew not what I should do, other than maintain the dignity of ordinary polite behaviour. That was how I had always behaved here at the Hall – and, I hoped, elsewhere. But until I had had a period of quiet – and prayerful – reflection, I resolved to avoid what papists call, I believe, the occasion for sin.

So I moved into the neighbourhood of her nieces, determined to extract as subtly as I might the details of their treatment of Miss Southey. Would they be prone once more to unseemly giggles? Or would what they had witnessed have brought them to sobriety?

'I trust you are none the worse for the distressing events of Monday?' I asked, in the low voice I reserve for invalids.

Lady Honoria responded with a simper. 'Indeed, sir, we have hardly had a wink of sleep since.' She added a great deal more, as if she were an ailing Bath dowager, not a strapping schoolroom miss.

Since both young ladies looked in the rudest of health, I suspected that this was a mere conversational gambit designed to elicit a compliment it gave me no pleasure to offer. 'Permit me to say, however, Lady Honoria and Miss Georgiana, that whatever you suffer within, without you are in the best of looks.'

Both bowed, concealing their faces behind matching fans – chicken skin, far too extravagant for girls not yet out.

'I was sorry not see Miss Southey before she departed,' I continued. 'Was it the shock of what she found that impelled her to quit the place?'

One shot a look at the other. 'It was found – she did not suit,' Georgiana managed.

'For what reason?' I asked, trying to keep my voice light. The last impression I wished to give was that I might be interrogating them.

Miss Georgiana gave a minute shrug of her silk-clad shoulder. My mother would have sent her back upstairs to change into sprig muslin, far more suitable for a girl her age. 'She did not suit,' she repeated. Her voice was as cold as her father could have wished.

'I am sorry to hear that. But I trust that her absence will not mean that your accomplishments will lapse?'

'We are to have a London dancing-master,' the elder sister informed me languidly. 'And an art-master from Leamington.'

I bowed. They were to construe that I was satisfied, even impressed, by the likelihood of their future attainments. 'I trust you will not let your more scholarly accomplishments lapse.'

'Pooh, as to French and the globes and such, we are no longer in the nursery, Mr Campion. We are to come out in the spring, provided that Aunt Chase will—'

Her younger sister cut in swiftly, 'Family circumstances being appropriate, Mr Campion. Now, if you will excuse us, I believe our mother requires our presence.'

I could conceive of nothing less likely, but rose and bowed them on their way. So the Bramhalls were hoping that Lady Chase would fund the extremely expensive business of a society launch. It was hardly surprising. What was surprising, however, was that both daughters were to be brought out at the same time, when the custom was for the elder to shine and catch her husband before the younger was allowed out of the schoolroom for anything more than informal dances. I wondered what Lady Chase would make of the idea when it was broached.

In the absence of the girls, I found a more pleasant situation beside Mrs Hansard, who, despite all her accomplishments and indeed her personal friendship with Lady Chase, was being patronised by our insufferable host. He surrendered her swiftly to me, and disappeared from the room.

She said quietly, 'May I suggest that you gentlemen agree to linger over your port this evening? It may well be that I might winkle out more of a girl's secrets than a young gentleman like yourself.' She patted my hand in a most uncharacteristic way with her folded fan, as if she had aged twenty years into an old lady like Mrs Powell and was treating me as an honorary son. 'But tell me, Tobias, how does our friend Jem?' she asked, almost under her breath. Clearly one did not speak warmly of the lower orders under the long faces of the Lely portraits of Lord Chase's ancestors.

I responded in kind. 'He compares his nose unfavourably with a pump. He keeps to his room, apart from sorties into my study for reading matter, and looks forward to your curry soup. I have hopes that he will be ready to return to the world by Friday.'

'Excellent. Ah, our hostess – our aspiring hostess, I should say – is preparing to gather us up for supper. Now, what will be the order of precedence, I wonder?'

'Order of precedence? For a family dinner?'

'You mark my words,' she said darkly, turning with a simper to Lady Bramhall.

Naturally, Sir Marcus led in Lady Chase. Then I was asked to give my arm to Mrs Hansard, whose husband led in Lady Bramhall. On any other occasion I would have been delighted by the arrangement, but on this occasion I feared it would limit my ability to interrogate the family subtly.

Even though we were dining *en famille*, the table had not been much reduced and the hideous epergne squatted determinedly in the centre of the table. As often before, I wondered why Lady Chase tolerated such intrusions into her routine. Did she not care? She had the authority to do anything in her late husband's home until the law decreed that her son was dead and that Sir Marcus was indeed the new Lord Chase. Or was she saving her powder for a more significant engagement? If that was the case, when might the next skirmish be?

A glance along the table told me that Dr Hansard was

deeply involved in conversation with Lady Bramhall, who was for once waxing quite loquacious. For all her faults I had not considered her a lady who indulged in imagined ill health, but from his expression of deep concern I could not imagine that she was doing anything but listing symptoms. With a blush I realised how little I knew about either of the Bramhall ladies.

My lapse in manners drove poor Mrs Hansard to seek conversation on her other side, a fact for which apology was certainly due – until I realised I might have afforded her precisely the opportunity she sought to speak with Lady Honoria. Without wishing to appear ill-bred enough to try to eavesdrop, I wished I could have heard the conversation, which was no doubt to elicit information that the young lady did not realise she was revealing. I prepared to concentrate on what was on my plate and in my glass. The former was excellent, as you would expect from Lady Chase's French cook; the latter, despite the care with which Lord Chase had laid down his cellar, was thin and sour. I suspected Sir Marcus's hand. I left it undrunk.

It became apparent that Lady Dorothea, seated the far side of the table, was preparing to flout convention, and even the epergne, to converse with me. My heart bubbling uneasily within my breast, I responded. I tried to persuade myself that had she been present the afternoon of Miss Southey's immersion in the stream, she would indeed have tried to comfort her. Soon I was listening to the latest musical news from London, and we had undertaken to attempt a new duet together.

Despite my desire to return to the drawing room and the piano as soon as possible, as the covers were removed, I recalled Mrs Hansard's advice that I must dawdle over the port. Since Hansard helped himself to a regular bumper, I assumed he was acting under similar instructions. My suspicions were soon confirmed. When Sir Marcus stepped from the table to relieve himself, the moment he was behind the screen, Edmund was on his feet too, emptying the greatest portion of his port into a convenient hothouse plant. A jerk of his head told me to follow suit.

I know not whether the wine benefited the health of the gaudy specimen. But at least we both kept clear heads, and encouraged our host to dip deep.

'Come, Bramhall,' Edmund urged at last, his speech a little slurred, as if he were half-sprung, 'tell me, man to man, what passed between you and that little governess of yours. I can't believe that either of your lads gave her a slip on the shoulder,' he added with a leer, implying that they would not have succeeded while an attractive older man might.

'That bracket-faced female,' he sneered.

'No need to look at the fireplace when you poke the fire,' Edmund cackled.

'Never had an eye for an ape-leader,' Bramhall declared conclusively.

'So you'll be looking for a prime article to replace her?' I suggested.

'No. Girls too old for a governess, they tell me. Two daughters. Glad to have them off my hands. Not in the basket, you understand, but not too flush in the pocket.'

'Good job her ladyship's full of juice,' I suggested. 'Keeps the duns at bay, at least.'

'Don't like living on the expectation. Don't like swimming in the River Tick.'

'So will you pursue a law case to have her son declared officially dead?'

'Why bother? Living here like lords, eating the fat of the land – any that's left, when her ladyship's fed the five thousand. And I blame you for that, Campion – all these charitable works of yours.'

I did not need Edmund's kick on my shin to keep my tongue in check. 'So you're just biding your time?'

'After seven years – declared dead. Why bother feeding those gull-gropers of lawyers? Just stay here. Sit it out.'

'Her ladyship will no doubt sponsor your daughters when they come out?'

'Swimming in lard – why wouldn't she? Both of them, with luck. Use her London House. Grosvenor Square, good enough for me.'

'But you have your own establishment in town?'

'Indeed.' He set his glass down on the table with a sharp rap. Drunk or not, he would not admit its location.

I made great show of leaving the table and then changing my mind. 'Damn near forgot. Friend of mine wants a governess for his girls. Wife says she's got to be fubsy-faced. Suppose your Miss Whatshername wouldn't want the post?'

He spread his arms widely, to the imminent danger of the decanter. 'How would I know? Upped and offed. Just like that. No idea where she's gone.'

'You did not dismiss her?'

'Wife did. Well, girls did. Gave her a month's notice. Got to do the right thing. Next I knew, she'd gone. No more idea than the man in the moon where she's taken herself. Honest truth. Honest truth. Where are you off to?'

Hansard had also risen to his feet.

'You said we were to join the ladies,' he lied. 'Been making indentures, Bramhall, all of us. Mustn't dip too deep or they won't like it, you know.'

'Me? Bosky? Never!' He lurched to his feet. The expression on his face changed with almost comical speed, and he covered his mouth with his hand. 'Damn me, if I'm not going to shoot the cat.'

CHAPTER EIGHT

I was surprised that even the considerable amount Bramhall had sunk had caused him to cast up his accounts, and to my shame wondered if Edmund might have slipped something into his glass to bring the interminable repast to a close. He, however, seemed as surprised as I by the sudden attack of vomiting, if rather less alarmed.

Bramhall himself dismissed any suggestion that he should retire to his chamber to recuperate, saying he would be well in two shakes of a bee's ankle. 'If I went to bed every time I spewed I'd be a poor fellow indeed – nor do I want physicking, thank you all the same, Hansard.'

'You are often indisposed like this?' Hansard asked quietly, taking the man's pulse, and insisting on looking at his tongue.

'Good wine, rich food,' Bramhall replied, waving a dismissive hand. 'A sip of brandy and I shall be as right as ninepence.'

It seemed he was. Having straightened his neck cloth and mopped his sweating forehead, he seemed improved rather than chastened by the bout of illness. His language became more suited to the drawing room than the stable, and we were soon able to join the ladies with a smile that must at least appear sincere. In the drawing room a sensible conversation about Miss Southey – not to mention about the man in the stream – was not possible, of course. It was as if death and disappearance had been written on a schoolroom slate, and wiped completely clean, lest the very notion disgust.

Accordingly, while nothings were quietly murmured in the rest of the room, Lady Dorothea, dazzling in that extraordinary gown, sang to my accompaniment, and appeared willing to sit apart from the others when the card table was suggested. Hansard, I knew, was so averse to gambling – or so addicted to it – that he would not expose himself to even the mild temptations of a domestic game of whist. As if eager for the privilege, I offered myself in his place, partnering Lady Bramhall. To my amazement, she was a very shrewd player, as acute as Mrs Hansard. Apparently now quite sober, Sir Marcus played with great verve. Much as I would have wished to pursue certain avenues of conversation, I was obliged to concentrate on the cards themselves. At last we lost, but not disgracefully.

The tea tray brought a further general exchange of trivia, and I for one was heartily relieved when we could at last say our farewells. We drove in tandem down the drive, Hansard's groom George attending to the gates himself to save disturbing Mrs Powell. As he closed them behind us he slipped round to my gig. 'The doctor's compliments, Mr Campion, and would you be kind enough to follow him and Mrs Hansard to Langley Park? I understand your bed chamber is ready for you there, sir.'

I saw no reason why I should accompany my good friends,

but would never willingly offend them, so I acquiesced. We arrived to find a good fire still cheering the drawing room, and Burns at hand with the decanters.

As soon as he had dismissed him, Hansard rubbed his hands together less with the cold than with satisfaction, I fancied. 'What a very useful and interesting evening, was it not? Including our *soi-disant* host's sudden bout of nausea, of course.'

'Useful? Interesting? You joke me.' I must, despite myself, have imbibed enough to make me forget my manners. 'In what way?' I added more humbly.

'We have learnt a very great deal we did not know before,' Edmund declared. 'I would never have thought that Lady Bramhall had any power behind the throne, for instance. I had her down as a mere cipher, but Bramhall insists it was she who selected Miss Southey and she who dismissed her.'

'So she will be able to tell us where her family live?'

He spread her hands. 'Let Lady Bramhall be asked to recall as simple an item as that and she reverts to her usual dizzy state.'

'But at least she will write to the steward in charge at their London house to ask him to find all the papers about the girl? Miss Southey must have come with recommendations – surely from ladies of Lady Bramhall's acquaintance. She must remember their names,' I declared.

'Alas, she has regrettably forgotten them too. But no doubt the London steward will have even those.'

'For someone so forgetful, she plays a remarkably cool game of cards,' Mrs Hansard said quietly, accepting with a smile a small glass of Madeira from her husband, who presented me in turn with his usual excellent brandy.

'Do you really think she knows nothing of what has happened to Miss Southey?' I asked. 'Sir Marcus assured us that *he* did not and I am inclined to believe him.'

'I do not think that she does, either. She seemed to think it a natural part of a governess's general awkwardness that she should decide not to work out her notice, and claims to have been surprised when she did not present herself in the drawing room as usual that evening. As for Miss Southey's trunk, she assumes it must now be housed in the attic – it would, she said, be too heavy for Miss Southey to have carried it away with her. But she did wonder that the poor young woman could possibly have left anything behind that she had always regarded as precious. Apparently soon after her arrival Lady Honoria and Miss Georgiana had decided that it would be amusing to ransack the trunk for garments for a schoolroom play and she fell into the strongest hysterics.'

'At which point the girls discovered they had power over her,' Edmund ruminated. 'And did you discover, my love, how Miss Southey came to be up to her waist in water when she came upon the corpse?'

'Lady Bramhall was careful to gloss over that. But my conversation with Miss Georgiana was not unfruitful. It was clear that they considered it amusing to cast poor Miss Southey's bonnet into the water and order her to fetch it – on pain of dismissal.'

'It was a bonnet hardly worth losing your position for,' I recalled. 'But why should she have been dismissed for abandoning her own property? Did they in fact threaten to betray another, different confidence if she did not do it? I remember such "dares" at Eton.'

'It would be useful to open the trunk, then,' Hansard

mused. He shot a sudden smile at me. 'Usually I criticise your want of logic, Tobias, but tonight I applaud it.'

'Open the trunk, Edmund? How will you do that?' Mrs Hansard objected.

'In my capacity of Justice of the Peace. I should have thought of it earlier, should I not?' Slamming a fist into his palm, he sprang to his feet and paced the room with ill-suppressed rage. But at the far end he turned, a smile softening his features. He looked around, and, spreading his hands, declared out of the blue, 'You have made this such a welcoming room, Maria. Welcoming, yet elegant. Occasionally, as tonight, when I am tempted to play cards, I think of losing all, as I so nearly did before. But what I have gained...'

Tears stood in his eyes. His wife rose and joined her hands with his.

Suddenly I realised the lateness of the hour. They did not attempt to detain me from my bed any longer.

It was a very formal pair that presented itself at Moreton Hall the following morning, asking for Sir Marcus and declining to accept the butler's information that his master could not see us until after noon.

'It is not a mere morning call, Timmins,' Hansard snapped. 'We need information of him, urgently.'

'Do not tell me that you wish to speak about this damned governess again?' Sir Marcus demanded, resplendent in a brocade dressing gown as he joined us some ten minutes later in the library. 'What is it now?'

'Sir Marcus, I might equally wish to speak of the man who inconveniently blocked your stream. Miss Southey was merely the person who discovered him. She will, however, be needed at the inquest that must undoubtedly be held. Unless you wish your two daughters to take the witness stand?'

As far as I understood the matter they might well have to anyway, but I remained silent.

Dr Hansard continued, 'Lady Bramhall has very kindly undertaken to obtain information from your London steward.' I could have sworn I detected a flicker of some emotion cross Sir Marcus's face. 'However, we cannot wait until his response arrives. We must inspect Miss Southey's trunk for information about her possible whereabouts. You made it clear last night you had no knowledge of her actions when she left you. So we must seek other means.'

Sir Marcus spread his hands in exasperation, but summoned Timmins again. He appeared with such alacrity I might have suspected him of attempting to eavesdrop.

With considerable – and possibly well-feigned – surprise, Timmins personally showed us up to the attics where Miss Southey's trunk might be expected to be stored. Other servants' boxes and the great pile of travel equipment that Sir Marcus and his family required were clearly visible. But of Miss Southey's poor trunk, there was no sign.

Hansard turned to Timmins. 'That trunk must be located. Do you hear? And before we quit the Hall.'

The butler bowed, removing imaginary dust from his gloves with finicking gestures. Such an expedition was clearly beneath him, but his loyalty to Lady Chase prevented him raising even so much as an eyebrow when he ushered us from the attic as if the steep steps we had to descend were the grandest of staircases.

'If you would be kind enough to wait in the morning room, gentlemen, I will set further enquiries in train.'

'And if he finds nothing?' I asked, impatient at kicking my heels for ten minutes.

'That in itself would be significant. I understand your frustration, Tobias – if only we could obtain all this information instantly. But a few minutes' wait may save us hours of jauntering around the countryside.'

I shook my head, taking an irritated turn about the room. 'We are allowing ourselves to get sidetracked, Edmund. Miss Southey may be an important witness but to the best of our knowledge she is no more than a witness. It is the dead man's identity that we should be seeking!'

'And do you not think I have had poor George careering about the village asking anyone who may have seen him – to have seen *any* stranger – to come forward?'

'I am sure you have – and sure that Jem would have been sharing his task, had he been well. But no one has given us any information at all. Unless—?'

'Unless I have been concealing an exciting development from you?' he asked, kind in the face of my anger. 'Nay, Tobias, you know me better than that.'

Dropping my eyes, I nodded apologetically.

'But I do have an idea to propose. You hold his funeral late this afternoon, do you not?'

I nodded. 'I decided to hold it so late in the day because it meant the men who attended would not have to lose any of their pitiful wages.'

He nodded. 'You have taught them to be compassionate, and those who are not may simply be nosy. I would like you to make an appeal at the graveside for information. You may even promise a reward – which would be gratefully received, in these unhappy times.'

'With all my heart. Edmund, I ask your pardon for my hasty words.'

He shook my outstretched hand, clapping me kindly on the shoulder. 'Too much of Sir Marcus's port, my boy – that is what made you hasty. And with a sore head and sick stomach, I make no doubt. No wonder Bramhall was ill.'

'I hardly drank, Edmund. What Timmins served with dinner was such sour stuff I avoided it. It is not Lady Chase's way to serve inferior wine.'

'But possibly Sir Marcus's way of countering what he sees as her extravagance in offering vintage champagne to her guests. But one may imagine what Timmins must have thought.'

'Of course. And when it came to the port, I followed your lead and applied it to the plants.'

Edmund went to remove his wig the better to scratch his head, but recalled that on their marriage Mrs Hansard had insisted that in future he present himself to the world with his own hair. He looked at his hand in surprise, then applied a finger to a sensitive spot anyway. 'How strange. I have been feeling bilious, too – and dear Maria, the most abstemious of creatures, admits to the headache this morning.' He said no more.

The door opened very quietly, as if Timmins were trying to catch us exchanging shameful secrets. But he too might have been scratching his head in puzzlement.

'With regret, Dr Hansard, Mr Campion, I have to confess that I cannot locate Miss Southey's luggage. I have, of course, enquired in the servants' hall.'

'Excellent. As a matter of fact, Timmins, it would be helpful to speak to those of the servants who helped her carry it downstairs and waved her on her way.'

Never could I accuse such a perfect butler as Timmins of blushing, but it was clear that he was sadly distressed.

'I fear that I have been unable to identify anyone who might have assisted her, Dr Hansard. It seems she had a poor farewell, from folk who should have known better,' he admitted, leaning forward confidentially.

I was unable to imagine him thawing enough to shake the lady by the hand to wish her well, but preferred to nod encouragingly to illicit further information. 'Did she leave on foot? Or was a carrier called?'

'On foot, I understand. In the hope, no doubt, of catching a coach at the crossroads outside the village.'

'A three-mile walk in the dark. No wonder she was unable to take her few belongings with her.'

'She had a bandbox and a cloak bag with her,' Timmins corrected me, adding belatedly, 'or so I am given to understand.'

'Not being a countrywoman used to making long journeys on foot, she would not have been able to make swift progress. And she was, after all, shocked and exhausted by the events of the afternoon. I wonder she was not compelled to take instantly to her bed – even Jem, my groom, has been suffering from a feverish cold.'

'Indeed, sir. I am very sorry to hear it.' Timmins clearly thought it best to bow himself out. 'I will send a message to you immediately I have located Miss Southey's remaining luggage, Mr Campion.'

Dr Hansard coughed. 'I think that despite what you have told us we will call again on Mrs Sandys. Would you be kind enough to announce us, Timmins?'

* * *

Mrs Sandys, whom we disturbed at her window pouring over swatches of fabric, was no more welcoming than she had been the previous time we had exchanged words, but in the presence of Timmins and Dr Hansard she could scarcely keep me standing in the corridor. She admitted us with subdued courtesy.

In Lady Chase she had found a generous employer, at least if her room were anything to judge by. In Mrs Hansard's days as a housekeeper to a noble family, her quarters had been mean and poorly furnished. Mrs Sandys, however, enjoyed a spacious and recently decorated sitting room, according her the dignity due to her position. It seemed that she even had her own serving-maid. At the ring of a bell, a child scarce old enough to leave home scuttled in, bobbing a curtsy. She was sent out to bring us tea and cake.

We waited until her errand was complete before we broached the matter of Miss Southey.

'We understand that you did your very best to make her comfortable,' I began, my smile meant to acknowledge her response to my request, 'but that your efforts were frustrated by people who should have known better – that your orders for a fire, for instance, were countermanded. Please tell us everything you know about Miss Southey, her life here and the manner of her dismissal and departure.'

Mrs Sandys opened her mouth, apparently to bridle.

'You may speak as freely as you wish,' Dr Hansard added quietly, 'knowing that nothing you say will reach other ears.'

In one swift movement she rose to her feet, opened her door, and closed it again, leaning against it for a moment. 'I need this position, gentlemen.'

'And someone has suggested they can persuade Lady Chase

to dismiss you?' Hansard asked. 'I am sure they could not, unless she herself had reason to be displeased with you.'

I nodded my agreement. 'And rest assured that should any attempt be made to get rid of you, Mr Campion and I would intercede. After all, you have been in her household for many years.'

'No, that I have not,' she said, blurting it out as if it were a confession to be quickly made. 'I have only been employed by her for the last few months. And I do not come from the village either, as most of the servants do – having lost their posts when Moreton Priory was left empty.'

So why had she, an outsider, been less than kind to another outsider? But I said nothing, not wishing to interrupt her flow.

'Servants take their lead from the top, sir. And when they could see that Lady Honoria and Miss Georgiana were making mock of her, others took it into their head to tease Miss Southey too.'

'The servants?' Hansard prompted. 'All the servants? From the very top?'

She managed the briefest of nods, but looked around in panic, as if the very pictures on the wall might betray her.

'Was there anyone in particular?'

She wrung her hands in something like agony, but declined absolutely to answer. Ours was not a clandestine visit, after all. Timmins had accompanied us down here – a very senior member of staff indeed.

At last we gave up the attempt. There was after all another member of Lady Chase's household who merited further questions – Furnival, the steward. I deemed it better not to mention to Mrs Sandys that I wished to speak to him, merely quitting her in her room with my thanks and my assurance that Mrs Trent, my housekeeper, would more than welcome a visit from her should she have time to spare.

'Very neatly done,' Dr Hansard complimented me when we had bowed our way out. 'And now to our rounds, yours to cure souls, mine to cure bodies.'

I raised a finger to interrupt him. Then in the manner of a schoolboy, I indicated with a jerk of my thumb that we were to head not for the outside world but back within the Hall – to Mr Furnival's office.

Furnival was seated at a huge rent desk facing the half-open door. Busy with a ledger and quill, he clearly did not wish for visitors. However, he stood and gave a formal bow, not forgetting, presumably, the last time we saw him, humiliated before her ladyship.

'Good morning, Furnival,' Hansard said, taking the straight-backed chair opposite, 'we come to talk about the enquiries that you were making on her ladyship's behalf about her missing son.'

I leant casually against the door jamb. Only as I loosely folded my arms, did I realise how threatening I must appear. However, I wanted no interruption to any narrative he might offer and there was no other chair unoccupied by papers, so I stayed where I was.

'Her *late* son. Gentlemen,' he continued, spreading arthritic hands, 'how can he be alive after all this time? It is three years since the skirmish in which he lost his life. Every officer has been questioned, even Sir Arthur Wellesley himself. Advertisements have appeared in every respectable journal in every respectable city. They have even appeared in Lisbon. But there has never been any response. I have tried times out of number to suggest that any further enquiries are a waste of time and money – her ladyship's pockets are deep but not bottomless,' he added.

Hansard's nod epitomised understanding and commiseration. 'But she will not let this go?'

'You saw,' Furnival said bitterly. 'But even assuming that the deceased man did indeed journey here with an advertisement in his shoe, I cannot see how that gets us any closer to finding Lord Wombourn – Lord Chase, I should say. The advertisement, after all, solicits information of his whereabouts – in fact, it could equally elicit confirmation that he is in fact dead.'

'But would anyone journey so far from London simply to bring bad news?'

'With the promise of a handsome reward, yes,' Furnival averred. 'You will recall that that was what the advertisement promised.'

'But an unspecified amount, as I recall,' Hansard reflected. He gathered himself together and half-rose. 'An estate like this must need a great deal of attention, Furnival.'

'It does indeed. And it is of course only one of the Chase properties. There are estates in Devonshire and Yorkshire, besides the Grosvenor Square house. I have deputies in each, of course, but I remain in overall control.' He straightened; his back gave an audible click.

'I can give you something for your aches and pains at least,' Hansard said. 'I'll get my groom to bring a bottle of linament over. And some drops. Do not mistake one for the other, Furnival, or we shall have another body on our hands. Now, pray, will you be attending the funeral this afternoon? In the absence of the poor fellow's family?'

For the first time in the interview, Furnival looked less than composed. Nonetheless, he smiled. 'I will do my best,' he promised.

Furnival's best was, however, not good enough, and he failed to join the thirty or so kind-hearted men from the village and the Moreton Hall estate who, as the day merged with the dusk, stood bare-headed in the light drizzle to bid their anonymous brother farewell. In my brief address, I invited them to attend the Inquest, due to be held in the great entrance hall of Moreton Hall at the same time the following day, a time chosen by our new coroner, Mr Vernon, lately of Nuneaton. I explained that any evidence at all was vital in establishing the identity of the poor man over whom Dr Toone had scattered the first handful of earth, and there was a general, if subdued, murmur of agreement that the man's family must be found and notified of its loss. The mention of a reward brought a brighter murmur.

The final words and deeds accomplished, Toone – invited to stay overnight with the Hansards – Hansard himself and I repaired to the rectory, where Mrs Hansard and Mrs Trent awaited us. The latter would be on her mettle, no doubt keen to prove as much to herself as to anyone else that the reason I took so many meals elsewhere was nothing to do with her cooking. We were equally keen to prove we meant no disrespect to her skills. She had refused point-blank to join us in the repast however, and Jem, who despite his lingering snuffles had insisted on attending the funeral, retired to join her and George, the Hansards' groom.

Truly Mrs Trent might have been catering for the Prince Regent himself, the meal was so gargantuan and so excellent in the quality as well as the quantity of its dishes. Dr Toone made more inroads into the wine than the food, a fact I suspect did not go unnoticed by Hansard.

'What next?' he demanded after his third glass.

'Wait patiently for the inquest,' I said. 'Much as I would love to leap on to Titus and gallop off in search of the missing Lord Chase, I fear my presence will be demanded on the witness stand.'

'Not in search of the missing Miss Southey?' he asked, with a meaningful lift of the eyebrow.

'It's an unfortunate truth, my dear Toone, that a man cannot be in two places at once,' Hansard said with some forbearance.

But it seemed I might have to be – indeed, that all three of us might. The front doorbell was rung with vigour. Susan was so struck by the untoward event that she bobbed a curtsy and left to answer it, leaving Maria clutching a tureen in mid-air.

She returned in a second. ''Tis Matthew, sir, wants an urgent word, he says.'

Matthew was a gamekeeper on an estate bordering Lady Chase's. Nodding apologetically to my friends, I dropped my napkin on the table and followed her into the hallway. Matthew, taller and broader than ever, filled the open doorway.

'Nay, Parson, I won't come in, not in all my dirt. But I think you should come and see what I've found, and come and see it now.'

CHAPTER NINE

'But it is dark,' was my foolish response.

Matthew blinked as his eyes met the candlelight. 'So it is. I had not realised when I found—'

'What have you found?' My pulse beat hard.

'I am sorry, Parson – this will wait till morning. After all, I can't see it going anywhere.' He started to back out. 'I've left Gundy.' Salmagundy was surely the most ill-favoured dog ever to enjoy his master's devotion. 'He'll guard it.'

The fact that he referred to this find as 'it', not 'he' or 'she' must be reassuring.

'What is it that you have found, Matthew?' I asked. 'Pray, do step inside.'

He shook his head, looking pointedly at his filthy boots. 'Nay, and in truth I was wrong to bother you.'

'What is a parson for, if not to be summoned at all hours?' I asked with a laugh. 'Or a physician, too, for I must tell you that Dr Hansard is with me.'

At this point Mrs Trent emerged – nay, erupted – into the hall. 'For shame, coming to the front door, Matthew, and disturbing good folk at their dinner.'

'And an exceedingly fine repast it is too,' I declared, wishing I had imbibed less.

'But I am sure,' Mrs Hansard declared, with a swift smile as she joined us, 'that if the menfolk must needs go out, Mrs Trent, the two of us together can save some, if not all of it, against their return. And if I might ask you about that wonderful quince preserve...' Taking her gently by the elbow, she drew her away just as the two doctors emerged from the dining parlour.

Matthew looked nonplussed. 'Indeed, I must be dicked in the nob to have made such a fuss. My apologies, gentlemen.' He made to withdraw.

'For God's sake, Matthew,' I demanded with some asperity, 'I do believe becoming a father has softened your brains. What is it that you have found, where is it, and is it truly imperative to retrieve it tonight?'

'I have found a trunk, sir, full of ladies' garments. To be honest, I fell over it in the dark. I would have hefted it here, sir, but I know Dr Hansard doesn't like things to be disturbed before he has seen them for himself – in...in...'

'*In situ*. Well done, Matthew,' Hansard said warmly, over my shoulder. 'Could you find your way back to it? Dr Toone here is not prepared for a walk in the dark, but Mr Campion and I can equip ourselves.'

I nodded. Edmund would never travel even to a social engagement without his boots stowed in his gig, but Toone could not have been expected to show such forethought. However, provided I left him with a full decanter, I presumed he would be happy enough to sacrifice a cold and dirty walk for a pleasant book by my fireside.

Jem joined the mêlée in the hall at this point, but was expressly forbidden by Dr Hansard, even now shrugging on his greatcoat, to venture into the cold night air.

'Not that you'll see much, even by lamplight,' Jem grumbled. 'Why don't you just put a rope round the place, and look more closely in the morning?' He went off, muttering under his breath, the gist of his complaints being that Matthew had more hair than wit and should have thought of that himself before dragging Christian men from their supper.

Had anyone taken any notice of his ill humour, I would have absolved him from blame on account of disappointment. But even as we trudged forth, stopping at the stables to collect the rope he had suggested, I began to admit – to myself, if not to the others – that he was in the right of it. I could only blame our lack of foresight on the effect of strong wine on empty stomachs, and each step away from my dining parlour and all Mrs Trent's efforts made me more regretful.

At last – it seemed many a mile into the woodland, but it was no doubt a mere few hundred yards – Matthew's brisk step became a slower pace. Had he been a hound I would have said he had lost the trail. But at last he plunged purposefully down what his eyes detected as a path, even if mine perceived it as a mere rabbit run.

'Short cut,' he said tersely.

And perhaps it was. Within a very few minutes we were standing still again, at the edge of a clearing. Matthew's cap and scarf hung from a tree like gaudy mistletoe, but it was not that that brought him up short. 'Gundy!' he cried. 'Gundy? I left him here on guard,' he insisted. 'He'd never have strayed from the spot. Not nohow.' He called and whistled, in vain.

I felt a fear so great I could scarcely bear to look about me. He'd raised Gundy from a pup and the two were inseparable. I might think him a brute, but Matthew always spoke to him as one might to another human.

'Over there,' Hansard snapped, pointing and raising his lantern aloft.

'Gundy? Not dead?' Matthew wailed, running straight across the clearing.

Hansard followed, with equal anxiety. In fact he reached the animal first. I followed more circumspectly, aware that we had come here with the specific intention of not disturbing the surroundings. My lantern showed an area of crushed grass some two feet by three – the size, I would suppose, of a trunk – and several deep muddy footprints, confused as if someone had danced on the spot. There were also some paw prints. Had Gundy tried to hold someone at bay?

Meanwhile Hansard had reached the prone dog, and was checking it for vital signs.

'He lives,' he declared briefly. 'But only just. See – he's been hit about the head, and has bled freely. We need to bind the wound before we attempt to move him. How could I have been so damned pea-brained as to leave my case at the parsonage?'

Despite the drizzling rain now blowing in the keen wind, Matthew stripped off his coat and tore at his shirt.

'Excellent. Now, hold him still, while I attend to him. Tobias, more light if you please. What are you doing, man?' he asked tetchily.

'Roping off what I think you will find most interesting.' I suited the deed to the word before coming and kneeling beside the stricken animal. 'Now, how may I help?'

'Seems to me the best thing you can do, seeing as you're on

your knees, Parson, is what you're best at. Have a word with the Almighty,' Matthew snapped.

I did not rebuke him. In the lamplight I could see tears trickling down his cheeks and dropping unnoticed on the dog's fur as he felt up and down each limb. Not wishing to get in either man's way I stationed myself at Gundy's head, hoping that both would get the maximum of the feeble glow. But then I lowered it, finding something of interest in my own right. Hooked on one of his evil-looking yellow teeth was a fragment of cloth. Wrapping my handkerchief firmly round my hand lest he regain consciousness, I grabbed the cloth and slipped it quickly away, wrapping it for safekeeping in the same handkerchief and stowing it in my inner pocket.

Any thoughts I might have had of fetching something to lay our patient on to carry him home were irrelevant. Matthew would carry him in his arms. I had rarely seen him with his new son, but I swear that he could not have borne him with any more tenderness than he did this ugly mongrel. When Hansard slipped his discarded coat about his shoulders, he shook it down so it covered Gundy too.

Meanwhile, I was despatched back to the parsonage to collect Hansard's bag, and to ride with it to Matthew's cottage. It was an eerie experience, one I certainly did not relish, walking through the utterly dark woods with only my night-eyes and a guttering lamp for company. Nay, there was more than that. Mine were not the only feet treading through the undergrowth. It seemed that every rabbit and vole in Warwickshire was on the move. As for my notion of studying owls, it was all very well to consider that in the comfort of my study, but in the open, as they dived and swooped on silent wings – indeed, that was quite another matter.

But I arrived home without incident, presenting myself at the back door so that I did not compound the felony of abandoning Mrs Trent's great feast by muddying her pristine floors. She handed over Hansard's bag with a grunt so disapproving I did not dare tell her that his patient had four legs, not two. Titus grumbled and fretted at being forced into the night air, but, thinking he was headed for the carrots and fuss that always greeted him at Langley Park, set off briskly. Only when he realised that he was bound for somewhere else did he try a little napping. Telling myself he was in fact taking his mood from me, I raised my voice in my favourite hymns, and thus we arrived at Matthew's home.

His wife was by the fire, suckling their baby. Matthew and Edmund had been relegated to the scullery, where they squatted on the floor.

'Will he survive?' I asked breathlessly, caught up in their emotion.

'Aye. He's like his owner, thick about the skull. Hand me my bag, there's a good fellow.' He received it with a smile. 'Now, I know that you're squeamish, so why don't you leave us here and return to the ladies?'

'Indeed I will not. I have already warned Titus to expect a double burden.'

'Well, tell the good fellow I should only be ten minutes.'

It was nearly three hours after we had quitted the dining table when, smelling strongly of lavender water, we at last returned to it. Mrs Hansard had spent her time in the kitchen with Mrs Trent, leaving Dr Toone to the decanter and his vinous dreams. Somehow the ladies' combined efforts had produced a reduced but still excellent array of dishes. By common consent no mention was made of the dog's treatment. I suspect there would have been none except Edmund to argue with Mrs Trent's evaluation of the patient. However, over our port and champagne, I did report on the scrap of cloth that I had found – and, more importantly, on the fact that there was no sign of the trunk or its contents.

'Nothing!' Edmund struck a fist into his open palm with exasperation.

'But to my mind there is evidence that it had been there.' I explained.

This time Edmund's gesture was a smack of applause. 'Well done, Tobias. You and Maria will soon be setting up your brass plate in rivalry of mine.'

'It is one thing to perceive a problem, another to deal with it. I shall leave that to you, my friend.'

Toone was swift to call for a toast. 'To observers all. *The observed of all observers*,' he added with a bow in Mrs Hansard's direction.

I caught, as he did not, an anguished glance between husband and wife. It was clear she felt that if Toone continued making indentures, he would end up under the table. Accordingly I offered a foolish smile, as if I were Lady Bramhall, whose hesitant tones I ventured to mimic. 'Shall we withdraw, ladies?'

Edmund laughed out loud, though I fear that my feeble jest deserved much less enthusiasm. 'Indeed you should, *your Ladyship*. And we gentlemen will come with you, instanter, will we not, Toone?' Since three of us were on our feet, he could hardly decline. At least the tea Mrs Trent swiftly provided and the chill night air might sober him enough for him not to rely on Turner and Edmund putting him to bed.

* * *

The following morning, I had scarce dressed before Edmund rang the front door bell. His bright eyes gave the lie to the previous night's activities. He had, he informed me cheerily, already visited his canine patient, to find him resentful of his bandages and eager for food. Since every time Matthew tried to leave him on his own, he set up a howling likely to be heard in Leamington, it had been agreed that Matthew must stay at home, Edmund making his excuses to his employer and – I suspected – surreptitiously making up his wages.

'Toone lies snoring in his bed, Tobias, and so it is to you and me that the honour of inspecting that clearing falls. It would be good to have something to report to the coroner this evening.'

'We already have something,' I reminded him. 'We have that scrap of cloth that I rescued from Gundy's mouth.' It was safely locked in my desk drawer.

'Of course.' He slapped his forehead. 'How could I forget? Too much port,' he answered himself dourly.

'Find,' I continued, flourishing it, 'a coat lacking this and we have found the one who stole the trunk.'

He shook his head with a pitying smile. 'Oh, you Cambridge men and your logic. Find that coat and we shall have found the one who removed the trunk from the clearing.'

I nodded, chastened. 'But not necessarily the man who put it in the clearing in the first place,' I agreed.

'And your logic tells you it was a man? Might it not have been a woman? Miss Southey herself? Miss Southey was a highly accomplished pianist. Her arms were as strong as a man's.'

I stared at him with amazement. 'But it was so heavy. You

might as well accuse Lady Bramhall of moving it.'

'I could indeed. Think how well-muscled her hands are.'

I could not tell if he was joking. So I continued seriously, 'Could it be possible that Miss Southey had a companion as she left the Court?'

'Very possibly. It is very hard to disappear so completely without assistance.'

We rode in a leisurely manner to the woods, apparently two gentlemen out for a constitutional. We had Toone as a topic of conversation, both of us worried by his hard drinking. He was, after all, no undergraduate to whom a state of inebriation was almost de rigueur. Amongst my father's cronies a state of total sobriety was hardly required after nightfall, but it was decidedly bad *ton* to be seen by your hostess in an addled state.

'The first time we met,' I recalled, 'Dr Toone struck me as an extremely able physician – is his skill impeded by his imbibing?'

'I hope and pray that it is not. Tobias – you knew him at school. What was he like then?'

'Always ready to fly into the boughs,' I conceded. In fact, he had been a vicious bully, at whose hands I had had many an unwarranted beating, and I sometimes wondered if his dedication to medicine might be a form of reparation for a decidedly misspent youth.

'Hmm.' He said no more as we rode into the woods, at first in single file and then dismounting and leading our horses, which eventually we tethered a few yards short of the clearing.

This was much as we had left it, the rope still around the place I had found the crushed grass. Hansard squatted and peered one way and another, but at last his conclusion was no different from mine – that Gundy had tried and failed to defend the trunk. Which might now, of course, be anywhere.

'My logic tells me,' Hansard began slowly, 'that anyone – man or woman – carrying such a weight would walk more slowly and make deeper footprints. Can we see any such?'

'Those there. Probably male? But they could equally well be Matthew's, staggering under the weight of his dog.'

'Let us see where they go.' He picked his way alongside them, tangling with brambles that he swished away with his whip. 'Ah, to the main ride. So they could be Matthew's. But are there any others, leading in another direction?'

Following his lead, I peered this way and that. 'If the miscreant did not wish to be followed, he would surely have made for the main ride too, knowing that the ground was beaten hard and would not betray him.'

'Would he be thinking so clearly? He would not have enjoyed the encounter with Gundy, and might in his panic...' Slowly Edmund returned to the clearing. He stood regarding my rope, as if it might hold the answer. Perhaps it did. 'Was there any blood on that fabric?'

'Not that I recall. Were you hoping for a trail of blood to lead us?'

'It would have been helpful. But perhaps it is not to be.' He lifted his arm, as if to fend off an assailant. 'How high do you think an enraged dog might jump?'

'Gundy? For the throat, I should think. And his intended victim would protect himself thus—' I crossed my arms in the air, a few inches from my face.

He sighed. 'If only we could inspect the forearms of all the men – and women – in the village. Well, Tobias, I cannot see anything to help us here. May I suggest we retrieve your rope and that we make our way back to our homes? We have daily duties to pursue, after all, and I have to sober up Toone for the inquest this afternoon.'

I coughed with embarrassment. 'The evidence about the mud in the dead man's nostrils – will Mrs Hansard...?'

'Take the witness stand? Have you taken leave of your wits, man?'

'I was going to say, be mentioned in Dr Toone's evidence? You must know that the villagers do not approve of "cutting decent folk up", Edmund, even when done by a man. And were word to get out of her part in finding such information, no matter how valuable, her reputation would be seriously damaged.' I did not add that there was enough unworthy hostility towards her from some of the village women, jealous of her translation from being a servant, no matter how elevated, to being the mistress of Edmund's not inconsiderable property.

He put his hand on my shoulder, 'You are right, Tobias. I must point this out to him. Thank you.' He spoke with perhaps more emotion than the occasion warranted. He made an effort to regain his composure. 'It seems to me that there is something else that should be kept out of the public domain for Lady Chase's peace of mind, indeed, her safety – the business of the ring and the newspaper advertisement.'

I hung my head. 'Much as I would like to agree,' I said at last, 'I do not see how we can avoid mentioning them – if asked. We swear, do we not, to tell not just the truth, but the whole truth?'

'Of course. But I tell you now, I fear the consequences.'

Breaking what threatened to become a long silence, I said tentatively, 'Edmund, there are others in the village with eyes more skilled than yours or mine. Should we not ask them to look along the rides? And more important even than tracks, might they even locate the trunk itself, discarded once its contents were removed?'

He clapped me on the arm. 'And who knows what else they might find? Well done, Tobias. Let us set some men on to it immediately.'

Although I had not neglected my duties as the world saw them, as a clergyman I had indeed fallen short: there is more to being a good parson than simply hatching, matching and despatching. So, once back in the village, I made my way to the church, there to kneel and lay my anxieties before the Almighty. Then I praised His Name with a psalm and the Collect for the day. I concluded in what I always found the most wondrous part of my prayers – simple, silent worship. Whatever this search might uncover, whatever the day held, my friends and I would not face it alone.

CHAPTER TEN

Mr Vernon, the coroner, did not give the grand surroundings of Moreton Hall a second glance, as if used to conducting proceedings under the blind eyes of Graeco-Roman gods, and was inclined to regard the gawping of some of the bucolic jurors with a slightly irritated amusement. He was a fashionable-looking man of some forty years, broad-shouldered and erect, with still-dark hair. He was dressed with elegance, his coat surely cut by Weston. He had been provided with an oak refectory table and a handsome but viciously uncomfortable Elizabethan straight-backed chair, both from the gun room. His clerk, sitting a few feet from him, occupied a much lowlier – but probably more comfortable – stool.

Vernon noted with apparent approval and a respectful bow the presence of Lady Chase, whom I had not expected to attend the proceedings. Presumably these would be very short, a question of my giving evidence of finding the corpse, a brief account of our attempts to identify the man, Toone's evidence that he met his death before he fell into the water, and then – pending other information – an adjournment.

I was indeed the first called to the witness stand, but scarcely had I begun my account than Mr Vernon interrupted me.

'You tell me you were not first on the scene, Mr Campion. Might I enquire who was?'

'Two young ladies were beside the swollen stream, your honour, and a third, their governess, was actually in the water.'

'For what purpose? Did she have some idea of assisting what she presumed was a drowning man?'

'I do not think so, your honour. She became exceedingly distressed when I indicated her proximity to him.'

'So what was she doing in the water? Where is she?' he demanded tetchily, looking round as if she might step down from one of the niches. 'Let her answer for herself.'

I coughed. 'Miss Southey is not present, your honour. It seems she left the Bramhalls' employment and indeed the district the same day. She has yet to be found.'

'This is disgraceful. Stand down, sir. Stand down this minute. And let Mr Bramhall step forward.'

His clerk whispered a swift correction.

'Very well, let *Sir Marcus* Bramhall step forward. Not here? Not here? Where the devil is he? He and his governess, flouting the court like this. Parson Campion, a moment, please.'

Halfway to my seat, next to the Hansards, I turned.

'These young ladies you spoke of – their names. And are they present? No need for the witness stand, sir – aye or nay?'

'I do not see them here, sir.'

'Where might they be? And what are their names? I warn you, sir, if you do not reply I shall hold you in contempt.'

Had I had a quizzing glass, I fear I would have raised it at that moment. Humble country parson I might now be, there was still enough of my father in me to resent such Turkish treatment. I permitted myself a frigid bow. 'Your honour, a simple enquiry would have sufficed. The young ladies are Sir Marcus Bramhall's daughters, Lady Honoria and Miss Georgiana. As I said before, they are not present in this court.' I bowed once more and sat down.

'And who might be representing Sir Marcus and the rest of his family?' Vernon demanded, scanning the courtroom.

Lady Chase rose to her feet. Tall, and still elegant, she cut such an imposing figure that I heard gasps. 'I do not claim to represent my late husband, Lord Chase's, family but I may inform the court that, though they are my guests, they do not appear to be at home today.'

Furnival got to his feet and scuttled from the room.

'Indeed,' she continued, 'I understand that there was talk of a carriage journey. My steward is even now seeking news of them.' She bowed slightly and resumed her seat.

'Thank you, Lady Chase,' Vernon said, clearly mollified. 'Now, although this will throw the narrative out of order, I would like to ask Mr Campion to return to the stand. If you would be so kind, Mr Campion? Thank you. So would you continue your account of what happened next?'

I had completed my evidence, and so had Hansard. The only information that caused a frisson was that the poor man had hair resembling that of an African's.

'And was his skin of an appropriate hue?'

'It was no darker than that of a man regularly exposed to the elements, your honour.'

'So he might have been of mixed blood?'

'He might indeed.'

'So the victim could not in fact have been the missing Lord Wombourn?'

'Indeed not, sir. The man in question had, apart from his unusual hair, perfect teeth. I happened to attend Lord Wombourn after a hunting accident in which he chipped an incisor – a front tooth,' he added, touching his own lest there be any doubt.

'What else can you tell us about the man?'

'He was poor. One of his boots was leaking, and he had stuffed it with folded newspaper. His clothes, once excellent, I would say, were threadbare. His drinking flask, which was located in a tussock of grass, was humble pewter, badly dented.'

Vernon looked up. 'Two questions, if I may? How was it found?'

Edmund told him about the search party.

Vernon nodded his approval. 'But I may deduce that this flask was not in fact upon his person?'

'No, sir. Further upstream, where I presume he originally lay.'

'Presume? Presume? Dr Hansard, you are a physician with an enviable reputation, but I must ask you to stick to the facts, not venture into the realms of speculation.'

I dared not catch Edmund's eye lest I explode with unseemly laughter. But, having been rebuked, would he then mention the ring?

He bit his lip, as if acknowledging his fault, and perhaps wrestling with his conscience. Would he tell the whole truth or protect Lady Chase? In the event, he did not have to make the decision for himself.

'Without indulging in theories about how it might or might not have arrived at the scene, did you find anything else, in what sounds like a commendably thorough search?'

'Not I, sir, but the village lad I have already mentioned. He found a leather bag containing a ring. The ring was subsequently identified as one belonging to Lady Chase's son, Lord Wombourn.'

Even the solemnity of the occasion could not prevent uproar at this point. Several women burst into tears, and two men threw their hats into the air with a loud cheer.

'He is alive! Thank God, he is alive! Her ladyship was right!' The room buzzed with comment.

With a most compassionate glance, at last Vernon insisted on silence. 'Let us pray God that this is one assumption that we can indeed make. However, all we may record is that such a ring was found. My profound apologies, your Ladyship.'

Now Dr Toone was speaking of the state of the deceased.

'Mud in his nostrils! What bearing does that have on the case?' Vernon demanded, clearly taken aback.

I shot a surreptitious glance at Mrs Hansard, who responded with what in anyone else I would have said was a wink.

'In my opinion,' Toone responded, 'it shows that the deceased lay face down in mud while he was still alive, dragging mud into his nose as he breathed. Whether he simply lay in the mud, or had his face pressed into it until he expired, of course I cannot speculate,' he added with a seraphic innocence that made me briefly warm to him. 'What I can add was that his lungs contained no water, which they would have done had he drowned.'

'And how did you discover this?'

Toone regarded him steadily. 'In the usual way, your honour.'

'By a post-mortem examination?'

The words cast a chill on those capable of understanding them. As comprehension dawned, a murmur of anger arose. Pray God that for Maria's sake Toone guard his tongue.

He continued, addressing Vernon, 'I should add that decomposition had already begun, of the facial features particularly. Perhaps it is fortunate that the young ladies left the scene before the body was recovered.'

'Very well, Dr Toone – you may step down. But do not leave the room. You may be needed later.'

Indeed he was – but not as a witness. He and Edmund were required in their capacity as physicians, both Lady Honoria and Miss Georgiana succumbing to the vapours as, having returned to Moreton Hall from their carriage-drive, they were summoned one after the other to give their evidence. In public, neither seemed able to explain why Miss Southey should have been in the stream; both retreated into hysterical spasms I for one considered entirely feigned. It seemed I was not the only cynic. Wafting the aromas of Hungary water and lavender vinaigrettes from his nose, Vernon ordered the girls from the hall, bidding the two medical men do what they could to silence them.

As their cries rang down the corridor, mercifully muffled by the huge mahogany doors, Vernon summoned their father to the stand. Clearly it was not to ask for evidence.

'I cannot understand how a man of sense, such as I supposed you might be, should allow a material witness to leave your household – I do not say house, as I understand that you are the guests of Lady Chase. Pray make every effort to find the young lady in question. I understand that Moreton has no village constable to assist in uncovering the identity of the deceased. Is anyone making an effort so to do? No? I am adjourning the case now, ladies and gentlemen, until a later date, but once the session is closed, I would like to speak in private to Mr Campion, if you please.'

Vernon sat in the armchair opposite me, sipping the sherry Mrs Hansard had swiftly provided before she excused herself and left us on our own. A tray of her best savoury biscuits lay at his elbow. It had been suggested that he pass the night at Langley Park, though the reason – it being less difficult socially than Moreton Hall, with the family he had so roundly castigated – was not spelt out. He had no sooner crossed the threshold, however, than Edmund had been summoned to a difficult childbed, and Toone had chosen to go with him, keen, he said, to learn from a master.

'Are you the only sane man in the village, Campion?' Vernon asked with a dry smile.

I shook my head firmly. 'Dr Hansard is both a fine scholar and an excellent doctor. We have a remarkably low mortality rate in this area, his skill in childbirth especially being exceptional. The mother he is attending now could not be in finer hands were Sir William Knighton himself available. If a man like that considers Toone his superior in matters dealing with the dead we must respect his judgement. Meanwhile, Hansard and I have not been inactive since poor Miss Southey disappeared,' I explained, concluding with the information that the search of the woods Edmund and I had yesterday set in train had so far proved fruitless.

'So why should anyone wish to run off with the young

woman's trunk?' he demanded at last, having listened without interrupting. Little by little he was shedding his abrasive manner. 'And risk losing some of his sleeve,' he added with a distinct twinkle. Perhaps I might come to like him.

'As to that, poverty is so rife in the countryside that many folk – and I do not exclude my parishioners – would be tempted by its contents, not to mention by the article itself. And a desperate man might well have tried to kill the dog he saw guarding his potential booty. However,' I continued, adding a further log to the fire, 'I think this is too much of a coincidence. All our enquiries about the young woman's departure have come to naught, and while Lady Bramhall has sent to the steward in charge of her London residence for all the details of Miss Southey's employment – her family, her references, and so on – as far as I know she has had no reply: certainly none that she has vouchsafed to Hansard and myself. You, of course, may have more success.'

He nodded grimly. 'I had wondered why Hansard suggested I return here. But I think he was right to do so. There is something altogether havey-cavey about the doings of the Bramhalls. And one can hardly dine *en famille* with a family of whom one harbours profound suspicions. However, I do think that tomorrow I should press Sir Marcus on the matter of Miss Southey – Lady Bramhall too, perhaps, reluctant as one is to question the fairer sex. But I believe our enquiries must spread further afield.' He rose, smiting one fist against another in exasperation, and took a turn about the room. 'I cannot believe that in these enlightened times you do not have a parish constable. Mind you, I suppose that even if you did anything more than a little poaching and minor theft would be beyond his powers.'

'The missing trunk would fall into such a man's purview,' I suggested. 'Both Hansard and I are professional men, with other responsibilities we cannot shirk. I for one would fain be on the road to London, to make further enquiries about the missing Lord Chase, but in all honour, even if I can provide my flock with a temporary shepherd, I would not know where to start.'

Vernon resumed his seat. 'There are the Runners, of course.'

'But with such a paltry reputation. And with such indolent magistrates in charge of the law.'

'Indeed. I had great hopes that Colquhoun might achieve something, but when he was overlooked and Richard Ford became chief magistrate at Bow Street the chances of turning London into a law-abiding city disappeared. Now all everyone looks for is Napoleon's agents! Oh, I grant you that the horse patrols and the river police have had successes, but where are the means to control those criminal refuges, the rookeries? To rid the streets of petty theft? Of prostitution?' He continued in the same vein for several minutes, reminding me that once I would have had, as the son of a rich household, such interest in the maintenance of the capital's law and order.

Now my concerns were parochial indeed, and perhaps in the worst sense of the word. Somehow, moreover, I needed to return the conversation to my main concerns. Who was the dead man? Where was Miss Southey? And, above all, did the young Lord Chase live?

It was Toone, at dinner served perforce late enough for the most fashionable London taste, who provided me with a sudden spark of inspiration. Or perhaps it was the Almighty, to whom I was able to give thanks not simply for the wonderful repast Mrs Hansard and her cook had conjured from nowhere but for the safe delivery of a lusty son to a mother neither doctor considered in any danger.

All servants having been dismissed, despite the presence of the distinguished guest, Toone was explaining his method of examining corpses – not by any means one's preferred topic of conversation over a green goose, with removes of saddle of lamb, roasted vegetables and macaroni. Apparently he made a sketch of the deceased before he started, with another sketch of each relevant body part as he examined it.

'So you have an image of the man from the stream?' I said, an idea forming itself slowly at the back of my head.

'I do indeed.'

'But it would not be fit for public display?'

'Indeed, it would be fit to show fellow doctors. But to the general populace, no. It would be too shocking.'

Vernon was looking at me as if I were mad. But Hansard gave me an encouraging smile.

'Would it be possible to adjust the sketch, to make it as if it were of the living person?' I pursued.

Toone shook his head frowningly. 'Why should one want to do that?'

'Because it occurred to me during a conversation with Mr Vernon that the majority of Londoners might not be literate – that the newspaper advertisements so assiduously inserted by Furnival on her Ladyship's behalf might indeed be almost useless. Agreed, the man in the stream might have seen and understood it, but what of his associates? If we are to tell his family, his friends, of his fate, we may need another means of communicating with them. We need a picture.' Embarrassed by my long harangue, I drew deeply on my wine.

Vernon smiled slow approval. 'What an excellent idea, Parson.'

Toone shook his head. 'My skills are limited to drawing – not well – from what I see before me. I am no artist, to breathe life into the dead. Sketching of that order is in general a female accomplishment, such as would be possessed by Lady Honoria and Miss Georgiana; and even if it were possible I would not expose such loudly lachrymose females to such as task.'

Mrs Hansard broke the ensuing gloomy silence. 'One task that they may have undertaken, gentlemen, is sketching their governess. She would be an easily available model. I dare swear that they have not so much as entered their schoolroom since her departure.'

'Allow me to congratulate you, Hansard, on such an excellent wife. Indeed, Mrs Hansard, I will send round my groom for them first thing tomorrow.'

'If I were you,' Hansard put in dryly, 'I would go yourself, with the full weight of your authority. They systematically flout my authority as a justice; they may try to do the same with yours.'

'We will go together,' Vernon declared. 'But Toone, having made these anatomical sketches, are you certain that you are not capable of turning them into something…more artistic?'

'I very much doubt it.'

I recalled dear Mrs Hansard's sitting room when she was employed at Moreton Priory. The walls were covered with silhouettes of her own making. Genteel young lady with a drawing master she might not be, but she had the skills and also the cool head to do what we needed. The only question was how to suggest it without betraying her part of the post-mortem examination.

I caught Mrs Hansard's eye, and raised an eyebrow. Having her attention, I mimed drawing and pointed at her. It took her a couple of moments to understand my meaning, but when she did, she shook her head minutely, rolling her eyes in the direction of her husband, as if to convey that she would need his approval. Knowing I could rely on her to seek it in private, I smiled warmly and turned the subject.

The hour was so late that there was no question of us sitting long over our port, although on this occasion Mrs Hansard had withdrawn from the table to allow us men to talk out our talk. Without her presence, however, conversation turned to the intricacies of medicine and it was hard to tell whether Mr Vernon or I was happier when the party joined her for the tea tray, which she summoned almost immediately.

As she poured, she said quietly, 'I have been giving the matter of the trunk some consideration, gentlemen. If we suspect that it was stolen because some poor soul was so desperate to buy his family bread, then perhaps a counter-attraction might win it back.'

'Are you speaking of a bribe?' Toone demanded.

'A reward,' she corrected him mildly.

'Excellent,' Vernon applauded. 'We must draw up some notices for prominent display.'

She shook her head, a twinkle of amusement in her eye. 'You need to tell only the servants here about it, and the news will be about the village by breakfast time. I dare swear the trunk would be found by noon tomorrow. Though with or without its contents I could not say.'

'I will offer a guinea forthwith,' Vernon declared. 'Bid your servants bruit it abroad.'

'They will need no bidding,' I smiled, as Edmund rang for

Burns, who received the news with a smile so superior it almost disguised his eager interest. He might have withdrawn at a funereal pace, but I would wager more than Vernon's guinea that the news would be in the kitchen within two shakes of a lamb's tail.

'Once we locate the trunk,' Hansard murmured, with a smile at his wife, 'what do we do with it then?'

'Guard it,' came her crisp reply. 'Until you have subjected it to the most minute examination.'

'Can you recommend someone?' Vernon asked.

'What about your verger, Tobias?' Maria asked.

'Simon Clark? What an excellent idea. Poor Simon could do with some extra occupation.'

'Indeed,' Edmund agreed. 'He's fading away since his wife was taken from him, God rest her soul. It seems to me these days he's afraid of his own shadow – how he'll manage to uphold the law I do not know.'

He voiced my own doubts exactly.

'But the responsibility might be the making of him,' Maria said.

And so it was settled. By common consent, we sought our bed chambers.

But I did not seek my bed immediately. My desire to set forth became stronger than ever, and spurred me to write to the young man who had cared for my dear flock when I had been called away once before. Trusting he would not be offended – and, more to the point, knowing that he could not afford to travel swiftly without some material assistance – I affixed a guinea under the seal. Feeling that I had at last taken a positive step, I slept as I always did in the benign setting of Langley Park, like a much-loved child.

CHAPTER ELEVEN

I had quit Langley Park before the others stirred. My hosts at least would understand that Jem would want to hear all about the previous day's activities.

I had already rubbed Titus down and was giving him what I suspected was a second breakfast when Jem entered the stable.

'You're up betimes,' he said, unwontedly surly.

Had I annoyed him? Or, knowing Jem, had he transgressed his own standards of punctuality? 'But not, like you, risen from my sickbed,' I said mildly.

'As to that, I am as well as you. And fresh air never harmed anyone as far as I know.'

'Unless I am very much mistaken,' I observed, finding a wisp of straw to wipe my hands, 'it seems to have harmed your temper, Jem. Or have I done something to offend you?'

'Nonsense. Who the devil is that?' He turned as a village lad sidled up, all eyes, wrists and elbows. Since he knew all of the village children, warts and all, as it were, his question was rhetorical.

'Will Pargeter, so please your honour.' Round-eyed, he backed a couple of paces before he remembered to knuckle his forehead. 'With a message for the parson, sir.' He glanced at me, not doubt fearing the same frosty reception.

With what I hoped was a reassuring smile, I put my hand on his shoulder. His bones, like those of many of the village children, were far too close to the surface. Even Lady Chase's largesse was not enough for growing boys. 'And what might the message be?'

'It be from Old Mother Powell,' Will replied. 'Her compliments, Parson, and would you be kind enough to partake of her cowslip wine when it suits you?'

'Thank you, Will. Now, pray run back and thank Mrs Powell for her kind invitation, which I shall be pleased to accept.' I held out a penny payment.

Temptation strove with honesty; the latter won. 'Parson, sir, she did say as she didn't need no reply – that you could drop by when your feet took you that way.'

'Thank you, Will. But please deliver my message anyway.' I pressed the penny into his grubby palm. 'Off you go.' I turned to Jem. 'It's best that he should earn it, isn't it?'

Despite that being his own precept, his nod was grudging.

'Have you breakfasted yet? No?' I persisted. 'Neither have I. Let us adjourn to the warmth of Mrs Trent's kitchen – I can smell the fresh bread from here, even if your woolly nose can't – and I will tell you all that has passed since the inquest.'

'You mean Ann Wood's baby? They both thrive – though I hear that Daniel misliked Dr Toone's presence in his wife's bed chamber. All those terrible rumours about him cutting up the dead,' he explained limpidly, as if he had never so much as looked upon a corpse, let alone used his keen eyes to assist Dr Hansard.

Without asking how he'd come by all that – truly, I sometimes believed that Rumour was the fleetest of birds, the swiftest of animals – I clapped him on the shoulder. 'Come on, man: if the Lord had meant us to be cold He wouldn't have let us have fine closed ranges to warm us.'

At last I let Jem accompany me and a bemused Titus to the gate-house, since Ben needed exercise and I was persuaded that a short ride would do Jem no harm.

Mrs Powell greeted him as if he had but lately risen from the grave. He said all that was proper about her wonderful blackcurrant wine, to which he attributed his swift recovery.

Before we knew it – and despite the earliness of the hour – we were pressed to partake, in Will's words, of Mrs Powell's latest brew, elderflower wine. We exchanged warning glances, but could scarce refuse refreshment altogether, for risk of offending the good woman. It was Jem who suggested he might prefer ale.

In fact, Mrs Powell's small beer was almost as potent as her wine, so we took very small sips. I knew that it was bad manners – and indeed pointless – to plunge straight into the reason for my visit, since she would know it anyway, and asked what I hoped were intelligent questions about her health, her husband's health and indeed the health of all her family, close-by and distant. One piece of good news was that Mr Powell's aches and pains were responding so well to his daily doses of rosehip gin that he had declared himself well enough to walk to market. I resolved to mention this to

Edmund, who was always keen to hear of local cures for all too common diseases.

Without her husband under her feet, she declared, she proposed a proper clean of her kitchen. The clear implication was that we were holding her up.

So – at long last – I could enquire if she had heard any interesting rumours.

'Funny you should be asking that, Parson.'

We all knew, of course, that it wasn't strange at all.

'That young lady governess – Miss Southey. Seems her trunk has turned up. Again,' she added with relish. 'It might be to do with the reward that gentleman from Nuneaton offered. The gentleman that put Sir Marcus in his place,' she explained with some glee. 'Only this time it's not likely to disappear. Crowner's made poor sad Simon Clark a temporary constable. Says if you trust him with the church, he can trust him with the trunk.'

I said nothing of my part in it. 'And the trunk is even now in Simon's possession?'

'Aye, but not at his cottage. They've taken it to Langley Park – I dare swear the good doctor will be sending for you as soon as maybe.'

Hansard had always sworn that the villagers knew what you were doing before you even knew yourself; once again he was proved right. Since I was eager to hear how he had fared at the Hall, I set about making our farewells, knowing that they would take at least as long as our greetings. We were almost on our horses when Mrs Powell recalled that she had promised Mrs Hansard a pot of her best damson conserve, and she tripped off to return with two, knowing, as she said with a twinkle, that I was partial to it too.

'But you must mind they stones,' she added, as I stowed them in my saddle bag, 'for my eyes aren't what they were, and I can't swear as I've picked them all out... But there I do rattle on, Parson, and I haven't told you the real news, have I? You'll be learning all the stuff about the trunk from the good doctor, won't you? But what he won't know, because I've not breathed a word to a soul, you apart, is that the poor governess wench was seen leaving the day she went off. Or was turned off. She left in a curricle, Parson, and that's the truth of it. I never saw her because they went through the other gates. The ones Sir Marcus has had opened up for tradesmen. And I do hear—' she gestured us closer and dropped her voice, lest the very trees betrayed her '—that it was someone very important driving it.'

'Someone very important? Sir Marcus himself, no doubt.'

She raised her eyebrows at Jem's tone, but replied, 'Him! Bless you, no – haven't you seen the way he handles the ribbons, young Jem? Cow-handed, he is,' Mrs Powell cackled. 'There, you didn't know such as I knew your cant, but I always was a downy one.' She chuckled, smiling reminiscently at all the young bloods who had no doubt carried on their loud conversations not realising that the good lady had ears. I hoped they had tipped her well.

'So who was it?' Jem urged, a sneer still spoiling his voice. 'Turning out in the dark of a November night? For a *governess's* convenience?'

'Now, young Jem, I'm only repeating what I heard. And even if you don't believe me, you've no call to take that tone. I'm more than seven! They were saying in the village you were like a bear with a sore head,' she added, looking at him with concern.

'I'm sorry, Mrs Powell,' he said swiftly. ''Tis true I've been blue-devilled these last few days. Indeed, Master Toby rang a peal over me before we set out.'

'Hmm. Well, you get some of that damson conserve inside you, and then we'll see.'

I interrupted their by-play as swiftly as I could. 'If not Sir Marcus, then who was the driver, Mrs Powell? It is truly vital that we know. Possibly a matter of life and death.'

'Don't you think I'm doing my best to find out for you? You young men, wanting everything yesterday…What you need, Parson, is a nice young lady to take to wife – and you, too, Jem.'

We tacitly agreed to ignore Mrs Powell's matrimonial plans for us, and indulged in a boyish race across country, that left us both pleasantly out of breath. As we crossed the water-meadow, we espied Edmund and Mr Vernon bowling back from the Hall, dressed as befitting gentlemen paying a morning call and honouring the occasion with the company of Hansard's groom, George, in his best livery. Naturally we turned our mounts and fell into step with them as they drove through the back entrance to Langley Park.

I knew that this would put Jem in an awkward situation. He ought by rights to assist George in the stable. But that would exclude him from our company, as we discussed the day's news, both from the lodge and from the hall itself. How I could manage it, I did not know.

I was rescued by dear Mrs Hansard, of course, who despite the chill wind rushed out to greet us all.

'For shame on you, Tobias, bringing Jem out on a cold day like this. Look how flushed he is. Do you want him to catch his death? Jem, off that horse this minute and into Edmund's study with you.'

Without prompting, Edmund joined in. 'Have you been taking that paregoric draught I left with you? I thought not.'

It would have been hard for Jem to so much as taste the draught since Edmund had left none. Without a word, however, he dismounted, passing his reins into my safe-keeping, and submitted to being shooed into the house like a recalcitrant chicken. Much as he would want to do his duty, he would have hated as much as any of us to be excluded from our counsels.

So George was left to deal with all the horses on his own. Somehow I did not think that he was deceived for one moment by the subterfuge. At least Jem's dignity was left intact, however.

Dislike Lady Honoria and Miss Georgiana though I did, I had to admit that the sketches they had made of Miss Southey were excellent. Vernon had laid them with a flourish on Edmund's desk. We had all joined the supposedly sickly Jem there, with Toone sauntering in as soon as he heard our voices. After his potations of the previous evening he looked far more in need than Jem of Edmund's professional attention. It was clear that the room would not hold so many in comfort, and Maria swiftly urged us into the library, where a bright fire fought with the greyness of the day. I harboured a hope that Hansard and Jem might return to the study on their own before we left – his current mood was so foreign to him that I was anxious.

Vernon fanned out the sketches on a *petro duro* table depicting brightly coloured birds. Smaller than those in my parents' London house, it was nonetheless my favourite of the genre, for sheer quality of workmanship.

I picked up a sheet of paper at random and looked more closely. Not only did the portrait give an accurate depiction of Miss Southey's features, it also gave a hint of the steel I was convinced lay beneath her consciously bland exterior.

'If only young women could be encouraged to keep up their accomplishments beyond the schoolroom,' Edmund sighed, as he looked over my shoulder. 'There is true talent in the bud here.'

'Indeed. And, should it be necessary, it will be easy to take an engraving from them to put on public display,' Vernon said briskly.

'There is still no news of her from Lady Bramhall? She has still not recollected which of her friends recommended Miss Southey?' Maria asked. 'I confess that I am reluctant to have the young woman's face blazoned abroad as if she were a common criminal, not just someone whom we wish to find for her own sake as much as any other reason...' She tailed off, with a surreptitious glance at me. No doubt we both recollected another young woman. Lizzie, whom I had so much loved, was supposed to have left the district but had been lying in familiar woodlands, murdered and alone. Unobtrusively Maria reached for my hand and gave it a gentle squeeze.

'Lady Bramhall tells us she has asked Furnival to deal with all the correspondence,' Hansard said, adding bitterly, 'as if her days were not filled with idleness and his crammed with as many matters as a man might wish.'

'But Furnival is Lady Chase's steward, not Lady Bramhall's personal secretary,' Maria objected. When she was a housekeeper, she must have been subject to similar impositions on her time from guests with their own servants.

'I hope the pressure of all his other business does not mean he leaves this on one side,' I said.

'I think after the conversation I had with him this morning he will regard it as a priority, his responsibility or not,' Vernon declared. 'I have told him that I shall expect to see all the correspondence by the end of the week.

'There is news of Miss Southey from another source,' I said quietly. 'Jem and I have heard Miss Southey did not creep hugger-mugger from the Hall, but was in fact swept away in some style – in a curricle, no less.'

'With "someone important" handling the ribbons,' Jem added.

'Who might your source be?' Vernon asked.

Jem shook his head stolidly, obviously less inclined to trust Vernon than I was. He was right. We must protect Mother Powell.

'Might it have been Sir Marcus himself?' Clearly there was nothing more that Vernon would have liked that to pick another quarrel with him. He veritably rubbed his hands in anticipation.

'At that time he was supposed to be at dinner with his family,' Maria said. 'You remember, Tobias, Mrs Sandys refused to interrupt the meal – and we were too cowardly to insist.'

'No matter. His presence can easily be verified,' Vernon declared optimistically.

'Would not Lady Bramhall – would not their daughters, in fact – lie if Sir Matthew told them to? And with work so scarce, would not the servants feel it safer to lie too?' Edmund put in.

'We will question them under oath,' Vernon declared.

'Our source is sure it could not be Sir Marcus.' I said at last. 'He drives so badly he could easily have been identified.'

There was a short, possibly disbelieving silence.

'If she did not slip away quietly on her own,' I said, trying to regain the initiative, 'why should her trunk be left behind, then disappear, then be found abandoned?'

'And then moved from where Matthew found it,' Jem added. 'Whoever did that must have wanted it very much, to half-kill Salmagundy.'

'Who fortunately appears as tough as his master,' Edmund put in, 'and will be back to normal within a few days.'

'Why do we not look at the trunk?' Maria suggested. 'It is here, on the premises, after all, and I am sure that Simon Clark will be delighted to surrender it to us while he adjourns to the kitchen to warm himself.'

'Let it be brought into the scullery,' Edmund said. 'It is never warm in there, but at least it is not as cold as in the old pigsty – Maria wanted the porkers moved further from the house,' he added, as he led the way, 'so they now have new, far more luxurious accommodation. Better than most of the villagers', truth to tell.'

If I feared we would find Simon Clark on the old pigsty floor, laid out cold, as Salmagundy had been, I was relieved to see him in one piece, if not a little chilly. Having deposited the trunk in the scullery, he slipped into the kitchen with alacrity.

Mrs Hansard smiled meaningfully at his retreating back. She waited till he had closed the heavy door before she whispered, 'Mrs Benn believes he needs feeding up. And if he had plenty of good food inside him, would he not prove a sturdy outdoors man? His wages would augment his church pittance, Tobias.'

'My dear, you are incorrigible,' Hansard said with a mixture of affection and asperity.

'I do not propose to consign a good cook to the rigours of his cottage,' she replied.

'So this is the trunk,' Vernon said, as one not involved with the villagers' intimacies.

'Who brought it in?' I asked.

'One of Matthew's friends – another gamekeeper,' Maria said. 'He has had his guinea, although he demurred. All he had done was find it, he said, in a tangle of brambles, along with some rags which might once have been a coat.'

'So our thief realised that the dog had torn his coat and disposed of the evidence. Confound him. And the contents?' Vernon prompted.

'I make no doubt that they will soon be keeping someone warm in a neighbouring village – I don't think any of Tobias's parishioners would be brazen enough to wear them, not to church, anyway.'

Toone peered at it. 'Hmm. 'Tis old-fashioned, but good enough. In fact, very good quality for a governess. I suppose one of her previous employers might have handed it down to her.'

I had a sudden vision of some able-bodied man slinging it idly down from the top of a coach to a young woman scarce able to carry the burden.

'Or her family might have fallen on hard times,' Hansard said. 'However it came into her possession, she was willing to abandon it.'

'Not much room for a trunk this size in a curricle,' Jem observed. 'And full it would be mighty heavy.'

'Full. But now it's completely empty.'

Maria had stooped, and was running her hands round the lining. It was still more or less intact, though the once brave scarlet cloth was now largely faded. Then she turned to the rim, giving particular attention to the protruding studs which slotted into holes in the lid to give a close fit. In turn she tried to press or lift them.

'When I had just started in service, I was fascinated by one lady's travelling chest. It was plain and serviceable – just like this – but in the bottom, operated by knobs – just like these – was a secret drawer for jewels, correspondence, anything her ladyship wished to keep safe.'

'But if someone stole the trunk, they'd have stolen whatever was in the drawer, too,' Vernon objected.

'A highwayman is usually in a hurry. He'd tip everything out, grab what he wanted, and flee. That at least was the hope,' she said, her voice slowing as she turned to the lid, subjecting it to similar pressure.

'Why not let me take an axe to it, and be done?' Jem asked.

'Because that would ruin a perfectly good...when...' Now her fingers were running over the exterior. She sat back on her heels. 'Oh, you may have to. But it goes against the grain to destroy something needlessly. And possibly, I have to face it, in vain.'

'Simon Clark is a skilled carpenter,' I said. 'Perhaps he—?'

But even as I turned to summon him, Maria cried out in triumph, and one of the side panels slipped down a neat groove. 'Yes, a secret compartment.'

'And what does it contain?' Toone demanded, like an excited boy. Where was the cool, superior man of the world now?

'Whatever it is,' Dr Hansard replied, 'may I suggest that Mr Vernon removes it and carries it back to the library. It is too cold to linger in here. Mr Vernon, will you do the honours?'

CHAPTER TWELVE

We were all in need of the wine and biscuits for which Mrs Hansard rang, but they went untouched while Vernon unfolded the papers he had so carefully carried.

'Pah! 'Tis nothing but some old bills! From Mr John Knight, Fishmonger, Honey Lane, near Cheapside...fresh herrings, full of roes...a barrel of oysters... And here is another. From Mr Wilson, Purveyor of... Do we really want to know about the man's tea and coffee?' He threw them down in disgust.

'Indeed we do not,' Hansard said quietly. 'But to whom were the bills sent? That might be of moment.'

'As to that – why, to a Mr Chamberlain, of Hanstown. A respectable, but scarcely fashionable address.' He waved the sheet of paper before our noses, and then set it down again.

'Is there nothing else?'

He leafed through them again. 'Some milliner's accounts, and here one from a haberdasher.'

'So we may conclude Mr Chamberlain has a female living in his establishment,' Hansard said.

'All we may conclude is that Mr Chamberlain *had* a female living in his establishment,' Vernon corrected him.

I smothered an inappropriate laugh.

'Are the bills dated?' Mrs Hansard put in quickly.

'All some six or seven years ago. 1803 is the earliest, 1806 the latest.'

I spread my hands. 'Why would someone wish to store old bills in such a private place? Are you sure, Mr Vernon, that you have missed nothing?'

'What did you expect?' he demanded, irascible in his disappointment.

'Something that would have been important to the owner of the trunk. A private letter. A miniature. A ring. A ribbon.' I smiled ruefully. 'I fear I am incurably sentimental.'

'You only voice all our hopes,' Mrs Hansard said firmly, as if daring the others to disagree.

None did, but there was a general reaching for biscuits and sipping of wine.

'Conceivably the bills might serve the same purpose as a letter, inasmuch as they provide us with an address,' Hansard mused. He gave first Vernon, then me, a rueful smile. 'If we enquire at Mr Chamberlain's, it is not impossible that we find Miss Southey once to have been living there.'

'I'll write immediately,' Vernon declared. Before anyone could speak, he turned his attention to Mrs Hansard's needlework table. 'And these? What are these?' He picked up a pile of sketches not dissimilar to those he and Hansard had brought over from the Hall.

But it was not a young woman's face upon them. It was a likeness of the young man whom I had had to bury. A likeness of the living man, not the worm-eaten corpse. I managed not to gasp – Mrs Hansard had breathed warm life into the cold features, and brought a sparkle to the lifeless orbs. Lest I betray her, I kept my eyes firmly away from the artist, but wanted to seize her hand in emphatic admiration.

'Toone, I thought you said you had no talent for bringing to life the features of the dead,' Vernon continued. 'But these sketches – while not as good as the young ladies' work – are excellent.'

Toone modestly shook his head at the praise, but did not deflect it. Clearly he and Mrs Hansard had agreed that her part in the task was best not mentioned.

'So we have someone who, while not African, has some of the features of an African,' Vernon reflected, leafing through them. 'Would he be the offspring of a slave, freed or escaped? Or of a sailor? By an English wench?'

Toone nodded. 'Probably. Which in my book means he hails from a port – Bristol, Liverpool, or some such.'

'Furnival tells us he recently confined his advertisements to the London journals,' I said, 'which would of course be consistent with your theory. So to London we must go.'

'But where in particular?' Vernon demanded, adding disparagingly, 'It is not some out-at-elbows hamlet like Moreton St Jude.'

'Perhaps the face will be known to the Runners,' I suggested. 'And we can have enough handbills printed to slap one on every street corner of every area, rich and poor.'

'But that will take time and money. While Lady Chase may have plenty of the latter, we certainly do not have unlimited quantities of the former,' Hansard said, smiling at me.

'As to that, I have already sent for young Rogers, who was my locum while we were in Bath,' I confessed. 'There were four of us then. But I have been thinking that if I, with Jem, of course, went as what I am, a simple clergyman, I might do better.'

'A poor clergymen might be even better – one without a servant,' Jem said.

I looked at him astounded. Surely he would not prefer to stay behind in the village?

'I reckon I know enough of the church to be another parson,' Jem said, a strange mixture of bashfulness and valour. 'We could work together or singly, Toby – what do you think about that?' he added eagerly.

Good though it was to see his eyes so bright at last, I could not be so enthusiastic about his plan.

But it was Mrs Hansard who asked, 'Of what use would that be, Jem?'

'The way I see it, if you want to go into the parts of London where we might see such folk as our poor late visitor, you need to be able to protect yourself. You're a gentle soul, Toby. I'd be afraid for your safety. But there are other tasks you could fulfil better than I. For instance, with respect, Mr Vernon, rather than your writing to Mr Chamberlain, do you not think it better for the Reverend Tobias Campion to visit this Mr Chamberlain in person? It would be easy for him to fob off any enquiry by letter, no matter how distinguished his correspondent,' he added, with a bow to Vernon, who looked as amazed as if the table itself had spoken.

'Jem is absolutely right,' Edmund said. 'Tobias's sudden and unexpected arrival would allow Mr Chamberlain less opportunity to prevaricate, indeed, to lie. So your plan would be to travel together for safety's sake, then, once you had reached London, split up, you, Jem, adopting Tobias's identity?'

'Or some other. I cannot think that anyone will ask me to prove my identity, can you?' His smile was dry, and that of an equal, not a servant.

And as such Hansard clapped him on the shoulder. 'You are in the right of it, of course.'

'I could simply add the title Reverend to my own name,' Jem mused.

'The Reverend James Turbeville – it sounds very good.' Mrs Hansard declared with a warm smile.

'Or maybe…Yes, I quite like the idea of becoming James Yeomans. That sounds reliable, you might say. Unless you think anyone might object to my pretending to be a man of the cloth?' Jem was suddenly anxious.

'You will not be conducting services?' Vernon said. 'So I can see no difficulties.'

Edmund agreed. 'Nor I. Indeed, I would dearly love to come too, in some capacity, provided Toone here can look after my patients.'

'And I, and Turner, and George, and no doubt Mr Vernon too,' declared Mrs Hansard. 'This is not a time for charades, my dear. If, as Dr Toone suspects, and this poor man –' she touched her sketches '– was indeed murdered, we are dealing with dangerous people. We must do nothing to make anyone suspect that Jem is not who he says he is, or surely his and Tobias's lives will be at risk. And furthermore, we must make no obvious exodus from the village. Perhaps it is best if Tobias sets it about that he has to attend a relative's sickbed. Naturally people would expect Jem to accompany him.'

'On the stage?' Jem asked, with a malicious grin. 'A country parson wouldn't have his own smart equipage, Toby.'

'The Mail?' I countered. 'Once we have arrived in London,

we could then sink into our anonymity at ease.'

'Hire a post-chaise and do the same,' growled Vernon, clearly piqued at his subtle exclusion. 'You want to arrive in one piece. And where will you stay? Grillon's? Brown's?'

'We can decide on that when we arrive,' I said, repressively. I was happy for Dr and Mrs Hansard to know that I proposed that our first stop would be at my family home, but I preferred him to think of me still as what I was – a simple parson. If he suspected my family connections he was likely to start toadying me, much as he expected to be toadied to himself. 'I will of course ensure that Dr and Mrs Hansard are informed of our location – Ibbetson's, in all likelihood.'

My abruptness – I heartily wished that I could rid myself of my habit of unconsciously slipping into my father's tones when I was irritated – was enough to make him raise his eyebrow. Soon we might have had a battle of the quizzing glasses, had I not long since abandoned my use of such things.

'Well, Parson,' he said, with just enough irony, 'if you are minded to travel post, and to do so anonymously, may I offer you a seat in my carriage when I return to Leamington? I can complete the negotiations for you myself so that your identity is never known.'

'I am sure we would be most grateful,' I said with a bow. I wished to make it clear that groom though Jem might be, he was entitled to as much consideration as the respectable clergyman he was going to become.

Jem bowed too, in absolute mimicry of me. As boys he had joined in schoolroom theatricals at my home, but I had never realised how well he could imitate others. He would easily pass for a man of the cloth. If there was a touch of the rustic about his accent, so there was about most of the country clergymen I knew. Better that than the affected drawl of what I could only describe as latter-day prince-bishops.

He now raised a minatory finger. 'It may well be that there is more in that chest. Simon is a skilled joiner and cabinet-maker. It was only when his wife sickened and needed his attention that he gave up the craft. Why not ask him to take one more look at it, before we do anything hasty?'

'Or indeed,' Vernon suggested, 'while you make your preparations. There will be valises to pack, servants to warn – and no doubt some farewells to take. Some feminine hearts are about to break, no doubt.'

'We should introduce him to Mrs Powell – they'd deal well together,' Jem muttered as we rode home together, his need for protection from the cold forgotten.

'They would indeed.' I was in truth wondering what to say to Lady Dorothea. I did not like lying, especially face to face. But I felt I could not simply slip away without some sort of farewell.

'You're not happy about this journey, are you, Toby, or you'd have dashed off days ago,' he said, slowing Ben to a walk. 'Does something misgive you?'

'Not in Hamlet's sense – I don't feel truly apprehensive about our safety in London. Perhaps I have grown lazy, here in this little backwater. Or perhaps I simply feel that there are still too many answers under our noses, if only we knew the right questions.'

'Meanwhile you will say your farewells to Lady Dorothea?'

'Don't make of that more than there is. She looks for a better marriage than to a country parson, and though we take pleasure in each other's company, despite my initial attraction to her, I feel I scarcely know her. Not as Hansard knew Maria before they declared their passion. I am allowed to look at her pretty face, at her figure in those fashionable gowns, but I know no more of her true self than I knew of Miss Southey's. Less. I knew that there was something that Miss Southey wished to conceal. I cannot say the same of Lady Dorothea. She could be one of those wooden figures my grandparents had placed in their windows when they were away from home to make the house seem occupied.'

'What did Miss Southey wish to conceal?'

I slapped my forehead, irritating both horses. 'Some bruises. Jem, one night she had bruises on her arms.'

'What – who – caused them?'

'As soon as she saw I had noticed them, she covered them. For the rest of the evening she made sure that I could not speak to her. At that point, to my shame I was more concerned with Lady Dorothea than poor Miss Southey.'

He shot a glance almost as impenetrable at Miss Southey's. 'She was not an easy woman to speak to. Whenever I addressed her, she made it clear that I was naught but an outdoor servant.'

Did this explain Jem's recent gloom? An unrequited passion? Or a simple resentment that someone just as much as dependent on others as he should treat him as an inferior?

'And now she has disappeared,' I said lamely. 'Driven by someone of importance. Why, Jem, when Gossip simply takes wing with trivial news, is it snail-like with vital information?'

*   *   *

Lady Dorothea was seated with the other ladies of the household. Lady Chase was nowhere to be seen. I knew she spent as long as she could in her private boudoir since she found all the other females irritating for a variety of reasons. Why she did not do the obvious thing and tell them all to return whence they had come I could not understand. My father would have held no truck with such unwanted guests. I once knew him instruct a set of other people's servants to pack their masters' baggage without deigning to mention their departure to the principals involved. My mother was more subtle: the supplies of coal and hot water steadily and inexorably dwindled in the rooms of those she wanted to be rid of. Perhaps the bad wine served at supper the other evening was Lady Chase's version of the ploy.

There was a general laying aside of embroidery and primping of lips. Neither Lady Dorothea nor her nieces was the slightest bit interested in me, but I was a male, and flirting with me was useful practice. I was spared the necessity of an embarrassing tête-à-tête conversation, into which far more than necessary could have been read.

'I fear I have to leave the neighbourhood for a few days,' I said, coming straight to the point as soon as the usual insipidities had been exchanged. 'One of my family is unwell, and I must away to her sickbed.' Had they been interested I could have supplied them with a great deal of invented detail about the good lady, whom Jem and I had decided was the respectable mistress of a select seminary for young ladies somewhere in Kent. But apart from a glib hope that her recovery would be speedy and that our journey would not be too onerous, there was no interest in the lady.

I made my bows, and then sought out Lady Chase, to give

her the same official story. Naturally she needed to know it, and in some depth, lest anyone show a belated interest in the reasons for my absence.

'But in fact Jem and I will be in London. First of all we will stay at my parents' house in Berkeley Square. Whether we remain there or move to more likely accommodation for two country parsons – ' I explained Jem's plan '– will depend on our progress.'

'How will the household treat Jem, if he stays as your guest?' she asked seriously, setting aside her stitching and peering over the spectacles she had but recently affected.

'With luck, since London will be exceeding thin of company at this time of year, my parents will have left at most a skeleton staff, none of whom will recognise him. Heaven forefend that my father decide to visit the capital – he is so high in the instep that the presence of his groom's son in the best guest chamber might drive him into an apoplexy.' I laughed, not entirely sure that I was joking.

'Perhaps he would not recognise him. Now, Tobias, you will take this for your expenses. I know you will be paying your curate more than generously, and that your stipend is mostly spent on the parish. When did you last collect your tithes?' she asked, raising an imperious hand. 'Quite so. So – since this errand is entirely on my behalf – you will accept what I offer. You may keep a strict account if it suits you. And you will make me a solemn promise: the moment it is safe for you to shed your disguise you will purchase for me every new book you can carry. If I am to spend the winter with…if I am to spend the winter here, then I must be entertained.'

'Surely the family will decamp soon,' I said.

'The longer they stay here, the more the threatened legal

case to declare my dear Hugo dead can be postponed. There is talk of my bearing the expense of my great-nieces' coming out. If I must, then I must inculcate some manners and conduct in them.'

'So they will stay with you till they have sucked you dry and then initiate action,' I said angrily.

'Not if you find Hugo first,' she said. Standing, she gave me her hand to kiss. 'God bless you in this noble endeavour, my dear Tobias.'

CHAPTER THIRTEEN

We arrived to find, as we had expected at this time of year, that most of the Berkeley Square house was shut up, with the bulk of the servants in Derbyshire to supplement the usual staff. My father and his cronies would be up there for the shooting I had once thought so important, and their wives would be chattering the sort of vacuous insipidities that drove my mother mad.

There was a long delay between my ringing the bell and the slow opening of the front door. Mitten, the butler, and his team of footmen were obviously in the north, and it was Mrs Tilbury, the housekeeper, who welcomed us. Indeed, her first welcome was hesitant, even reluctant.

'Mrs Tilbury? Tilly? Surely you remember me?' I said, taking her poor gnarled hands and kissing them.

'Master Toby, is that really you? Oh, behave yourself, do,' she added, as I gave her a child's embrace.

Thereupon she fell on me as if I were the Prodigal Son indeed, swearing I had not changed by so much as a whisker since she last saw me. However, her screwed-up eyes and need to hold her face within inches of my own told its own story, and Jem – in his guise as the Reverend James Yeomans – was spared more than a cursory inspection. For several years now my mother had wished to pension her off, but the poor woman clung to the idea that she was still essential to the running of the household. Soon, my father insisted, Mama would have to find some way of – in his terms – putting her out to grass, before she fell down the grand staircase and broke her neck.

'You'll have to take us as you find us, Master Toby,' she declared, gesturing at the Holland covers in the Green Salon. 'Alterations,' she added in a stage whisper. 'One of *those* closets. I tell a lie. Four of *those* closets. And a proper bathroom for her ladyship, he said, though improper's the word I'd use, and another for himself.'

'Bramah water closets?' I asked

'Yes, indeed. But there's no need for you to worry, Master Toby – there's no call for decent folk to strip themselves off in some great empty room, not when they can have a hip bath in front of their bedroom fire. So just you tell your valet that.'

'As a matter of fact,' I said gently, 'now that I am a man of the cloth I have no valet, and neither does my friend, Mr Yeomans, here. We make but a short stay, Tilly.'

'I'll have a fire set in your room this instant, Master Toby, and one in the best guest chamber. Young Wilfred's a decent, hard-working lad – he'll look after your needs. But a rare lot of noise those builders make, Master Toby.'

'I doubt if we'll be spending much time here, Tilly. Cook will be up in Derbyshire, will she not?'

'Aye, and Pierre, the chef your father's had set on.'

'So we'll dine at my club.'

There were two reactions. Beside me Jem tensed and Mrs Tilbury's face fell.

'But first we will come down to your room,' I said quickly, 'and you will pour us a glass of wine and tell us all your news. How is Mitten's back? And is there news of his son – the one in the navy?'

In fact, since neither of us had brought evening dress, we repaired not to Boodle's but to Brown's Hotel for our supper. No one looked twice at two respectable clergymen dining there, and we partook of an excellent meal.

Jem threw himself into his new role, only after a glass of Burgundy dropping his voice and admitting that he found, after the stillness of the country, the noise and bustle of the city no longer to his taste.

'You echo my very sentiments,' I said. 'But it is the squalor and the stench of the streets that I found most distressing. To be poor in the country must be bad enough, but here, with no kind landlord to help in times of hunger! To think I once considered that London was the only place to live. But you will be finding far worse tomorrow, Jem – James – when you make your way to the east of the city.'

He nodded. 'Toby, I've been considering...' He paused as the waiter removed our soup plates. 'If I'm to be a poor clergyman, I can't be living in Berkeley Square, not even as a guest. I have to be living amongst the people from whom I hope to obtain information.'

'You are right, of course. As it happens, the same thought had occurred to me. But where you live must be as respectable as it is poor, and not for anything would I have you sleeping in some infested rooming house while I enjoy the luxury – not to mention the new water-closets – of my home. I write occasionally to a man who was up at Cambridge at the same time as I. He too was subsequently ordained, but was not as fortunate as I in obtaining a generous patron.'

'Generous indeed,' Jem observed, with a twisted smile, as he and I both considered the fate of that lady.

'Touché. But Charles Frane is curate in Southwark – the vicar in charge holds several benefices and makes sure that he serves only the most fashionable.'

'Which Southwark is not.'

'Exactly so. Charles and his wife have not been blessed with issue, as yet, so they have room to spare and I am sure that they will be more than happy to earn a few pence by offering you board and lodging.'

'Well, Southwark is just the sort of place I would want to start displaying those bills you've had printed. Excellent, Toby. Yes, I'd be grateful if you would write to this Charles Frane to put the idea to him. And you – you'll be going to Hanstown?'

'Hans Crescent, to be precise. But not until you're settled with Charles.'

'Wearing these bands?'

'Why not? That was what we agreed.'

'But as for you – I wonder if you might not do better to act as the sort of out and outer Mr Vernon aspires to be. If Mr Chamberlain of Hans Crescent is a cit, he'd more likely to pull his forelock for that sort of man than for a clergyman.'

'You may be right... I'm not dressed for the part, however.'

'Don't tell me your old valet – what was his name, now? Held his nose far higher than you ever did!'

'So I should hope. A valet aspiring to the heights can't

admit to serving a lowly divinity student. Cumberbatch. Can you imagine his face if he saw the rectory? Anyway, what about him?'

'He may have been toplofty, but I wager he did his job properly, and that all your clothes have been properly stored against your return.'

'But they'll be three years out of fashion. Though I suppose that's all the better – country clothes always takes a while to catch up with London modes.'

'Exactly. You may smell of camphor, but at least you'll look the part of a country gentleman.'

'So that's settled. I'll try it.' I waited for the waiter to remove the cover and offer us brandy. 'No, Jem, I propose that tomorrow we enjoy ourselves – in a modest way, befitting two men of the cloth, but enjoy ourselves nonetheless.'

It was only right that we should visit Westminster Abbey and St Paul's. I was glad I had suggested that we do them in that order, Jem uneasily suggesting that the former was too crowded with memorials to rich people to be truly the House of God. St Paul's was much more to his taste, despite a hackney carriage journey during which the jarvey so unmercifully whipped his horse that I feared Jem would if needs be engage in fisticuffs to restrain him. However, the fury in his eye was sufficient to quell the villain. Once within, he raised his eyes to the glories of the dome, and knelt in prayer beside me as to the manner born. I believe his prayers for the success of our venture were as devout as mine, and his demeanour certainly did not want for reverence as we explored the rest of the awe-inspiring building.

* * *

Knowing that for several days afterwards there could be no thought of pleasure, for Jem at least, I privately asked young Wilfred to obtain tickets to the play that evening, and book a table afterwards at the Piazza. Remembering how well Jem acted in Shakespeare, it was natural to select something by the Bard. I only had to glance at Jem's face during the performance – *Othello* – to know that I had made the right choice.

Since we were in town incognito and I was anxious lest such extravagance might offend him, I made no mention of our family box and we took our places with the groundlings. The audience was as well behaved as I had known, and the performance by all the actors one to stay in the memory forever. I might not miss the filth of the Metropolis, but I realised with a painful pang how much I missed some of the other things it had to offer.

As if stunned, Jem hardly spoke, even when I hoped to loosen his tongue by ordering champagne with our supper. Every time I made a gesture such as that I was on tenterhooks lest he feel patronised, lest the difference between our lots in life were to become unbearable. Perhaps they would, did he not know almost to the penny how much I lived on, how much I gave away, in my new, my *real* life in the village.

Though we had forbidden her or Wilfred to wait up, Mrs Tilbury had ensured that there was a bright fire in the Small Saloon when we returned, with brandy and port to hand. In truth, however, we were both weary after our day's dissipations, and sat no longer than ten minutes, making our plans for the morrow. Charles Frane had responded promptly to my letter, assuring me that any friend of mine would be a friend of his, and only reluctantly accepting my offer of payment for his hospitality. However, his wife was now – and even as he wrote the words, his hand had trembled – was in an interesting condition, and he feared he must avail himself of a few shillings.

'Can the Church be no more generous towards its clergy?' Jem demanded.

'It is very generous indeed to some of them,' I said dryly. 'At least the rector holding Charles's benefice has bothered to introduce and pay for a curate. Others do not trouble even with that. Pray God that one day everyone will find pluralism as offensive as I do – if a man cannot look after the souls of all in his care, he has no right to call himself their shepherd, and absolutely no right to all the pecuniary advantages of his many parishes, no right to the tithes, the pretty vicarages, all the other privileges...' I preached to the converted, of course.

But Jem raised a finger. 'Pray continue, Toby. If I am to pass as a man of the cloth, I must needs be aware of all these controversies.'

Five minutes later, however, when I looked to him for agreement on some point, he was already asleep. It was nearly three in the morning, and both of us were used to country hours. Gently I removed the brandy glass from his grasp. He jerked back to consciousness.

Stretching apologetically and hauling himself to his feet, he smiled. 'Thank you, Toby. This has truly been one of the best days of my life.'

CHAPTER FOURTEEN

The next morning, heavy-lidded but still basking in the recollection of the previous day's holiday, Jem donned his garb as a poor parson, and in the clothes I had once worn every day I became truly the country justice of the peace. We looked each other up and down.

'I'm afraid you look too strong and healthy, Jem. But we can't remedy that.'

'I'll try to look hungry, shall I? And worried? But anyone living in the country will look healthier than these poor grey-skinned city souls. As for you, Toby, you need to strut a bit more. Think about that relative of yours that thinks he's God Almighty: remember how high he holds his chin. Come, give that quizzing glass of yours a bit of exercise.'

Jem trying to look hangdog, and I sneering down my nose in the manner of my least favourite cousin, we summoned another stinking, but suitably anonymous, hack. It crossed London Bridge and lumbered through streets deep in ordure and rotting vegetables to take us to my friend Charles Frane's home in Southwark. This was in sight of the cathedral, which rose above an ill-assorted mass of manufactories, breweries and timber-yards. The vicarage, but for an extensive but ill-maintained glebe, would have been almost swamped by the noisome tanneries and skin markets emitting their nauseating stench.

Despite the fine features and proud bearing that would have made him an excellent dean, Charles Frane cared for the souls attending not the historic cathedral, but the small and comparatively modern church of St Stephen the Martyr. Try as one might, one could not envisage this poor house of God remaining upright much longer. Damp was seeping up its walls, and the south transept clearly needed a buttress or two to support its outer wall. But that was as nothing compared with the state of Frane's parishioners and their accommodation. Even the poorest of my flock would have found it in them to pity these wretched souls, who seemed to rely on gin to survive their brutally short lives and ease them into the blessed oblivion of death.

In the midst of this, Frane and his wife lived in a house perhaps fifty years old that was decent but little more. I was sure Mrs Frane, an anxious-looking woman in her later twenties, only achieved the neatness and no more than adequate cleanliness through constant toil. She was assisted by a slatternly cook, and a couple of girls who seemed scarce out of the nursery. How she would manage when her babe was born I knew not.

Then inspiration struck me. My mother had constantly entreated me to take up one of the benefices within her gift – tonight I could write to her urging her to offer one of them to the Franes. Perhaps it was possible for two strong young people to survive here, but no one should be condemned to raising a longed-for infant in such a place. I briefly contemplated the idea of inviting Frane to join me as a permanent curate, but that would mean I could not give as much as I wished to my flock – in material or spiritual terms.

While Mrs Frane prepared the nuncheon she would press upon us, we three men adjourned to what she hopefully referred to as the morning room. Presumably if the sun was ever brave enough to shine in this district it would illuminate the smoke-stained walls and scuffed woodwork.

I had of necessity explained to Frane something of our motives for both speed and secrecy, but had omitted to reveal that Jem was my groom. Nor had I confessed that he wore his bands as a disguise. Much as I preferred the truth at all times, it occurred to me that the second piece of information would be more palatable than the first, which I still withheld.

Frane received my admission with so little pleasure that I was glad I concealed the truth about Jem's usual employment. In fact, his fine nostrils flared with indignation, a reaction that accorded ill with the japes that he had constantly played at Cambridge and that would probably have resulted in permanent rustication but for the intervention of a convenient uncle who was an intimate of the college master.

'Pretending to be in Holy Orders? Indeed I have never heard of such an outrage. Such a want of reverence, such... Every feeling is revolted.'

I bit my lip. Perhaps in his place I would have felt a similar revulsion. And how dared I condemn his spiritual volte face when I too had changed profoundly since our undergraduate days?

It was left to Jem to speak. 'I am sorry that you disapprove,' he said calmly, setting his understandably scarce-touched glass of sherry on a convenient but greasy table. 'But you must know that sometimes it is necessary to balance two evils. To my mind the greater evil lies in letting a murderer go unpunished, and if, by spending a few days in the attire of a profession I admire and revere, I help achieve that end, then so it must be.'

Since he spoke with the calm and authority – indeed, the exact intonation – of Dr Hansard, it was unsurprising that Frane was slightly mollified.

'Indeed,' I added, 'we believe that our own lives might be at risk, not to mention those of other good people, should our activities be known. Jem – James, I should say – will become a parson and I return to my old idle ways, as a man about town.' I shot a smile at Jem to acknowledge his idea.

'I cannot see why this double impersonation should be necessary,' Frane insisted. 'Campion is perfectly capable of asking any questions. He made a perfect nuisance of himself in tutorials at Cambridge doing precisely that.'

'For one thing, Charles, I lack the common touch – and try as I might I cannot rid myself of my wretched Eton drawl.'

'Furthermore, can you see Tobias defending himself in a fist fight?'

'I understood he was taught his science by the great Cribb himself,' Charles objected.

'He was indeed, and has plenty of bottom. But he would fight fair. And by your leave, Mr Frane, I do not expect our still unknown adversary to fight that way. I would deal with him in any way necessary.'

'Mr Yeomans, you tell me that you would have no compunction in...?' The rest of the sentence hung accusingly in mid-air.

'In dealing a bit of the home-brewed? None at all,' Jem said firmly. 'I wish to harm no one, Mr Frane. But if anyone has to defend himself, I would rather it were me than Tobias.' He bit back whatever he had meant to say next – presumably an allusion to the physical strength required by our respective lives. After a moment's hesitation, he asked, as if prompted by our dear Dr Hansard, 'Would you put the same question to a Bow Street Runner?'

At last Frane shook his head, but rose from his seat to take a turn about the room, finally stopping to look out at a lifeless garden. His view was obscured by the thin but penetrating drizzle trickling in grey rivulets down the dirty window.

'We have the authority of the coroner investigating the suspicious death of an unnamed man to place these handbills in prominent places,' I said, flourishing a handful.

He gave a cold glance, raising a disdainful eyebrow. 'A reward? That should bring them like flies to a midden.'

'That is what we hope. As you can see, there are spaces left for me to fill in – to whom information should be brought and where. The Reverend James Yeomans' name will fill the former. In the absence of a midden, can you suggest a place where James may pass his time a few hours each day – a respectable hostelry?'

Seating himself once more, Frane gave a bark of laughter. 'A respectable hostelry? Did you never hear the term *oxymoron*, Tobias? Here there are dark alleys, low taverns – nay, even the front steps of sordid dwellings – where drink is taken.'

'Is there none less vile than others?' I pursued. 'Or would you prefer his informants to call here?'

He blenched, visibly. 'Good God, no. It is one thing to

exhort the pitiful few who occasionally come to church to mend their ways, quite another to bring them to the doorstep of one's own house.'

I dared not catch Jem's eye. 'Should we suggest they come to the church itself, then? To the porch? Where can I purchase a few apples and nuts, to persuade children to spread the word?' Lest he suspect I intended him to pay for them, I produced a couple of guineas.

'Our maid will do that,' he said curtly, trying not to eye them.

What proportion of his stipend that little pile of gold would represent? Clearly his distinguished uncle was making little or no contribution to the household's finances. Yet even as I planned my letter to my mother, I worried about Frane: would he make a good pastor in any parish, if he loathed his congregation here so much?

At this point we were bidden to nuncheon. I must not criticise the poor food, since it was presumably all – more – than they could afford. But I shrank from using the cutlery and china, which still bore traces of previous meals. How I refrained from wiping the rim of my glass I do not know.

When had I become so pernickety? When I took refreshment with my parishioners it was not as if I did not share the peck of dirt they said they ate in a lifetime. Was country dirt somehow better than city dirt?

Or was it the lack of effort I felt? In my parish there was not a single person, in no matter how mean a dwelling, who would not wipe a mug before filling it, even a chair before offering it – or even the windowsill, in hovels where there were no chairs.

'If Mr Yeomans is to use St Stephen's as his base, as it were, where will he spend the rest of the day?' Frane asked.

'I shall slip from boozing-ken to boozing-ken – see, I have the cant already,' he said. 'Taverns and alehouses, Mrs Frane,' he added with an apologetic bow.

'Drinking, no doubt. Now I see another reason for your exchange,' James said with a thin smile. 'You never could hold your ale, could you, Tobias?'

It was easier to agree than argue that it was he who constantly dipped too deep, and if it made him feel happier about the deception, so be it.

At last I bade them all farewell, promising to send a daily messenger for Jem's reports. In response to my blessing, he clasped my hand and said earnestly, 'Remember that I am not the only one asking inconvenient questions, young Toby.'

Impulsively and – given the chaotic state of the roads – foolishly, I hired a curricle to drive myself to Hanstown. It was what Vernon would have done, and it also spared me another journey in a hack, enclosed with nothing but the odour of mothballs.

As Jem had predicted, all my garments had been carefully preserved, perhaps on the instructions of my father, who had never truly believed that I would keep to my chosen path. He had probably expected me to return to them much more quickly, and indeed more permanently. At one time I had needed my valet to ease me into the beautifully cut coat. Now after my period of rural abstinence, I could slip it on with little difficulty – a fact I must never admit to either Mrs Tilbury or of course Mrs Trent, lest they see it as their mission to feed me up. My boots were still miracles of mirror-like polish. They fitted so well I resolved to take them back to Warwickshire with me, though I doubted if they would retain their gleam without Cumberbatch's arcane mix of blacking and champagne.

Hans Crescent was the natural habitat of people my father would have dismissed as cits and lawyers, respectable enough but not the sort of place one of the *ton* would expect to visit. Indeed, although they had not long been built, the rows of brick houses were already looking out at elbows. One stood out: Mr Chamberlain's house, its paint gleaming bravely in the wintry sun.

Leaving the curricle to the care of the diminutive tiger whose services I had also hired, I ran up the steps and addressed myself to a gleaming knocker. The door was opened by a pleasant-faced woman, who wore a clean lace cap over her sandy hair. Her apron was equally clean.

'Might I speak to Mr Chamberlain?' I asked, Eton accent a little to the fore, but tempered by what I hoped was an encouraging smile.

'Mr Chamberlain?' Her face froze. 'You are mistaken. No Mr Chamberlain lives here.'

I stepped forward, stopping her shutting the door in my face by putting my foot between the door and its frame. 'But a Mr Chamberlain used to?' I pitched my voice halfway between a stern statement and a question.

She flushed, the colour ill-becoming to one of her almost white complexion. What do you know of Mr Chamberlain?'

'I found some property of his and wished to return it.'

'But – But I—' She took her hand from the door and clasped its fellow. The knuckles gleamed with white against the red of the compressed flesh.

I doffed my hat. 'I represent Mr Vernon, the South

Warwickshire coroner. Perhaps we could talk in more discreet circumstances?'

'My husband is not at home – it would not be appropriate…' She turned at the sound of footsteps coming down the corridor behind her.

The child – she must have been about six or seven – tugged at the woman's skirt. 'Mama. Mama!'

I was surprised at the relationship. The little girl was almost as dark as a gypsy, her black hair and flashing eyes so very different from the woman's ginger and hazel.

I smiled, temporarily abandoning the haughty and peremptory mien of a coroner's representative for the avuncular geniality of a village clergyman. Indeed, I did what I usually did when encountering a child that age: I dropped to my haunches, so that our eyes were more or less level. 'And who might you be, young lady?'

'My name is Emma Harriet Larwood.' She dropped a polite curtsy. 'And who are you, sir?'

Her mother seemed torn between wishing to hear my answer and wanting the child out of the way.

'I am Tobias Hampton,' I said, having decided to adopt the name of one of my brother's more obscure estates. I put out my hand to shake hers.

But this her mother would not tolerate. 'I can only suggest, Mr Hampton, that you return at a more convenient time. My husband is likely to be here between four and five.'

'But it is not your husband I wish to see. I merely wish to enquire about Mr Chamberlain.'

'Nonetheless, it is to my husband that you must address yourself. Good day to you, sir.'

* * *

To the tiger's amazement and delight, I dismissed him with a large tip and a request to drive the curricle back to its stable. I meanwhile slipped to the back of the row of houses, in time to see a thin lad possibly ten years old emerge from the Larwoods' scullery door. As discreetly as I could – oh, for the skills of one such as Matthew – I tailed him through a variety of streets heading ever towards the dome to St Paul's. In other words he was making for the City, where, no doubt, Mr Larwood would be found.

Although he never once looked back, the boy seemed to sense that someone was in pursuit. He sped up, dodging down alleys and slipping into doorways. After a mile, perhaps a little more, I had to admit that he had given me the slip.

So, lost and uncomfortably hot in my fine feathers, I had only one thing to do – to ask why my visit to Hans Crescent was so important as to warrant a messenger to Mr Larwood's place of employment. And so much effort to make sure that I did not know what it might be.

Retracing my steps, discovering, of course that my elegant boots were not as comfortable as I expected, I found a tavern and pondered my next move over a glass of surprisingly good ale. The landlord was keen to press refreshment upon me and, reflecting that I could do nothing until Mr Larwood's promised return at four, I accepted some excellent spiced beef.

It was exactly four when I presented myself again in Hans Crescent. This time my assault on the knocker went unheeded. Where the shutters were not up, the blinds were drawn. The house as not only empty, it was deserted.

There was not even a servant to admit me when I slipped round to the back door. I stood staring at it in disbelief.

Dusk was deepening swiftly. I was in an unfashionable and

ill-lit part of London. I had been thoroughly gulled. My misery was complete, I thought, when rain began to fall on my fine feathers. I would to turn round trudge my weary and embarrassed way back to Berkeley Square.

But it was not. There was someone else in the yard. Someone emerging from an outhouse. I bethought me of Cribb, and tried to recall all his precepts as I heard the swift footstep. I braced myself, lashed out hard. But as Jem had feared, I tried to fight fair. After a bruising blow to the head, I felt nothing.

CHAPTER FIFTEEN

It was hard to persuade poor Mrs Tilbury not to summon Sir Henry Halford himself to attend my injuries, but I was constant in my assertion that little apart from my pride was truly damaged. Eventually she withdrew, muttering something I did not quite catch. Meanwhile Wilfred did not put in an appearance, which – even in my befuddled state – I found strange.

Feeling lamentably sorry for myself, in due course I contrived to shed my fine plumage. My coat, unlike my hat, which appeared to have been jumped on, was largely undamaged, and I was sure that Wilfred or Tilly would contrive to remove the odd spots of blood. My shirt collar was another matter altogether; the cuffs were also badly stained. At least the shirt itself was reasonably intact. But not even a needlewoman as skilled as Mrs Trent would be able to restore the torn knees of my breeches.

As for myself, lump on the back of the neck apart, I was really no worse a schoolboy who had taken a bad tumble and had scuffed and bruised more skin than was comfortable. The only source of real pain was in fact my feet, and I set about easing off the confounded boots. I believe I groaned. In some irritation I rang for Wilfred, only then recalling that the Reverend Tobias Campion would have had to manage himself, not withstanding a little discomfort. But rung I had, and I might as well ask for some brandy.

There was an immediate tap on my door. Had the lad been lingering outside waiting for my summons? What a fearsome master I must have seemed. But even as I bade him enter and turned to apologise, a familiar voice declared, 'No need to announce me, lad.'

Wearing but one boot, I sprang to my feet. 'My dear Edmund: can it really be you? What brings you here?'

'Curiosity. I ever desired to see your family's town house.' His bland smile was a replaced by a frown. 'And it seems I came at the right moment.' He knelt to yank off the second boot. 'That Wilfred of yours has seen to the jarvey – who did his best to bamboozle me into paying far more than my shot until Wilfred told him he was doing it too brown and to, er, cut his slum. He's just brought up my baggage and is even now unpacking. I will ask him to leave everything where it is and to bring hot water and towels here. Then I will see what I can do to make you presentable.' He slipped from the room, returning on the instant. 'Bend your head, if you please.' He looked at but did not yet touch the back of my neck. 'Hmm. What was stolen?'

'Very little. They left me my money. But they took my watch – not the one my grandfather gave me – and my fob—'

'Fob, Tobias? I thought you eschewed such fripperies.'

'I thought I should truly play the role of a man of fashion,' I said, 'in case I needed to browbeat Mr Chamberlain. As it was, I so thoroughly misjudged the situation that I have let his whole family slip through my fingers. They have flit the coop, as Matthew would say.'

'How did you manage to annoy them enough to have you set upon?' There was a tap at the door. As Wilfred entered, Edmund smiled. 'Thank you. Just put everything there on the washstand, if you please. Now, in my valise you will find some lavender water. Would you be kind enough to bring it?' The astonished young man withdrew, and Edmund applied himself to washing his hands. Only then did he fall to prodding and poking my injuries.

He was so engrossed that he did not notice Wilfred's return.

He coughed politely. 'The lavender water, sir. And I have taken the liberty of bringing some bandages.'

'Good man. Now, I think you should lay out his lordship's clerical garb for this evening, do not you? And then we will ring for you.'

'Very good, sir. My Lord.' Wilfred did as he was bid and left obsequiously.

'How strange to hear that mode of address,' I said, as if speaking would take my mind off the contusions he was intent on cleaning. 'The Reverend Campion – how infinitely more mellifluous are those words. I never want to be a lord again,' I added. 'I cannot, will not, return to my old life, Edmund. Almost these injuries could be God's judgement upon me for my folly and vanity.'

'In that case, given the character of some of the clergymen I know, I must expect to see a great deal of broken heads and torn clothes,' he said, washing his hands afresh. 'You are not a thing of beauty, Toby, but you will pass. If you pull down your cuffs a little no one will detect anything amiss – except you, of course. Do you need any drops for the pain? No? Good man. I can see we must ask Cribb to engage in a couple of bouts with you, to remind you of what you should have done.'

'Hard to do anything if someone creeps up behind and cudgels one!' I bleated, wishing I had asked for just a little of the laudanum of which he so disapproved.

He snorted in amusement or disgust, I knew not which.

'But where is Mrs Hansard?' I asked belatedly. 'Did she not accompany you?'

He said, with a bravery that sounded more like bravado. 'She says she can spare me for a few days – but a few days only. This is the first time we have been apart since our wedding, Tobias...' He coughed, and continued, 'She insists that there are enquiries to be made in the village – of Mrs Powell, for instance – which she can do quite safely. And, since she has promised me never to go unaccompanied, on this occasion I let her have her own way.'

Privately I wondered if Mrs Hansard was unhappy at the prospect of assuming the role of one accustomed to life this side of the baize door. If only she could know that Jem seemed to be achieving it with no problems. 'She will take no risks?' I pressed.

Hansard struck one fist on to the palm of the other. 'Damn it, Toby, do you not think I worry about her safety every moment of the day? We all feared – Lady Chase included – that it would look quite singular if we all decamped at once. Toone will look after her – as long as he is not as drunk as a wheelbarrow.' He took a turn about the room. At last he turned. 'Where do we two bachelors dine tonight?'

I had forgotten that he must be both weary and hungry

after his journey. It was time to be host again.

I managed a smile. 'Did Wilfred show you to your room, Edmund?'

'To the best guest chamber.'

'Then I am afraid he must remove you to another – to the second-best guest chamber.'

'Second?' he demanded, an ironical gleam in his eye.

'The best is awaiting the return of the Reverend James Yeomans, Edmund,' I responded with an answering gleam in mine. I added seriously. 'And for nothing on earth would I slight him by demoting him—'

'Can you even think of it? I anticipate, of course, a battle royal when he returns and begs to sleep in a coal scuttle rather than a decent room. What is his news?'

'There is none yet. He spends the night in Southwark, where I suspect a coal scuttle would indeed be more comfortable than the chamber he occupies. Tomorrow I send a messenger to enquire – though now I have scared off the Larwoods, there is no reason for me not to go in person. With you as my escort, no doubt,' I added with a mocking bow.

'We may have other things to occupy us. I think we should lay this information before the Runners. *They* most certainly have the authority to run these Larwoods to earth, and moreover they have men enough to do it. I suppose it is just possible that the attack on you is entirely unrelated to the Larwoods, but on the other hand someone hit you about the head and trod on your hands, and did it on their premises. Enquiries might as well start with them.'

'But what if Jem needs help too? How ironic that it was he who went to Southwark because he thought it too dangerous for me, and it is I who – in a quite respectable yard – suffer this.' I touched the back of my head.

'What I cannot understand is this deviation from our plan,' he declared with asperity. 'You were both to be clergymen.' He sat on the day bed and stared at me.

'As I told you, we thought a gentle enquiry from a clergyman might be to no avail, that a man in the mould of Vernon might be sufficiently intimidating.' I would not implicate Jem. Perhaps we had both been pot-valiant when we had hatched the scheme.

He gave me a shrewd glance, but said nothing. 'And to repeat my question, where shall we dine tonight? Thank goodness Sir Marcus and his tribe have inured us to town hours. Even so, I could eat a stalled ox.'

'I'm sure we shall find some herbs to go with it. But not here. I told dear old Tilly – the housekeeper – that I should fend for myself this evening, though I know she is longing to cook for me. Tomorrow, perhaps... Did you bring your evening gear? Well, then, may I suggest Grillon's...'

'You set the Runners after an innocent family?' Jem repeated, in tones mixing disbelief and doubt.

We had been shown by one of the Franes' little maids, apologising for her mistress' absence, into the same dismal morning room as before. It did not respond well to the sun, enfeebled though it was by misty cloud which would become fog by the end of the day.

'They may be far from innocent. Do not blame Tobias – it was my doing,' Edmund insisted. 'We cannot run all over the country looking for the family.'

'But what if they are free of all blame? After all, to have a

strange man presenting himself at your door and demanding
to see someone—'

This was in fact exactly what Jem had recommended.
However, there was no point in repining, and I would
certainly not apportion blame, since I had acquiesced more
than willingly in the change of plan. Even to the boots.

Edmund replied, 'Then at very least we shall be able to
speak to them about what made them flee. And how do you
do, Jem? It does not seem to me as if the Reverend James
Yeomans slept well.'

Jem looked about him, as if he could detect ears pressed to
the door. He dropped his voice. 'Mr and Mrs Frane do their
best, I suppose. ' He stopped short, pulling back his cuff to
reveal the unmistakeable sight of flea bites.

'Which is the most damning condemnation one may make,'
growled Edmund softly. 'And have you had any luck with
your enquiries?' he asked in his normal voice.

'None, as yet. But Toby's bribery encouraged many children
– and some older people – to come to the church porch at
four. I told them what I needed to know, asked if any of their
acquaintance had gone missing – which aroused considerable
black mirth, I fear – and promised a reward for hard news. I
was just about to set forth about the taverns when you called.
I accompanied Mr Frane to matins,' he said, as if needing an
excuse for not having set mouth to tankard before now.
'There were just the two of us and the churchwardens. I left
the three of them discussing a funeral. There are so many
there is talk of obtaining more land to extend the graveyard,
but Mr Frane suspects that many families simply dispose of
their kin in the river, to save expense.'

'It is, alas, not just those who die in what pass for their beds who fetch up in the river,' Dr Hansard observed. 'It behoves us to make sure that you do not inadvertently become one of them.'

'Amen,' I agreed.

'As to that, it would be better if I were not seen in your company,' Jem said, with a smile I thought was forced. 'Deviating from our plan had ill results yesterday, Toby, and I am sorry for it.'

'Nay, my assailants might not have been deterred by my bands,' I said hastily.

'What I fear, Jem, is that yours may not be either,' Hansard said grimly. 'Might I make one suggestion? I understand that you will send a messenger with any news. Pray do not go into any detail. The simple word *Eureka* will suffice. I have it,' he explained.

Suppressing a vision of Jem, like the great philosopher, hurtling naked down the street, I said, 'And pray God we have it soon – the sooner we return to the safety of our village the better.'

They both looked at me. 'Safety? In Moreton St Jude? There was none for the poor man in the stream, Tobias,' Edmund reminded me, 'and there may be none for us, once all this comes out.'

'If only we could unlock its secrets,' Dr Hansard declared fervently.

We stood before the Rosetta Stone, which I had seen back in '01 or '02 when it was first put on display. Dr Hansard, however, had not visited the British Museum since his return from India and evinced a desire to see this wonder of the ancient world. I had suggested a tour of the museum to take our minds off Jem's possible trials, realising all too strongly that much as we wanted to protect him, our very presence might endanger him further.

'I believe that there is already a young French scholar hard at work on just such an investigation,' I said, dredging the information from some gossip conveyed to me by one of my mother's regular chatty letters.

'French? I suppose it is fitting, since it was French soldiers who discovered it in the first place. How such works of art come to be spoils of war, allocated under a treaty, defeats me. God knows what we would have to cede should Napoleon conquer us.' He looked at his watch, for perhaps the fourth time in the last half hour. He, too, was wondering if our friend was still safe.

I strove for something that would divert our thoughts, preferably an occupation that made no further demands on my feet. The smart boots might remain in my chamber, there being no need for a respectable clergyman to embrace anything other than comfort, but they had a lasting revenge. We would both enjoy a performance at Drury Lane that evening. Should I bespeak our vacant family box or pay for a lowlier place? I explained the situation to Edmund.

'I think that you were in the right of it as far as Jem was concerned,' he said at last. 'And I rather think we should continue to eschew the comforts of the box. I do not want him to have the slightest idea that you treated us differently, and I am sure that, careful as we might be, we might let the secret drop. Let us go with the crowd, Tobias. Then if the performance is bad, we can hiss it off the stage.'

The performance was neither good nor bad. We had promised Mrs Tilbury that we would afterwards return to

Berkeley Square. Just as Mrs Trent would have been piqued not to show off her skills, so dear Tilly wished to show she was still the mistress of a bachelor supper. Given the state of her poor eyes, I dared make no predictions as to the quality, but I would wager that the quantity would be equal to Mrs Trent's.

We pushed our way through the crush in the foyer. It was thronged with brightly garbed and painted Cyprians all plying their trade. Taking Edmund's arm, I hurried us through.

'You are turned Puritan?' he asked with a smile.

'I am indeed filled with disgust.' And who would not be, at the lewd propositions even now being whispered in my ear?

'With the men who use such women or the women themselves?' His voice was sterner.

'What woman can stoop so low as to sell her body?' I demanded.

'Those with no alternative.'

'Alternative? Surely there must be alternatives? Think of the good women of our village, toiling night and day to keep their families together. Would *they* ever stoop to such a trade?'

'If their husbands had left the land and come to the city in search of a decent wage – what would the women do then? Oh, they can become servants, milliners, I grant you. But say their men die, or are seized by press gangs, or simply disappear? How is such a woman to survive?'

'There is always poor relief…the workhouse…' I blustered.

'Tobias, you are truly scraping the barrel of argument. Do not our very laws begrudge poor relief, despatching applicants back to their home parish? And the workhouses? Why, you know how desperate your own flock are to escape such a fate.'

'Indeed...' I bit my lip. 'I am still repelled by the very notion of that most pure of God's creatures, a woman, should...'

'Pure? Consider what harm a woman is capable of, Tobias. We have seen it in our own village. I grant you that such a trade is repellent, as vile as slavery. But to every trade there are two partners, the seller and the buyer. Look at those bucks ogling the women, just as if they were so many paintings in a gallery. And I tell you, they would look after a painting better. Not discard it after looking at it.'

'I feel soiled in their very presence, Edmund. Both buyers' and sellers'. Let us quit the place now.'

I waited for the ubiquitous Wilfred, now unaccountably grand in a butler's tail-coat two sizes too large for him, to serve us Madeira in the yellow saloon and withdraw. Encouraging smells had wafted from behind the green baize door to welcome us on our return. The very moment we rang, supper would be served in the family dining room, Wilfred declared as he bowed himself out.

'It seems to me,' I began nervously, aware that my achievements in the capital had not been great, 'that there is still something you and I – more particularly I – might do to discover information about Mr Chamberlain, and possibly even the Larwoods.' Encouraged by Hansard's bright questioning look, I continued. 'If I returned to Hans Crescent in what is now my proper attire, I could present myself as what I am – a country clergyman eager to trace the family for – some purpose or other,' I concluded lamely.

'You do not think that anyone saw you approaching the house and being turned away?'

'They might have seen an aspiring country sprig, with a

particular brilliance to his boots, but they surely would not associate him with me. I do not think the Larwoods would have time to make their escape and communicate the reason to all and sundry. Indeed, they would want to conceal any motive for their flight.'

'And you think that as long as you are rustic in your choice of footwear and clerical in your garb, you might cajole information from unwary householders or their garrulous servants. And what would your pretext be?'

'That is something we could perhaps discuss over supper. I fear that that blow sadly addled my brain, Edmund, but perhaps some of Mrs Tilbury's beef pudding will restore it.'

CHAPTER SIXTEEN

In the end, Edmund and I decided that when I questioned the Larwoods' neighbours or their servants, the nature of my search would be vague, limited to such discreet hints as 'a family affair'. Let my interlocutors interpret that how they would. Initially I would go not to front doors, with knockers gleaming or otherwise, but to the servants' entrance, as befitted a humble parson.

Edmund, meanwhile, would lurk in a hack just down the street, reading a long letter handed to him as we left the house. It was from Mrs Hansard. It seemed that she had promised to write every day, giving every domestic detail. Since there was no one to frank her mail, I imagined that this would prove an expensive separation, even though she had crossed and recrossed the lines.

We agreed that if I did not emerge after what he thought a reasonable interval, he would come in search of me. With his fighting prowess, not to mention his repellent-looking cudgel, I could think of no more efficient guardian angel.

My first visit, earlier than it would be acceptable to pay

morning calls to the householders themselves, was to the left of the Larwoods' house. My informants, a blowsy cook and insinuating manservant, would have worried their employers by their general garrulity, which ate into their time and mine, but brought me no nearer details of the Larwood household. I signified to Edmund that I had abandoned that house, and would move to the neighbour on the right-hand side. These servants were clearly too harassed to indulge in the sort of general conversation likely to lead tactfully to the information I sought. In fact, it was only when I reached the house three doors further down that I struck gold in the form of the nursery maid, a girl of about twelve, applying diminutive pinafores to the washboard.

"'Tis strange you should be asking about them, your honour, because their little Miss Emma is bosom bows with our Miss Augusta.' She paused in her labour, wiping her reddened hands on her apron. 'According to Nurse – Nurse Stoughton, that is – they're like sisters. Stands to reason, being the same age and both on their own.' She dropped her voice. 'Master Frederick was taken from us last year by the putrid throat and Miss Thomasina called to the angels with measles.'

Rigidly suppressing my unholy imagination, I made suitable noises of sympathy. 'Does Miss Emma have no brothers or sisters?'

'No. And no sign of any, either, if you take my meaning.'

'And what sort of a child is Miss Emma?'

'Like Miss Augusta – awake on every suit, and as pretty as paint.'

I nodded, hoping she would tell me something I didn't know. 'Like her parents, Miss – er...?' I asked vaguely.

'Betty. Betty Ewers at your service.' She dropped a curtsy,

continuing as if there had been no interruption, 'Lord bless you, no. Two carrot-heads, they are. Auburn, I *should* say. And she as dark as the devil.'

Would Edmund deduce anything from that?

'Except there isn't anything impish about her,' she continued. 'Quite the little angel, she is.'

Since what she said accorded with my brief impression, I smiled encouragingly. 'But little children are often naughty – in their way.'

'Not Miss Emma. Her nurse – Miss Fowler, that is – says she knew her letters and her numbers before you could credit it. And she'll sing a little hymn as sweet as a bird.'

'Did Nurse Fowler leave with the family?'

'Now that I don't know. She may have, because I've not seen her since, but that doesn't mean anything, does it? They cast you off, these people, leaving you to find another position as if they grew on trees,' she said with the bitter wisdom of one twice her age.

'Miss Betty, would Nurse Stoughton know where Nurse Fowler's family might live?' I chinked a couple of coins encouragingly.

'I could go and ask her, your honour.'

The coins slipped from my hand into hers. She ran off like the wind.

Nurse Stoughton was an altogether more stately lady of forty summers and few teeth, greeting me with a stiff bob and something of a sniff. It was hard to tell whether she considered she was rising in the world or falling, when she took a position with a family in a street like this. It was a nuance that dear Mrs Hansard would have discovered in a minute, but I was not sufficiently attuned to. It was clear that she priced my garments and found them and my boots, on which her gaze lingered, authentically shabby.

'Nurse Stoughton, it is imperative that I speak to Mr and Mrs Larwood. It is possible that Nurse Fowler may still be with them. But if she is not, she may know their whereabouts. Do you have her address?' I floundered in the face of her silence.

She smiled grimly. 'She is the daughter of a vicar like yourself, sir, up in Northumberland, so it would trouble you to speak to her urgently if she were up there.'

'Indeed it would.' I tried the smile with which I was used to charm older ladies. 'So it is not her family's address that I need, but her employers' – assuming that she is still with them.'

'I know not any reason why she should not be. She is devoted to Miss Emma and she to her.'

'Has she been with the family long?'

'As long as I have been with Miss Augusta, give or take – I was with Madam when she gave birth,' she added proudly.

'And was Miss Fowler able to help at Miss Emma's delivery?'

Her eyes narrowed. 'As to that, I think not. Miss Emma was born at Mr Larwood's family home, she said; she must have been about three months old when they moved here.'

I knew not why, but I sensed she had said something of importance. 'Is it possible that you know where that place might be? As I told you, it is vital that I speak with them.'

She was about to speak but stopped abruptly. 'I think you ought to ask the master about that,' she said at last.

'And is he at home?'

'At work.'

'His wife? I must impress on you that this is of the utmost
urgency.' A coin found its way from my hand to hers.

'Indisposed.' She was ready to go and close the door. But by
some means she must have divined the value of the coin and
she thawed enough to say, 'He works in the City, sir. At a big
bank near Charing Cross.'

'At Drummond's?' My heart lifted.

'That may be the name.' She made to return to the house.

'One last thing, Nurse Stoughton – what is your master's
name?' I allowed myself to offer her what I was beginning to
think of as my old ladies' smile. 'I can scarce present myself at
the bank and ask for a gentleman living in Hans Crescent, can
I?'

She responded with an indulgent sigh. 'That you couldn't,
Parson. Ask for Mr Thorpe. Mr Edwin Thorpe.'

'My father has banked with old Mr Drummond since before I
was in short coats,' I explained to Edmund, as I came running
back to the hackney carriage and urging the jarvey to spring
the horses. With persuasion, they managed a desultory trot.
'He will have no objection to my speaking to his employee, I
am sure. At last we will have a reliable informant!'

'Whom the Runners may already have questioned. But I
have news for you – this mass of verbiage was not, it seems,
simple gossip.' He opened Mrs Hansard's letter and tapped it.
'Oh, my dearest wife, why did you not tell us this in your very
first paragraph?' he apostrophised her in what sounded like
exasperation.

'Tell us what?' I prompted. It was the first time I had ever
detected a note of criticism of his wife.

'That they found another secret drawer in the governess's

chest. This one contained a lock of hair, folded into paper. Blond – probably baby hair.'

I covered my face in an attempt to concentrate. 'So we are looking for a blond child in the Chamberlain household?'

He shook his head. 'If only nature were as straightforward as that. I have seen babies with hair so fair as to be white growing up into people as dark as our late friend. But we know – we *suspect* – a child to be involved.'

'The Larwoods' child was dark,' I mused. 'And, according to the servant I spoke to, the father as ginger as the mother.'

'Really! So the child is at very least a sport of nature. It would be interesting to meet this little family. Now, there is something else concealed in this mess of crossed lines.' He turned the pages in irritation.

'It could be that she was being cautious,' I said. 'Anyone rapidly scanning the letter might miss the information.'

'Exactly. But this was negative, not positive information. It was that Lady Bramhall's steward has been unable to lay his hands on the papers pertaining to Miss Southey's appointment. It seems he claims not to have access to her private papers. So now – now! – she is sending him express authority to search her escritoire. God knows when we shall have everything made clear...Ah, is this Drummond's?'

It was – but there was such a press of carriages it was minutes before we could be set down outside the august premises, minutes that clearly irked my friend. 'All this rainbow chasing, Tobias, when we both have our daily work to do.'

But he was happier when we were shown straight into Mr Drummond's sanctum.

'Good heavens, 'tis Master Toby.' Mr Drummond greeted

me warmly, as if it were only last week that he had found sugar plums for me in the depths of his great safe. 'I beg your pardon: I *should* say—'

'You *could* call me Parson Campion,' I said, wringing his hand. 'But I would be just as happy with Master Toby.'

He looked my up and down in that familiar appraising way. 'So the story is correct, that you have become naught but a country vicar.'

Naught! 'I did what I had to do,' I said mildly, but, I hoped, firmly.

'A life of poverty, when as a lad you liked nothing better than sitting on my lap making heaps of golden guineas into shining little towers…Well, well.' He turned belatedly to Dr Hansard, and I effected introductions, soon sealed with a glass of fine sherry and some excellent biscuits.

It was a matter of minutes before Mr Edwin Thorpe entered Mr Drummond's office, a cautious but not quite apprehensive expression on his face. Without Mr Drummond's assurance that we were eminently respectable, and asking for the best of motives, he was able to supply us with the ghost of an address.

'All I know is that they have spent holidays at a farm in Devon. Between Newton Abbot and Dawlish, I think. He has mentioned both towns. I am sorry that I cannot be more precise, gentlemen,' he said with a bow and half an eye on his employer, 'but the address of a friend's parents-in-law is not something one normally requires.'

'You have been more than helpful,' I declared, with more enthusiasm than I truly felt.

There was a general shaking of hands before we quit the building.

*   *   *

'Somewhere near Teignmouth,' Hansard mused as we strode to the hack still waiting for us. 'Well, for my part, Tobias, I say we inform the Runners of the Larwoods' possible whereabouts and leave them to do their work. We cannot be haring hither and there when it is just as likely that the Larwoods are in Tunbridge Wells or in Timbuktu. To Berkeley Square, if you please.'

The jarvey nodded, his eyebrows saying quite clearly that if these eccentric countrymen wished to be ferried haphazardly about the capital it was none of his business – so long as they came up with the dibs. His horses returned to what I suspected was their usual dawdle.

I could not argue. My friend was right. Furthermore, if we left London, we would leave Jem alone, an idea quite insupportable. Pray God we would soon have news from him, and we could all return to Warwickshire together. From the way my dear friend kept fingering the letter in his pocket, it could not come too soon.

Mrs Tilbury had provided a light nuncheon in the morning room, Wilfred announced as he took our hats. Since I knew that the simple declaration carried a great deal of import, I thanked him and declared that we would take sherry beforehand in my room.

'It seems we have but just eaten,' Hansard grumbled as he joined me there a few minutes later. 'Thank you, Wilfred.' He gestured with his glass.

'Wilfred knows the amount of effort it has cost Mrs Tilbury – and possibly Wilfred himself – to set the room in order,' I declared, also taking a glass. I looked at the young man enquiringly.

'Indeed, Master Tobias, she has set on three extra servants to help her. That chandelier's come up something lovely, though I says it as shouldn't.'

'So you assisted too? Thank you very much.'

He bowed low. 'Not a sign of a Holland cover will you find, nor any drugget on the carpet. She's done you and the doctor proud, sir. And you'll find the Crown Derby set and the Stourbridge crystal on the table, sir.'

'Pray tell her that we are on our way down.'

I waited until he had bowed himself out. 'And now we must prove good trenchermen indeed,' I said. 'The poor lady is all but blind, Edmund, and this represents effort and devotion in equal measure.'

'Blind? The least I can do by way of thanks is to look at her eyes, then. I know a very good man in London, Tobias—'

'I am glad of it. My mother has been pressing her this age to consult someone. We must see if your charm will do the trick.'

My ribs veritably squeaking after the repast we had consumed in the august setting in which dear Tilly had placed us, I sat back with the newspaper to savour a last glass of wine alone as Edmund disappeared backstairs to work his magic on her, preferring to do it in private, he said. I had hardly perused more than the first pages of the *Morning Post*, however, when an urgent peal of the bell made itself heard, as did Wilfred's scurrying feet.

I declare I was already on my feet, my hand held out, when, after a most perfunctory tap, he came in with a salver bearing a folded, unsealed note.

You wreaker, it declared.

I threw it swiftly on the fire – not even Edmund would ever know Jem's problems with Greek – and rang the bell, Wilfred returning in an instant, as if he had been hovering outside the door for such a summons.

'Summon a hack, please, Wilfred. I will find Dr Hansard myself.'

With no more than a nod, he was on his way. I would suggest to my mother, next time I wrote, that she found a way of ensuring that such a quick-witted and willing young man found speedy promotion.

The inevitably sluggish horses took us to the Franes' vicarage with a speed that suggested they might have sensed our urgency. Mr and Mrs Frane received us with cool politeness and the news that *Mr* Yeomans – not *Parson*, I noticed – was out. A lad whom they had left kicking his heels on the scullery step was much heartier in his welcome, when we identified ourselves as 'the bang-up coves what he was wishful to take to the God-botherer down Marsh Lane way'.

'Willum, at your service, gents.' He even managed a jerky bow.

Just as we were about to follow him, however, Frane emerged, with a turn of speed I had not seen in him since he escaped from an irate Cambridge bag-wig.

'Tobias, Dr Hansard – pray return instanter.'

Had Mrs Frane been taken ill? We dashed back to him at full pelt.

'Inside – both of you. Now, divest yourself of your valuables.' He produced a large box. 'For God's sake do not attempt to take more money or property than you need. Even a handkerchief is a desirable object, to be unpicked and sold.'

Astonished, we did as we were told, Frane locking everything in his box, which he took off with him.

It was clear the lad reckoned he deserved another vail for the delay, but we urged him on, promising him fourpence on our arrival.

'A groat? Go on, guv, make it a sow's baby.'

'Done,' I agreed, not at all sure what I had promised.

Our way lay through alleys hardly worthy the name, they were so narrow and full of stinking matter I for one did not care to look at lest my stomach revolt.

'Green about the gills, ain't you, mister? Tell you what, we'll stop at the next boozing ken and you can have a ball of fire. No? A drop of daffy? That'd go down well.'

'Just get us there, lad,' Hansard said with authority.

The child shrugged, his thin shoulders emerging briefly from the holes in his shirt and subsiding again.

At last, after twists and turns that so disorientated me that I doubted I could ever find my way back to the vicarage without his assistance, clearly worth at least a florin, he came to a halt outside a rooming house. It must once have been a farmhouse, perhaps two hundred years old, but now it was cheek by jowl with lowbuilt slums, already falling into desuetude. From inside came the sound of rough swearing, of feminine tears, and the wail that children give when they are almost beyond hunger. It was into here that Willum wished us to proceed.

The stench of unwashed humanity and its detritus assailed us, like a physical force. Dr Hansard had no compunction in pressing his handkerchief to his nostrils, so I did likewise. We followed the child up a staircase that could have been grand, had not someone purloined the newel post and half the banister rail, presumably for firewood.

'You there, Bess?' Willum yelled.

'And where the hell should I be?' came a squawk of a reply.

'It's them nobs for you. Nah, that reverend's cronies,' he said, overriding a comment so lewd I cannot repeat it. 'After Lanky.'

'They'd better come in then. Come on, Lanky, perk yourself up a bit.'

By now we stood in the doorway. We were greeted by the sight of Jem, at the barely open window. Sleeves rolled up, he was applying a wet rag to the face and hands of a tall young man, whose dark hair sprouted at odd angles from his head, who was cowering away from the door. Jem dried them with his own handkerchief, the object, it was soon clear, of Bess's cupidity. She, wearing what was left of a crimson and black velvet robe some ten years out of fashion, was squatting on a pile of rags that might have concealed a mattress. Although she was much thinner, there was no doubting her relationship to the poor man who had made his way to Moreton St Jude – her hair was as black as his, with the same kink, and her features broad. The skin was an attractive pale olive, but marked by the small-pox and far from clean. As to her age, she might have been anywhere between twenty and thirty.

'That's Bess,' Willum said, adding, 'Miss Bess Monger, sister to 'Enry Monger, deceased.'

'Parson Campion at your service, ma'am. And Dr Hansard,' I said, not quite knowing how to greet a woman in such a position but nonetheless holding out my hand as if she were a duchess born.

While Hansard made his bow, she gripped my hand and I

found myself not engaging in a social courtesy but levering her to her feet.

'This 'ere's my brother's mate,' Bess declared, with a jerk of a curling thumb. ''Enry. The one what's dead, 'e says.' She showed no immediate sign of grief. 'Looked after Lanky there ever since he was hurt in Spain.'

'How very good of him,' I breathed.

'Not just you toffs as have debts of honour,' she said sharply. 'Seems Lanky saved 'Enry. What must 'Enry do but nurse him back to health and then bring him here. Then he sees this advertisement about him, and does as he's told and goes off to the country to claim his reward and there he goes and snuffs it. And left me without support,' she added, pointedly.

'I'm so sorry to hear that,' I said.

We stood like an ill-mixed tableau, all staring towards the window.

Jem stepped forward. 'Gentleman, may I introduce Hugo, Lord Chase?'

CHAPTER SEVENTEEN

Having achieved what we had set out to do, we all, I suspect, felt a similar sense of anticlimax. In the thrill – or otherwise – of the pursuit, none of us had considered what to do next.

'I am sure you are right, Jem,' Hansard said. 'But we must have evidence. Sufficient to convince any lawyers Bramhall has engaged to have him declared dead.'

Without a word, Bess crossed to the fireplace and shoved a hand casually up the chimney. She dusted the soot from a small box before handing it to Edmund. 'Your mate there took it on trust, but if you want to cast your beadies on that lot, feel free.'

A miniature of Lady Chase; a letter from his father; a pencil sketch of a building I did not know; a note from his commanding officer.

Acting as devil's advocate, I made myself say, 'I fear the lawyers will say these could have been stolen.'

'There is one piece of evidence that cannot have been stolen,' Hansard declared. 'My Lord, will you smile, please?'

It took a word from Bess to produce the desired result.

'Look at that chipped tooth, Tobias – it is Lord Chase indeed. Or, as Hamlet might have said, a part of him.'

It was Bess who spoke next. 'Dunno where you're planning to take him, gents, but I doubt if he'll go quietly. He's hardly shifted from the room since poor old 'Enry left. And he won't go nowhere without me, I'm telling you.'

That turned out to be the simple truth. The barest hint from Jem that Lord Chase might quit this foul place was greeted with a terrified wail. The poor man dashed to the shelter of Bess's arms as a child might seek comfort of its nurse, despite the nits visible in the tangle of her hair.

Reaching up she stroked his cheek with remarkable tenderness. Now we could see why the hair grew strangely – a network of scars, some horribly deep, crisscrossed his scalp.

'Miss Bess,' I asked, 'what would your advice be?'

She reflected. 'You could leave him here and pay me to look after him. The only time I leave him, see, is to go and earn enough for our bread. Isn't it, Lanky? I goes and whores for you, so you can have your bit of supper.'

I could not meet Edmund's eyes. I said, my voice cracking, 'Miss Bess, you could have raised a great deal of money had you sold that miniature.'

'Wasn't mine to sell, was it? Nor that great ring my brother took with him.'

Somehow my stuttered promise of a reward was deeply inadequate.

None of us, I was sure, could imagine taking Hugo, stinking and rough-dressed as a beggar, or Bess, in her tawdry rags, back to Berkeley Square, no matter how poor Mrs Tilbury's eyesight. Even Frane, and perhaps especially Frane, would baulk at their presence, no matter how temporary.

But it was more than time that someone said something. 'Madam, I promise you that you will never again have to whore to buy your supper,' I declared flatly. 'Indeed, you may have to quit this room for a while, but it is only to buy yourself and – er – Lanky – some decent clothes.' I might have used the word in its general sense, but indeed she showed far more of her flesh than can have been seemly even in this part of the world.

Her eyes gleamed. 'And how am I to pay for them? You tell me that.'

I turned to Willum, who had occupied himself with chasing down vermin and squashing them between two overgrown thumb nails. 'How much would it cost, Willum?'

'A couple of yellow boys, your honour.'

Bess protested. 'Come on! Them parsons' pal looks full enough of juice, even if they don't!'

'*And* a few hogs' change for you, Reverend,' he declared inexorably.

'Will you go with her?' I asked humbly.

He weighed me up, observing that I had not offered him money, no doubt.

'You may keep two hogs for yourself,' I said. 'And Bess may keep the rest.' If only I knew how much a hog might be.

The two exchanged glances.

She acquiesced. 'Now, you stay here with these gennelmen for a bit, Lanky. They won't do you no harm. And Bess'll bring you back a nice glass of porter.' She pushed him away, chucking him under the chin.

We took advantage of her absence to strip the rags off him, washing him in the cold water Jem fetched from a pump in the yard. I would have set to myself to pare his toe– and fingernails, but my knife had unaccountably disappeared from my pocket.

'I fear Frane was right,' Edmund observed. 'My spectacles have disappeared too.'

Jem, with a dry smile, produced a knife from his boot. In the absence of eyeglasses for Edmund, I knelt on the floor and got on with the job. Jem attacked the nits. At last, having done the best we could, we swathed the silent and unprotesting man in my greatcoat while we awaited the return of the others.

At least in their absence we were freer to talk.

Hardly to my surprise, Jem took the lead. 'A cheap but respectable tavern is the answer, I think,' he said, although the question had not been spoken aloud. 'I will stay with them until you decide where to take them next.'

I nodded. 'You are right. It must be *them*. See, he is already getting agitated. Presumably she has not left him alone for such a long time before.'

The moment we had released him, Hugo had pressed his face to the filthy window panes, and was now tearing his hair in an anxiety so great it was almost madness. He slapped away Edmund's gentle reassuring touch.

'And it cannot be back to Moreton Hall,' Edmund said. 'Not yet.'

'You fear the effect on her ladyship of seeing him like this?' I asked.

'She will do whatever is needful, I warrant you. No, I fear the effect on him. Consider the end of his strong and healthy friend, Henry. Hugo would be as vulnerable as a baby. I will stay with Jem, at whatever inn young Willum suggests. You, Toby, will return with all speed to the village.' He clicked his fingers in irritation. 'No, not the village. To Leamington.

Thence you will make a calm and unhurried journey to your home, and when you have seen Maria and Mrs Trent, *then* you will pay your respects to her ladyship. She must make no sign whatsoever that she has received this news. Instead, she will decide to make a trip to one of her other estates – a distant one. And she will tell no one, no one *at all*, why she is going. I would rather they did not even know where, but I can see that secrecy might in itself arouse suspicion.'

'How will she receive the news that initiates this journey?' I asked.

'Oh, I will write – I will disguise my usual hand. Between you, surely, you can devise some excuse. You may even wish to escort her to her destination, as she is so fond of you; probably my dear Maria will. When you have settled where it will be, Jem and I will convey Hugo and Bess there, and I will find a doctor skilled in such cases to treat him. And we will all return to our normal village lives. All of us. Even Lady Chase. Do I make myself clear?'

Willum and Bess had chosen some respectable artisans' gear for Hugo, and for Bess something she clutched tightly to her. We withdrew, waiting on the landing as Hugo would go no further without her, while she carried out the ablutions we insisted on. She swore fluently and audibly as the chilly water met her flesh.

At last she presented herself for our inspection. She wore a silk dress almost fashionable but for its cherry and apple-green stripes: no doubt some old gown had been unpicked and reshaped. Her bonnet bore a startling array of fruit, and her battered velvet pelisse was a green that did not begin to tone with the green of her gown.

'I told you you'd look like a bleedin' tart,' Willum moaned.

'Well, that's what I bleedin' am,' she responded.

'But you're not supposed to look like a bleedin' tart. I told you. You're supposed to look respectable, like.'

'It'll do till tomorrow,' Jem intervened. And then you may take her out again, Willum, with the same reward for yourself, and trick her out like a decent servant girl. As for you—'

'You don't need a tiger, do you, sir? Always wanted to be a tiger.'

Jem laughed, but very kindly. 'Working with me would take you a long way from home, Willum.'

'I ain't got a home, have I? I'd scrub up good, too, you know.'

He sounded eager rather than pleading, but my heart was wrung. Dear God, how had I forgotten to include him in my largesse? 'How long would it take you to get kitted out – nothing fancy, mind?'

His eyes lit up. 'I could do it on the way to the Bear, your reverence? Only take a tick.'

'Then a tick it shall be. But Jem—' I stopped, my face aflame with embarrassment. 'But I will hold you under the pump myself when we get to this Bear of yours – understand?'

In the event it probably was Jem who applied himself to the task of sluicing the lad. Edmund returned with me via the Franes' home, where we collected all our property and what little Jem had left there. They were handsomely reimbursed for their minimal and – it seemed to me – grudging trouble.

As we hunted down a hack, I said quietly, 'It seems we have given too little thought to poor Bess. She has lost her brother after all. Her protector—'

'Or possibly her pimp. Jem and I will have the opportunity to speak to her this evening. I, for one, would like to know how Lord Chase came to be there – indeed, how long he has been with them.'

Once back at Berkeley Square, Edmund wrote a letter for me to deliver to Maria; then he took all his things and the rest of Jem's to the Bear. 'We will make an interesting supper party, my dear Tobias. I wish you could be there.'

Wilfred applied himself to packing for all three of us, eyes bright with questions he steadfastly did not ask. Even as I kept silent, I wondered what it must be like to be so vital to others' affairs without being considered important enough to know what they were.

All too soon I waved Edmund off in the hack Wilfred had procured and returned to the house. Wilfred closed the door silently behind me.

'We put you to such trouble,' I said with a smile. 'And yet you never complain, or demand the explanations that are due to you.'

'Not at all, my – Mr Tobias,' he said woodenly.

How could I argue? That was how we behaved, how they accepted their lot. I said, 'Believe me, Wilfred, your tact and discretion are valued more than you know. And when I *can* explain what has passed, believe me, I *will*. Now, while I make my farewells to Mrs Tilbury, I want you to do one more thing. I must needs return to Leamington this very night, and it is too late to catch the Post, is it not? I want you to hire me a swift team of horses, with postilions. Spare no expense. I shall set forth in an hour.'

The trouble with grand words such as those is the need to

follow them up with a grand gesture, the casting of a full purse upon the servitor's shocked hand, perhaps.

As it was, Wilfred replied with no drama at all, 'If speed is vital, Mr Tobias, then why not send round to the stables for your brother's post-chaise?'

I was a mere whipster, but Charles was a nonpareil, whose horses were always matched thoroughbreds.

'His lordship's team of greys are eating their heads off, with the grooms and postilions doing likewise, I make no doubt, and no one calling on them these six weeks. There are no better bits of blood in the whole of London, I'll wager.'

I regarded him quizzically. 'So it is a choice of hiring an unknown equipage with an unknown team, or setting out in immediate luxury with a hand-picked team of men and horses.'

'Outriders, too, Mr Tobias.' He permitted himself the ghost of a grin, to which I gladly responded.

'Would you be kind enough to ask them how soon they can be ready?'

Mrs Tilbury looked aghast at the news of my precipitate departure, and more to please her than anything, I ate a scrap of the chicken she'd hoped I might fancy for my supper – alongside a great deal else, I would wager.

'Now you've found your way back to us, pray, Master Tobias, don't leave it so long before you come again,' she said, pressing me to her as if for the last time. And indeed, it probably would be the last time she *saw* me, Edmund having sadly confided to me that the condition was so advanced that no surgeon would be able to cure her poor eyes.

I made a rash promise. 'I will come again, very soon. And

give you better warning, dear Tilly.' It must be kept. And I must see her regularly after my mother persuaded her to retire. I wondered where she would be accommodated. I could trust mother to see that she had every comfort, every attention – but I must do my share.

And so I set forth in a style that would have rounded little Willum's eyes. Something must be done for him, too – an apprenticeship, or even that job as a tiger. And for Bess. Try how I might, however, I could not imagine her donning the demure garb of a servant or even a milkmaid.

Somehow, with thoughts such as these swirling about my head, I let my head fall back on the luxurious squabs and to my amazement passed most of the night asleep, woken only by the changes of horses. Having sped at something like ten miles an hour, we were able to wheel at last into Leamington in time to bespeak breakfast at the Angel.

I was so keen to follow Edmund's instructions to the letter that, using the rough paper, vile pen and muddy ink that the landlord provided, I wrote to him confirming my safe arrival in Warwickshire, my note returning with my brother's team. Then, to ease my unaccountably aching limbs, I walked about the town to do a little shopping before returning to a hired hack, on which I jogtrotted easily home. I went via Langley Park, knowing how anxious Mrs Hansard must be.

It was my good fortune to find her in the garden, in conversation with the gardener. She soon abandoned him, and, tucking her arm in mine, was ready to return to the house. I bent our footsteps towards their pretty wilderness, however, lest we be overheard. Pressing Edmund's note into her hand, I attempted in the privacy of the grove to tell her all our adventures.

At length she nodded her understanding of my garbled narrative. 'And Edmund wishes me to accompany her ladyship on this journey?'

'He thinks you might prefer to. But cudgel my brain as I might, I cannot think of the reason you might give for doing so. Certainly she will need a lady's support when she sees her son, and loyal as we must believe all her household must be, Edmund was reluctant to let any of them into the secret.'

'I will speak to her and see how it may be arranged,' she said firmly. 'And you want the same discretion in our household, too?'

'Absolutely. And even in mine. Though Edmund did not explain how three of us should suddenly take it into our heads to travel to the same far-flung part of the kingdom.'

She squeezed my hand. 'Lady Chase and I can ponder the matter. Meanwhile, I suppose you must go post haste to the Hall?'

'Indeed no. My orders were quite explicit. I was to be seen going about my normal tasks, making my morning call tomorrow.'

'And will you retain your locum? Alas, poor Mr Rogers cannot be easy with the villagers, nor they with him.'

I laughed. 'But, as Mrs Powell would say, he has only been here five minutes. How long did it take me to acquire a decidedly grudging respect? And I am sure it was Edmund's sponsorship of me as a friend that tipped the balance. They like and respect him, so they must try to do the same for me.'

'You do not do yourself justice. However, you do not answer my question.'

'I fear he must go home, or it will look as if my journey is premeditated. Poor Rogers – he needs both the country air and the money.'

'You can always summon him back again?'

I shook my head. 'In truth, I trust it will not take us long to reach whatever estate Lady Chase selects. Then we are to return immediately – I, at least.'

'Ah, ha – you do not like to be away from Lady Dorothea.'

'I wish I could keep her out of my thoughts, dear Mrs Hansard. I do during the day when I can keep my mind occupied. But who can control their dreams? Emphatically she would not make a clergyman's wife – but when her bright eyes gleam with amusement at something I say or do...Yes, I confess, I still carry the tiniest of torches for her. Were she to know where I stayed in London, how I travelled to Leamington – but that would mean she loved my family and its accoutrements, not me, would it not?'

'Come and have a glass of wine, Tobias. And then everything will seem much better.'

As I had promised, I did not make my morning call at the Hall until the following day, having sent Rogers on his way with many thanks, two baskets of fruit and vegetables from my cottage garden, one of Mrs Trent's matchless cakes, a fine ham, and, though he did not know it, a couple of extra guineas folded into a scrap of paper at the bottom of his valise.

I was shown directly to her ladyship's private bookroom, where she was going through her accounts with Furnival. We exchanged commonplaces, and I was able to reassure her that my relative's illness had been much exaggerated. Since this personage's very life was an extravagant fiction, it could scarcely be otherwise.

At last, with almost a girlish flounce, she pushed away her papers and declared that she had had enough of tedious figures. Furnival might present himself, should he think it necessary, the following day, but she would take a turn about the knot garden. Since the day was sunny, despite what the locals called a lazy wind, blowing not round but straight through one, such a decision was hardly likely to raise the most suspicious eyebrow. Accordingly the old man bowed himself out, and Lady Chase gripped my hand almost painfully.

'Well?'

'With respect, your Ladyship, I think we should put your plan into operation. The day is cold, but a turn in the fresh air never did anyone any harm.' I kept my voice as even as I could, my face bland.

'How dare you keep me thus in suspense?'

I touched my finger to my lips. 'Pray ring for your maid and ask for your pelisse and bonnet. Perhaps even a muff.'

We were scarce out of earshot of the house when I said, very quietly, 'You must walk and talk as normally as if we were discussing the black spot on that rose.' I pointed. 'Do you understand?'

At last she bent towards the same plant.

'Your son lives, your Ladyship. But he is far from well.' I gave the briefest explanation.

'Bring him here this instant! I can nurse him back to health.'

'Alas, no. Dr Hansard believes – we all believe – Hugo to be in great danger should anyone discover his whereabouts. Think of the fate of the mere messenger.'

I thought she would faint, as she staggered almost drunkenly. But I took her arm and held her upright. 'Is there a stone in your shoe, your Ladyship? Let me assist you.'

She looked at me blindly, but at last realised what I was trying to do, and, still leaning heavily on my arm, slipped her shoe from the patten she was wearing and shook it vigorously.

'Excellent,' I said. 'Now this is what Edmund proposes we should do...'

It was not to be expected that she take everything in immediately, and I had to repeat details several times before she was able to absorb everything.

'You fear that Hugo will never be himself?' she asked bleakly at least.

'Your Ladyship, I am not the one to ask. Even Dr Hansard confesses himself unsure. But he will seek out the finest medical man in the land for you, if that is your wish – nay, I do not need to ask. The finest and the most discreet, of course. He warns that you may have to turn whatever is your choice of estates into what may be virtually an asylum for him.'

'He has – had – happy memories...'

'And may have them still, my Lady, simply waiting to be aroused. He has suffered injuries to the head, I know not how severe. He seems to have lost his power of speech, but not of understanding. He is anxious but biddable. My apologies – you were about to speak of a place he loved.'

She nodded. 'My own nurse is retired to the dower house of one of the estates that formed part of my jointure. It is in Shropshire, somewhat south of Shrewsbury. Perhaps its very peace and tranquillity will bring healing.'

'Amen.'

'I will tell my people that poor Mrs Rooke is dying of a painful female complaint. Does Mrs Hansard have family there, and would benefit from a seat in my carriage?'

'I am sure she does, my Lady. And if she does not, we can obtain one from the same source as my relative in Kent.'

CHAPTER EIGHTEEN

Edmund once told me that there was an oriental proverb to the effect that travel with hope in one's heart was often better than what one found when one arrived. So, I fear, it seemed with our various journeys to Ditton Priors, the village in Shropshire nearest to the remote manor house that had formed part of her ladyship's dowry. As Lady Chase had said, her own nurse, Mrs Rooke, a sprightly dame not much above sixty, lived in retirement in the dower house, but the manor itself had been shut up for years, since the late Lord Chase found it intolerably damp and gloomy.

We were not surprised. Hardly did it seem that we could ever make it habitable in the short time before the other party reached us, although they were travelling more slowly and, of course, much further. Indeed, at the very sight of it, Lady Chase, for the first time in our acquaintance, succumbed to an attack of the vapours. We had to convey her back to the dower house, where she was bustled into bed by Mrs Rooke.

'For shame on you, bringing the poor lamb here at such a

miserable time of year. Well, you have your reasons, no doubt?'

'We have indeed. And her ladyship will no doubt explain more fully when she is recovered.'

There was very little room at the dower house, which was in truth far less grand than the name implied. Mrs Rooke gave up her own room for her ladyship, accommodating Mrs Hansard in the best guest chamber, and, on my insistence, taking the only other bedchamber herself. Her cook and maid-of-all-work, on whom so much extra work would fall, could not be asked to leave her quarters. Accordingly, rather than share with Mrs Rooke's outdoor man, I was relegated to an attic, which did not boast a fireplace but was wonderfully scented with the apples she was storing there.

As we prepared the manor, Mrs Hansard came into her own. Since her marriage to Edmund, she had truly become a lady of fashion, having despite her years retained a neat, indeed youthful, figure. Now she divested herself of her elegant attire, almost literally rolling up her sleeves the better to work. She began by hiring a small army of local women, paying enough for them to keep their mouths closed even if – in this remote part – anyone might be interested in their activities.

As for Lady Chase herself, Mrs Hansard reasoned that the best cure for her melancholy was not to sit watching the seemingly unremitting drizzle, but to join in the improvements. Accordingly, the grieving mother was given fabric to cut into curtain lengths. That done, she was to hem them. Although she was reluctant at first, I truly believe that doing something so visibly useful helped restore her spirits.

Meanwhile I made myself useful by journeying to Ludlow

or Bridgnorth to buy anything from paint to clothes pegs. My only attempt at sweeping a chimney ended in so much mess and an equal amount of derision that thereafter my only contribution to the fires was to chop endless quantities of wood so that every room could be aired.

With all our efforts, when the invalid and his friends arrived late one afternoon, they could be welcomed into something very closely resembling a home.

There was, alas, no question of a dramatic and touching reunion – Lady Chase must have realised that as soon as she saw her son's condition, even as she held open her arms and called his name. It must however be said that the combined attentions of Jem, Edmund, and Bess, not to mention the medical man and his assistant whom they had brought with them, had decidedly improved his appearance. But Chase, like all the group, was bone weary; unlike them, he was too weak to do anything other than retire to his room.

'Done to a cow's thumb, he is,' Bess declared, shoving him willy-nilly up the fine old oak staircase. 'So don't look so Friday faced, Lady C. I'll have him tucked up in the twinkling of a bedpost.'

As they disappeared, Lady Chase's voice came as no more than a hoarse whisper; she fought with understandable tears. 'He does not recognise his own mother.' She added, appalled, even though Willum had found more appropriate apparel for poor Bess, 'And he smiles at That Woman.' She sank into a chair by the welcoming fire lit in the great hall.

Edmund found hartshorn in his valise and mixed it with a little water. 'Already there is some improvement, my Lady,' he insisted, pressing the glass to her lips. 'He has now recalled, without prompting, that his name is Hugo. And as we drove into the grounds, he said something about a rope swing.'

Her face lit up. 'He remembered that? It used to hang from an oak in the paddock. Let it be restored tomorrow.'

'Let it indeed.' Edmund looked around for Mrs Hansard. Finding her, he crossed the room and kissed her hand. He did not need to say anything. Nor did she, as she blushed rosily as a girl.

'Dinner can be served as soon as everyone is ready,' she said, struggling to regain her composure. She beckoned two of the new servants. 'Owen, Mary – remember your duties. Show our guests to the rooms we have prepared for them, and then bustle about with the hot water. Off you go now.' As they went, awkward in their new uniforms and new responsibilities, she smiled with a mixture of exasperation and amusement.

Though Lady Chase insisted on moving up from the dower house to her old chamber in the manor, there was not room for all of us to follow suit. Dr Hansard suggested that Mrs Hansard should remain there, to supervise, he said, the inexperienced staff's morning activities, a proposition with which she did not argue. But after supper Jem and I returned to the dower house, and the apple-scented attic.

'Is there likely to be a happy ending?' I asked Jem.

'Possibly for some. But it seems too much to hope for one for everyone.' He extinguished the candle.

What did he mean by that? Had his taste for another life made him dissatisfied with his old one? I would hardly be surprised. The only question was what occupation he might take up. Even as I opened my mouth to ask, his breathing slipped into snores.

* * *

Once he had assured himself that Hugo was in the best of hands, Dr Hansard declared it was time for the party to break up. Mrs Rooke undertook to do whatever housekeeping was needful, so Maria and Edmund set forth first, visiting friends in Droitwich en route to Langley Park.

Bess insisted on staying with Hugo, who clearly depended on her far more than Lady Chase liked.

''Ow could I not? 'Enry left him in my care, after all,' she said reasonably, coming down to my makeshift timber yard for ten minutes' fresh air. Jem, to whom the task would have fallen at home, was amused by my pretensions, and spent his time bringing the stables to his exacting standards. He had discovered a useable gig, and had managed to buy what he declared was a reliable, sweet-natured cob. 'Lanky – his lordship, I *should* say – wouldn't be alive now but for 'Enry. Well, you can see those scars, can't you? Pity you gentlemen don't wear wigs no more, 'cos far as I can see that hair of his is never going to grow anything like. But he wouldn't have survived without me neither. Not since 'Enry went.' Her voice changed from the almost unremittingly cheerful. 'D'you reckon he suffered, Parson? 'Enry? At the end?' She frowned back tears.

I laid aside my axe. 'Hardly at all. There was no sign of a struggle where we found his flask and Hugo's ring.'

'Got hisself drunk and just keeled over? And then the stream flooded and took him off? Come on, Parson – I've cut my eye-teeth, you know. All this secrecy.' She looked around her and spread her hands. 'You think someone done him in, don't you? And you want to make sure no one does Lanky in.'

I looked her full in the eye. 'Or you, of course. If they think you have information about his whereabouts.'

'I reckon that's the only reason his old ma puts up with me,' she said, sitting on a log. 'She thinks I'll blab if I go back. But I wouldn't, Parson. I wouldn't.'

'I know you wouldn't. You have behaved extraordinarily kindly, generously, towards the young man. I honour you for your loyalty and devotion, Miss Bess.'

She gave me a self-deprecatory grin. 'I got fond of 'im, didn't I?'

'And you want to see what becomes of him?'

Her head went to one side as she reflected. 'Yes, I suppose that's it. If he'd been a common soldier boy, it'd have been better for me, you know. 'Cos if he'd got better, he'd have stayed with me and looked after me for a change.' She sighed. ''Ere, put your weskit back on – you'll be froze to the marrow.'

I obeyed. 'And as it is?'

'I s'pose I shall have to go back to me whoring. Ain't much else for the likes of me.'

'I promised you you'd never had to do that again – if indeed, you want to go back to London. Her ladyship will make provision for you for life, Bess.'

'Not without you nagging her, she wouldn't. Can't bear knowing he'd rather it was me kissed him goodnight than her.'

I suspected that that was a euphemism, but could scarcely ask. 'She will be generous,' I insisted. 'Would you prefer a pension for life or a position?'

She regarded me, hands on broad hips. 'I can't see me working at some great house, can you? Except the gentlemen want a spot of...No?' She laughed at the shock on my face. 'But going back to London, to that room... I dunno, Parson, I dunno.'

Who could wonder at the poor woman's doubts? 'Were you never apprenticed?'

'Tried me hand at being a milliner, but it's me eyes, see – not up to it. Either that or the mother's ruin giving me the shakes of a morning. Trouble is, Parson, you gives me a purse full of money, I shall booze it all away, and soon find myself in dun territory.'

'A weekly or monthly allowance? No? The more the money, the bigger the bender?' I smiled sadly. 'We shall think of something.'

'Well,' she said, pulling her shawl tightly round her shoulders and standing up, 'no point in us both hanging round here catching our deaths, is there? He'll probably be awake, a-calling for me.' She shook her shirts free in a gesture her ladyship would have recognised. If only I could persuade her to converse a little with the poor creature.

'Wait a moment, Bess. What would you really like for the future?'

She stopped short and turned, shaking her head. 'I dunno. You see, Parson, no one's ever asked me that before. Things sort of 'appen to me, if you knows what I mean.' As if faced with an insoluble conundrum, she chewed on a thumbnail and shrugged. She took a couple of paces away from me. 'Maybe I shall stay here,' she said, over her shoulder. Before I could respond, she returned to the house.

I lifted my axe again, with all the more fervour because of my inability to see a future for her. At least, I told myself, for the time being she was useful, clean, well fed and learning – from Mrs Rooke's example – how to conduct herself with decency and sobriety.

'You won't leave *me* here, though, will you, Parson?'

Willum demanded, coming on me as I weighed into the next log.

'Heavens, boy, I nearly chopped off my fingers!' I shouted, for I had indeed stripped a long slice of skin from a finger. There was a great deal more blood than there should have been, soaking quickly through my handkerchief. As the blood flowed, so did my fierce words. As it eased, I said more gently, 'My apologies, Willum. I didn't mean to ring a peal over you. But you must never make anyone jump when they are doing something dangerous – no creeping up on a cook, for instance, when she's wielding a carving knife. Do you understand?'

'Or a man when he's loading a gun?'

'Exactly. So you don't want to stay in Shropshire, Willum? It's very beautiful round here.' To be honest, I did not really want to take him back to Moreton St Jude. I feared he would let slip enough hints about his recent adventures to put everything at risk.

'Quiet as the grave, more like. Everyone as blue as a megrim. And now you're in a dudgeon and going to leave me here, so help me.' Occasionally – at a time like this – his self-assured mask would slip and he would become the child he was: anxious, vulnerable and indeed inclined to tears.

I smiled and shook my head. 'I'm not in a dudgeon – except maybe for the same reason as you. I'm missing my home.'

'Not missing mine, 'cos I ain't got one to miss – I told you.' Lower lip a-tremble, he left the silence to grow.

At last I succumbed, as he must have known I would. 'Would you like to come and live in the rectory with Jem and me?' What work we could find for him I had no idea.

'Bit of a rum touch, isn't it, a village having two parsons?'

'Jem is only a parson when he's in London, Willum,' I said, hoping that would be the end of the matter.

'I'm more than seven, you know. You can't be a parson only part of the time.'

'The rest of the time Jem works with horses,' I said, not attempting to argue.

He would as long as he stayed, at least. Jem had had itchy feet a while back, after a disappointment in love. Probably he realised, as I did, he could be far more than a simple groom. To be sure, he could not read and write in Greek, but he was lettered in English, and wrote a good hand. Perhaps if Willum relieved him of some, if not all, of his other duties, he could teach in the school Lady Chase proposed establishing for all the village children. He was patient enough, and firm, and would set an excellent moral tone – after all, he was not just my groom, not just my friend, but also my mentor.

'I'm good with nags. I always wanted to be a tiger.'

'I don't need a tiger. Not in the country.'

'Not need a tiger? You're a bang-up cove for all you're a man of the cloth, aren't you? Stands to reason you need a tiger.'

'Not in the country. It's different there. But what I will do is ask Lady Chase's coachman if you may ride on the box on the journey back to Warwickshire.'

His face lit up. 'Can I handle the ribbons?'

'With her ladyship inside? Willum, you joke me.' I softened. 'If you make me a solemn promise, then I undertake at least to ask if you may sit beside James.'

'Feed me liver to crows and let ravens peck my eyes out if I let you down, guv.'

I managed not to shudder. I had seen what birds could do

not just to sheep, of course, but also to humans. 'I'm sure you won't let me down. Because if you do it's straight back to London with you. I want your most solemn oath never, under any circumstances, unless you have my express permission, never to reveal what happened in London and what has happened here in Shropshire.'

'Nor any of the journey in between?' he prompted.

'Exactly.

He spat in his palm. We were to seal the bargain by shaking hands. 'Done. I won't tell no one. Not that I shall know anyone to tell, shall I? You and Parson Yeomans apart, that is.'

'Oh dear, Willum, you've made a mull of it already. He's only a parson in London, remember. From now on, he's Mr Jem.' I would not confuse him with the Turbeville or Yeomans problem.

Willum gave a parody of a salute. 'Mr Jem it is.' His face troubled, he added, 'But you're still Parson Campion, aren't you?'

'I am indeed. Now, will you stack these logs while I go and find a bit of clean rag for this cut of mine?'

As Dr Hansard insisted, we all settled quickly back into our old ways back in Moreton St Jude. Dr Toone had delivered two more babies, whose parents wanted them christened immediately, before the cold of winter set in. Old Mr Jakeman had died in his privy, which gave rise to certain jokes best not repeated in company. The mummers were deep into rehearsals.

Lady Chase, however much she would have preferred to be in Shropshire, was much to be seen about the village dispensing charity; only three of us knew that she received regular reports of her son, which were sent either to the rectory or to Langley Park, never to the Hall.

Receiving her in my study two or three days before Christmas, I presented her with the latest. Absently she sipped a glass of Madeira, brought with a respectful curtsy by Susan, reading and re-reading the document as if studying her son's face. She did not speak until Susan had left the room and quietly closed the door behind her.

'The weather has been fine enough for him to sit on that swing we set up for him,' she said. 'And he has started to recall other events that took place there. He walks as far as the village now, and there is talk of him riding again. And – yes – he asked about his regimentals last night.'

'That is excellent news,' I began, but raised a finger as I heard a commotion in the hall.

Susan knocked on the door. 'There's a strange man arrived,' she announced. 'And there's nothing for it but he sees you, although her ladyship's here.' She bobbed another, lower curtsy.

'Ask him to wait in the morning room, if you please, Susan. Offer him some refreshment and tell him I will be with him shortly. Well?'

'It's just as – he looks very rough, sir. And he talks very funny, so I can hardly understand him. Like Willum,' she added, with a burst of inspiration.

I had an inkling who this might be. 'Even so, do as I tell you,' I said gently but firmly. 'And bid Jem join us there.'

With another bob, and a rosy blush, she left us.

Lady Chase rose to feet. 'I will leave you to this intriguing person, Tobias.'

'Thank you, my Lady. But you forget one thing.' As inexorable as Edmund would have been about destroying any news of Lord Chase, I pointed at the fire. 'The missive, my Lady.'

CHAPTER NINETEEN

The visitor rose, treating us to a bow and an affable smile. 'Alfred Mullins of the Runners at your service, gents.'

Susan was right. Mr Mullins did speak like Willum, presumably because he came from the same part of the country – London. In fact his accent was his only defining aspect: he was indeterminate in appearance, build and even age. Was that how a Runner eschewing his distinctive red waistcoat should look? Such anonymity might be needful in some duties, where to be recognisable might be a hindrance. But I found the studied nothingness unnerving, not knowing what it might conceal.

'Like manna from heaven, that,' he declared, running his stubby finger round the plate he held, as if to endure that not a single scrap of whatever refreshment Susan had brought should elude him. His tankard, which had held ale, was no doubt as clean as the plate.

I gestured him back to his seat, refilling the tankard. Jem, taking his favourite chair, also accepted ale; I helped myself to wine.

'You have news for us, Mr Mullins,' I prompted. 'But first, I wonder if you could prove that you are who you say you are.'

Raising an eyebrow, he showed me his warrant. 'There's not many as has the rumgumption to ask that,' he said, as if undecided whether my wariness merited suspicion or respect.

As for me, I became ever more convinced that Mullins was not the mutton-headed fool he would like us to believe him, but a man of considerable native intelligence. 'Thank you. And what do you have to report?'

'I been the length and breadth of the country,' he affirmed. 'And the roads getting deeper and dirtier by the minute. Durham one day, Devon the next. I tell you, I'm worn to a frazzle – and me piles getting worse by the mile. Begging your pardon, your reverence.'

'Parson Campion will do,' I said. 'And what news do you bring me?'

He made a great show of reaching out his notebook, but I thought he had the information by heart. 'I have not yet spoke to the party on whose premises you was robbed in broad daylight, sir, but I understand that he – or even they – are expected any moment in Dawlish, down in Devon, that is, for Christmas.'

'Not yet arrived? So where have they been since they quit London in such haste some three weeks since?'

My question had been rhetorical, but he responded with a shrewd one of his own, with nothing of the rhetorical about it. 'Why are you so wishful to know, if I might make so bold?'

Feeling that I was suddenly the one under suspicion, I temporised. 'From London one may reach Dawlish in three or four days – Devon is hardly the end of the earth.'

'Why, as to that... But I grant you, Parson, their route has been unusual, given their destination. And they have done mortal strange things, like bespeaking rooms at one inn, but staying at another. You sure it ain't the crown jewels they half-inched?'

'Not from me, at least.'

'Quite so. As for the nurse, she does indeed come from Northumberland. But she will not, according to my informant, be returning there because she is still in the employ of the Larwoods, who will be requiring of her services over the festive season. And the first snowflakes are falling,' he added plaintively and not at all irrelevantly.

I rang for more refreshment, not least because however much I had expected, nay, hoped for this news, I needed urgently to reflect. It had come at a time when I simply could not act upon it. How could I leave my flock, neglect divine worship, during the second most important festival in the church calendar? The simple answer was that I could not.

Susan, round-eyed with curiosity, brought more of Mrs Trent's excellent biscuits and another jug of ale. I would have to invent some explanation for Mr Mullins' visit, because, whether or not I swore both housekeeper and servant to secrecy, everyone in the village would be talking about it before dusk.

Mullins was used to practising discretion; he made no attempt to speak till she had left us on our own once more.

'Will you be wanting me to go to this 'ere Dawlish and apprehend the party on suspicion that one of their servants robbed you?' he asked, mouth not quite empty.

Put like that, the venture seemed absurd. I temporised. 'It is Christmas, it is not? The time of good will to all men. And I am sure you have a home to go to.' I smiled persuasively.

'Aye, that I have. And a Mrs Mullins and a whole quiverful of nipperkins a-waiting for me.' He applied himself to his tankard, but his eyes were ever observant.

'Be so good as to furnish me with the address that you have discovered, Mr Mullins. Then I can decide what action to take. And you, my good friend, may post back to London, happy in the knowledge of a job well done.'

'You're no longer wishful for me to question them? Well, if that don't beat cockfighting!' He fixed me again. 'I suspicioned all along you just wanted to know their whereabouts – that all that stuff about a robbery was cock and bull.'

I raised a chilly eyebrow. 'Indeed I was robbed in the Larwoods' very backyard – and your colleagues at Bow Street saw my injuries with their own eyes. But as a Christian, I must practise forgiveness.' I allowed a sanctimonious note to warm my voice, not daring the while to meet Jem's eye.

'So what would you be wanting to know their whereabouts for? *If* I might make so bold?'

My smile verged on the unctuous. 'Just because I do not wish the miscreants to be pursued with the full force of the law, Mr Mullins, does not mean that I am happy for them to retain my watch. I shall write to them asking them to return it; if they do, than I shall consider the matter closed.' Glancing out of the window, I observed, 'Oh, dear, now the snowflakes come not as single spies but in battalions.'

'Like sorrows, according to the Bard,' Mullins reflected, his chin at a slightly challenging angle.

I bowed my appreciation. This man was no less a scholar than Jem.

He plainly thought of me as no more than his equal. 'Seems to me it's very strange that you should only have bethought yourself of a bit Christian forgiveness when I've done all the hard work for you. But then, I'm not man of the cloth, so I wouldn't know about such things, would I?'

'How I would have liked to employ Mullins further,' I confessed to Jem as we waved the Runner on his way. 'He knew that while I might have been telling the truth, I was far from telling the whole truth. I nearly made a mull of the whole thing, didn't I?' I added frankly.

Jem kindly ignored the last question. 'He's a downy one, awake on every suit, no doubt about it, for all he feigns to be a buffle-headed clunch. It was a good idea,' he conceded with a grin I had not seen for some time, 'to bring him into Leamington and see him on to the coach. It would not have done for him to go sniffing round the village, making enquiries about our activities. He'll be pleased to return in some luxury to his family for the festive season – but I doubt we've seen the last of him, Toby.'

'I fear you are right. I just hope we reach Dawlish before he does.'

'You're not thinking of setting out before Christmas?'

'Indeed no. And not in this snow, either.'

'They say in the village it will not last above two days, and not lie then. Where they get this intelligence from I know not, but they always seem correct in their predictions. If they are, her ladyship's Christmas party should be safe, thank the Lord.'

'As to that, amen. But as soon as the festival is over – assuming the roads are passable – we must be on our way.' I looked at the shop fronts, lit by flambeaux. 'I think we have time, before we must return to the rectory, to make a few purchases for all the children, do not you? Their parents will have no money to spare, and what little they scrape together will be for useful and sensible items like boots.'

He clapped me on the shoulder. 'I see oranges over there. And tops and whips...'

All too many landlords thought that by giving a single lavish Christmas party they made up for underpaying and badly housing their labourers for the rest of the year. A little largesse in the form of copious quantities of beef and ale was supposed to compensate for the inadequacies of the diurnal diet. Lady Chase, of course, personified bountiful generosity, but nonetheless accepted my suggestion that an extra celebration might not go amiss. I thought planning the event might take her mind off Hugo, still residing in Shropshire.

Furnival had presented his usual gloomy face when apprised of her decision, but now the mummers were engaged and the carol singers particularly invited to sing at the Hall. The party itself was to be held on Christmas Eve, all those able adjourning afterwards, at Lady Chase's suggestion, to Midnight Communion. To my enormous pleasure, Lady Dorothea even asked if she might augment the little band playing for the service by taking her place at the organ.

Ashamed of my lingering folly, I was yet impelled to solicit her hand for one of the dances at the estate party, as she stood with the other ladies of the household receiving our guests. There rose from them all an overwhelming odour of mothballs and damp. The females' gowns were so garish as to suggest that old garments had been recently dyed to lift the mood. In contrast, and such a contrast, Lady Dorothea wore a soft green overdress over a slip of a slightly paler hue, and carried an ivory fan. Her curls shone with brushing and good health.

With my enquiry I might as well have pulled a blind down over her face. After a moment, however, she recovered her gaiety. 'Surely you should be engaged in leading a rustic maiden through the dance. Polly Freeman now – she would be what I hear the lads call a fine armful. Or Lucy Croft – if you do not object to her squint, of course.' She made play with her own fine eyes to ensure that I noted the difference.

I could not forbear laughing. And yet even in the heady moment I wished she had not made a butt of the girls who had made such an effort, far greater than hers since they lacked both her beauty and her purse.

'Indeed, I will dance with as many maidens as I can, provided their swains do not monopolise them – they are unaware that one should not dance more than two dances with the same partner. But I would be more than honoured if you would grant me the privilege of leading you into a set.'

Perhaps Furnival, standing behind us, blamed me in part at least for the revelry on the floor and the bounty on the tables. I could not otherwise explain what for a second appeared to be a look of cold hatred in our direction. But it seemed he was merely suffering one of his arthritic twinges, for he hobbled across to me to shake my hand and wish me the compliments of the season.

'I have not welcomed you back after your travels,' he said. 'I trust your relative is recovered.'

'She ever enjoyed indifferent health,' I said with a deprecatory smile.

'And her ladyship's old nurse?'

'A doughty dame, who resented our anxiety as much as she welcomed our presence. Thank goodness her ladyship has you to rely on when she has these strange starts, Furnival.'

'Thank you, sir. I do my poor best.'

Lady Dorothea and I joined with a will in the first of the country dances she had promised me. However, she suggested we sit out for the second, and she led the way into the blue saloon, where refreshments had been set aside for the family – a break with tradition of which I did not approve, preferring that on one day at least we should all be social equals.

'When you look so fine in evening dress,' she said with a flirtatious smile, 'I wish you would tell me what persuaded you to become a clergyman. I asked you once, but you were notably evasive. Now, pray tell me. Was it simply because that is the lot of the youngest son?' She took a glass of champagne from a convenient tray and toasted me with it, her eyes shining above the rim.

I returned the gesture, but with a heavy heart. 'Do you think the church is never chosen for its own sake?' I could not but wonder why she had chosen this particular night to question me again. Had some rumour of my activities somehow reached her, in particular my free use of my family's house?

'*Never* is a heavy word. But yes, in the *never* of conversation, which means *not very often*, I do think it. For a man should distinguish himself. A man might distinguish himself in the army, better still the navy, but not in the church. A clergyman is nothing.'

'Does *nothing* have the same gradations as *never*? I confess,

Lady Dorothea, that I shall always be *nothing* as far as leading the *ton* or making a fortune on 'Change are concerned. But I cannot call what I am doing in the sphere in which I find myself *nothing*. I am entrusted with my Master's work: caring for my flock, both individually and collectively. I am responsible for inculcating good principles, distributing the necessities of life—'

'As to that, a schoolmaster could do the first, and Lady Chase makes it her business to do the latter.'

'But would either endeavour to teach not just good manners, but the difference between good and evil? Lady Chase offers earthly comfort, may God bless her for it, but I am privileged to offer the promise of heaven.' In an attempt to reduce the tension between us, I added with a smile, 'Which you shall hear tonight, when you play for our service.'

'Oh, as to that—' For a long moment I feared that she was about to break her promise. Perhaps she was. But the petulance faded. 'Oh, as to that, I shall be too embarrassed by my mistakes to listen to any sermon. Who is operating the bellows for me?'

'Simon Clark – a good reliable man. And musical, too, if his performance in the dance is anything to judge by. Did you not see him almost whirling Dr Hansard's cook off her feet? Do you not think that they will make a match of it?'

She looked at me quite blankly; it was clear she did not know of whom I was speaking.

'Perhaps we should return?' I offered her my arm, all too conscious that the unchaperoned conversation was entirely unsatisfactory to both sides.

She took it with a smile, but drew me to an immediate halt. 'If a church, a parish, you must have, why not a London one, where your light may shine? Surely your family has influence.'

I chose to ignore the last sentence. How she had discovered what I preferred to keep hidden, I knew not. But it was a topic I was not prepared to engage in. 'Were I a fine preacher, perhaps I might be tempted. But as to setting an example, getting to know one's congregation, the city – any city – offers infertile ground. I would be lost in the crowds in London. Here I am known and – I like to think – observed. My manners, indeed, my conduct, must at all times be above reproach.'

'Like Caesar's wife,' she agreed, without enthusiasm, or, I fear, comprehension. Or perhaps she understood all too well. 'And what is to be the topic of your sermon, Parson Campion? Will it keep those rustics awake?' She pointed to two old gaffers, nodding over their jugs of ale.

The church was crammed, the warmth of the braziers Simon had set up being supplemented by the press of bodies. The ancient building was decorated with garlands Edmund assured me derived from an older, pagan tradition, but since the beauty brought smiles of joy to the faces of folk who had all too little to admire in their lives, I was sure the Almighty would look down with approval – just as He did on the occasional discords from the little band and the strained breathiness of the choir. What He thought of Lady Dorothea's performance I cannot tell. Even to think of the lady caused me such a confusion of anger and yearning and desire, all fuelled by champagne, that I kept my mind resolutely on the purpose of our gathering. Even during my sermon, when I tried to look into the face of each in the congregation in turn, I averted my gaze from her.

At least, God willing, I would be able to put a safe distance between us very shortly. The weather had set in fair, as the villagers had foretold, and Jem and I had resolved to set out in but two days. Perhaps it was the thought of our journey that made my references to the Slaughter of the Innocents and the Flight into Egypt all the more heartfelt.

Even Furnival thanked me as he left the church, in particular congratulating me on my sermon. To him and too all the others alike, I wished a most joyful Christmas and prosperous New Year.

CHAPTER TWENTY

'So that is stage coach travel,' I observed, easing my cramped and chilly limbs to the terra firma of the yard of the London Inn, a spacious modern building, clinging to a hillside only yards from the sea at Dawlish.

As the villagers had predicted, the snow had gone as swiftly as it had come, and we had set off for Devon accordingly.

We had spent more hours than I cared to recall aboard a vehicle apparently determined to stick in the snows of the uplands, or get bogged down where the thaw had set in. The forbidding hills of Dartmoor, which we could see in the distance as we crossed the smaller but hardly less awe-inspiring Haldon Moor, were still swathed in snow.

'It is indeed,' Jem said as he joined me joined me. The experience was new to him too, but was at the opposite extreme from mine. I had been used to making my journeys in the comfort of one of our family's luxurious chaises; his had been to accompany them, sometimes with what all too frequently in my family became a veritable luggage train, or leading my horses.

There had no question of his appearing as my groom on this trip. He was Mr James Yeomans again, my friend – though not this time feigning holy orders. Lady Chase's Christmas present to him, a mark of gratitude, she insisted, for his tender care of Lord Chase, had been a fine suit of clothes, with appropriate shoes and boots. Dear Mrs Hansard had made him some shirts with her own hands.

'Do you think we shall ever get rid of the smell of onion?' I asked. We had sat for sixty miles beside a farmer's daughter with the ear-ache and a baked onion pressed to her head.

'I doubt it. I believe it has permeated my very skin!'

'For a complete cleanse, we should try the sea-bathing,' I agreed, to have my suggestion greeted by the derisory snort of laughter I had hoped for. Dawlish might be milder than Warwickshire, but the afternoon sky over the brilliant sea was that deep clear blue that in winter presages a sharp frost. 'Pray, Jem, would you see if you can unearth our baggage? I will bespeak rooms for us.'

The serving maid who greeted us pulled a doubtful face when I requested a private sitting room in addition to two bed chambers. I resorted, as sometimes to my shame I did when I wished to win an argument, to imitating my father. Such a sudden access of hauteur sent her scurrying for the landlord. In welcome contrast to the girl, Mr Veale was all that was courteous and obliging.

Both the rooms his wife curtsied us into were clean and well appointed, and I had no doubt that the sheets had been properly aired. Ordering dinner, we set forth swiftly to take advantage of the fading light to see what there was of Dawlish, leaving the sea to our left as we headed inland.

'The whole place is a veritable builder's yard,' he said in

disgust, surveying the work in progress all around us.

There were many fine new residences wherever one looked, with many more half built.

'Indeed – but with these marshes lying between the village and the sea one could not imagine it to be a healthy place.'

Even as we stared down from a convenient bridge at the stream bisecting the town, a gentleman we took to be a resident accosted us pleasantly, inviting us to see how much work had been done to repair the damage done by what he referred to as the floods.

'To be sure,' said he, in the slow warm accent of a Devonian, 'it was hoped that by confining Dawlish Water – or as the villagers call it, the Brook, as if there were only one in the kingdom – to a single stream we would make a pleasant park. But we had terrible floods two years back, and all the good work was undone. But now we are trying again, with weirs – do you see that one there? – to stem the flow.'

'You are doubly at risk, I take it,' said Jem, 'from the waters coming down from the moor, and the sea making incursions inland?'

'Exactly so. And there are other streams too – those propelling our watermills. But if we are to develop the town to its fullest – and we have wonderful sea bathing here for gentlemen such as yourselves, with bathing huts along the eastward shore – we must improve the air.'

'And while you have marshes, you have miasmas?' I observed.

'And many rheumatic complaints. There is quite a little pilgrimage from here to Bath every winter. 'Tis much easier now the stage comes here – why, only two years ago, the nearest the stage stopped was Chudleigh. The rest of the journey had to be made by horse.'

I snorted. 'If the invalids' journeys are anything like ours, they will need to recuperate on their return – from bruises and bangs.'

'Dr Penhallow holds such agitation of the vital organs to be extremely healthy,' our interlocutor assured us, perhaps offended.

It was now so dark as to give an excuse to move away. As we doffed our hats, he produced a pasteboard card. 'Samuel Twiss, Builder, at your service,' he declared, swiftly recovering his composure in the interest of potential profit.

We said all that was proper, returning to the inn to be greeted by a roaring fire and a welcome bowl of hot punch.

The following day being the Sabbath, there was nothing we could do to pursue our enquiries. We took the path beside the brook, on which the bright sun made dazzling patterns, to St Gregory's, a church in a quite alarming state of dilapidation. There was a very small congregation for matins: I hoped and prayed that there was a better attendance back at Moreton St Jude, where one of Toone's friends, a man with a fine reputation as a preacher, was standing in for me. The harassed-looking parson was a man in his later thirties. Identifying me by my bands as a brother clergyman, he greeted me warmly, but with such an apologetic air, I truly felt for him.

'There must – shall – be a subscription started to repair, even replace this poor House of God,' he assured me.

'Indeed, you must have many new residents who will be delighted to assist you,' I observed.

He spread his hands in a speaking gesture. It was true, I had to admit, that not many of the occupants of the fine houses had wanted to commit their presence to the old church, as if it were beneath them, let alone their money to a new one. 'All too many of the properties are merely to be rented out for the summer,' he continued, 'to people leaving London when it becomes too hot and unhealthy there. I understand that a great number of naval officers are also likely to grace us with their presence, here and in Teignmouth, over the great hill, there, or across the river in Exmouth. Some will be true gentlemen, of course, but others will merely be fighting men laden with prize money.'

We spoke for a while about the village, and in particular about the curious redness of the soil.

'If you were minded to walk along the shore, you would see an even stranger phenomenon – the cliffs are decidedly rosy as they tumble to the sea,' declared a familiar voice.

Our conversation had been interrupted by our acquaintance of the previous evening, Mr Twiss, who swiftly introduced his wife and two daughters, Catherine and Julia, bearing us from the church on a tide of further encomiums about his beloved village. My father would swiftly have depressed the pretensions of such a mushroom, but it occurred to me, Sabbath or no Sabbath, that Mr Twiss might well be a source of information about the Larwoods, whose house we still had to locate. In any case, had I wished to decline their company, I was too late: Jem already had Miss Twiss on his left arm, and Miss Julia Twiss on the other, and was showing very sign of being charmed by the feminine attention as he was led towards the sea.

One could readily understand why Mr Twiss and his builder colleagues might wish to control the Brook and institute pleasant walks beside it. The beach it concluded in was truly excellent, with firm golden sand on which one might envisage boys kicking a ball or playing at cricket. To the west end of the beach fishing boats lay safely beached. Beyond the outcrop that sheltered them lay another fine cove, with two strange-shaped red rocks off-shore.

Mr Twiss roared with laughter when I asked about them. 'They are statues of you and Mr Yeomans.'

Mrs Twiss, a gentle-faced lady of much quieter disposition than her husband, shook her head in some embarrassment. 'Nay, Parson Campion. Take no notice of him, I pray you. We do call them the Parson and Clerk, indeed. Mr Twiss refers to a legend that an ambitious man of the cloth was led into the sea by the devil himself and there he sits to this day, his anxious clerk before him.'

Twiss, called thus to order, blushed and coughed and hoped we had not taken offence – 'For none was meant, I do assure you.'

'And none taken, my dear sir,' I assured him heartily.

The path being too narrow for three, Jem had to surrender Miss Catherine Twiss to my care. She was swathed like her sister and mother in a fur-trimmed velvet pelisse – hers was the deep rich green to which poor Bess might have aspired. With a pang I realised how little thought I had given since arriving in this pleasant place to Bess, still in Shropshire caring for Hugo, or to young Willum, who had insisted on coming to Warwickshire with us, and was presently caring for our horses under the careful eye of the Hansards' groom. How strange it must be for both of them, to have spent the festive season, no matter how luxuriously compared with their existence hitherto, so far from all that was familiar, if not loved?

But it would be uncivil not to make pleasant conversation

with the pretty damsel beside me, who was mightily forthcoming on the matter of assemblies here, in Teignmouth, Shaldon or even Newton Abbot. Lest I feel she was dwelling too much on the western side of the town, she enumerated the charms of Exeter, Exmouth and far distant Lyme. Clearly she was well travelled in the pursuit of pleasure, and highly discriminating between the dancing of one company of militia and another.

'As for Dawlish,' she assured me, 'although we could be considered a little thin of company, it is not often that we stand up with fewer than ten couples when my parents have a card party.'

I was beginning to regret that neither of us had brought evening clothes, with an agonising realisation that Jem did not possess such garments. But no invitation was forthcoming. Relinquishing her hold on my arm, she darted off up the hillside waving vigorously.

Her sister followed suit, leaving her parents to apologise to us for their being such sad romps. Secretly I suspect that Mr Twiss was proud to be able to declare that the couple they were racing towards were London friends of the girls.

Although the Londoners were swathed to the ears, my heart beat strongly. Surely a lock of ginger hair was escaping from the bonnet Miss Julia pushed back as she embraced her friend. For one precious moment it appeared that two groups might merge into one large party, but it was clear that the girls' hail was also to be their farewell. The young man and woman were pointing up the hill and again at the sky, as if to warn that there was very little daylight left. Waving, their laughter carried in the still air, they retraced their steps up the path they had but two minutes ago descended.

The sun having sunk suddenly behind the headland, we were plunged into instant dusk, and as the Misses Twiss ran back I was in terror that one might fall and break a well-turned ankle.

But all was well, and we too wended our way from the shore – but not to the inn. At some point – I knew not how, I knew not when – it had become understood that we should be their guests for dinner.

'Nothing grand,' Mr Twiss protested. 'Nothing hot. Just a cold collation, it being the Sabbath. And I would take it mighty fine, Parson, if you would lead us all in a prayer this evening before we read from the Good Book. Indeed, were you to say a few words, it would make a marvellous change from one of Mr Blair's sermons, though Catherine reads them aloud very pleasingly, I do assure you.'

I did not doubt it for one moment. Catching Jem's amused and assenting eye, I was happy to accept on behalf of us both.

Cold collation it might have been, but there was nothing of the hair shirt about the evening. The food was excellent and the wine well chosen, with no ostentation. In trade Mr Twiss certainly was, but in his elegant new home he behaved and spoke like a gentleman, not changing his attire himself lest we felt out of place in our breeches and boots. I suspected the Misses Twiss might have pouted a little when their mother gave instructions that they were to eschew evening wear too, but their walking dresses were replaced by the most modest and tasteful of gowns, as was Mrs Twiss's.

Over an excellent sherry, with ratafia for the girls, I was able – without appearing particular in my enquiries – to ask who the young couple were that we so nearly encountered.

'As I said, they live in London town. He has a position with the East India Company, I think, and is well on his way to making a fortune. Mr Larwood's parents live here – they farm out Holcombe way. Little Miss is their first grandchild, so you may understand how pleased the Larwoods are when they all make the long journey down here.'

'And Miss Marsh, as was, her parents come from up at Ideford, so they share the pleasure too,' Mrs Twiss added. 'They're second cousins, once removed, though you'd never think it to look at them – almost brother and sister they might be, with their guinea-gold curls.'

If I thought that that was carrying euphemism too far, I did not say so. Neither could I observe, as I wished, that their daughter must seem like a foundling. I cast round for something to say. 'I think I may have heard of young Mr Larwood,' I mused. 'I believe he is the friend of someone working at the bank my father patronises – Drummond's. And once I briefly met Mrs Larwood, and Miss Emma.' It was painful so to mislead such good people.

'You'll be wanting to call on them then. I will furnish you with their direction before you leave,' Mr Twiss declared.

'I am scarce on visiting terms,' I protested truthfully.

'They are such hospitable folk they'd want you to call. Old Mr George Larwood, Mr John's father, is housebound with the gout much of the time, and loves new faces. With the lanes so dirty at the moment you can scarce drive a gig up them, he doesn't have as much company as he would like.'

'Is it far?' I asked, almost despite myself.

'For a young man like you, not above the half hour,' he declared with finality.

Perhaps sensing my discomfort, Mrs Twiss interposed. 'Now, Parson Campion, it is at about this hour I ring for the servants to join our evening prayers. I believe my husband has already asked if you would be kind enough to lead us...'

CHAPTER TWENTY-ONE

I did not feel I had time to pursue the usual courtesies of leaving my card before making my call upon the Larwoods, so I presented myself the very next day at the house near Holcombe that the Twisses had indicated. Perhaps manners were freer here, for the rosy-cheeked servant had no hesitation in showing me into the morning room. Half of me was full of shame that I had imposed on the friendly family; the other half was pleased that at last I might ask a direct question of the parties I believed to be involved. Jem had insisted on waiting outside – perhaps he thought that the Larwoods might try to run for it, or perhaps he preferred not to lie yet again, even by implication, about his identity.

Guilt was uppermost when I was offered refreshment by Mrs George Larwood, a kindly old lady, a lace cap perched perilously on hair thick, springy hair still showing traces of the original auburn. I declined it swiftly, explaining apologetically that my business was in fact with the younger Larwoods. I remained on my feet.

'The matter is, alas, confidential,' I added.

With a shrewd look, she rang the bell, bidding the young servant, whose mousy hair looked almost abnormal in the household, to fetch Mr John. His wife was not mentioned.

Mrs Larwood did not quit the room when he appeared, but retired to the window seat and her stitchery.

Mr John Larwood, whom I judged to be in his late thirties, was a strong man of military bearing and a coat almost certainly cut by Stultz, although I had heard no suggestion that he might be engaged in anything other than commerce. His eyes, as blue as the previous day's sky, were set under brows, like his hair, almost orange in hue.

Now wearing my bands, I could be no less than honest, introducing myself under my own name. 'A few weeks ago I called at your house, Mr Larwood. My enquiry about the whereabouts of Mr Chamberlain caused your wife a great deal of anxiety; indeed, I think it made you flee the city.'

'I had received some bad news,' he blustered.

'I think that I myself was the bad news. But I came merely to ask a question, not to threaten you in any way. I assure you that you have nothing at all to fear from me.'

Despite my softly spoken and sincere words, his white skin became if possible even more bloodless. But he did not flinch from asking, 'Why do you want Mr Chamberlain?'

'I wished to restore some property to him. However, that was but part of a larger mission, Mr Larwood, concerning a death and a missing person.'

He nodded me to a seat, himself remaining on his feet, the better, I suspected, to control the situation. 'I deserve an explanation.'

After a moment, I sat down, thinking to reduce the tension crackling about the room. 'An explanation you shall have –

provided, Mr Larwood, that you reciprocate. I had arranged with your wife to speak to you at four. When I arrived to keep the appointment, I found no one at home. Calling at the back door of your house, in the hope of speaking to one of your servants, I was knocked down by someone emerging from your brew-house and robbed. Was this at your behest? In which case,' I continued, reading the answer in his face, 'Would you be kind enough to restore my watch to me? Its value is sentimental only.'

'Yes.' It was impossible to tell whether he was agreeing with my estimation of its value or acquiescing in my request. He made no effort to summon a servant or to leave the room himself.

'May I ask why you should do such a thing?'

'I wished...to deter you from following us. I hope your injury was not serious.' He sat heavily on a chair opposite, its legs so spindly that I wondered how they would support him. 'I repeat, what is Mr Chamberlain to you?'

'I do not know him.' I raised a placatory hand. 'Nay, I promise you that I tell the truth. But I think he knows a young lady who disappeared in most mysterious circumstances after a death in my parish. His address and a little property were found in the trunk she abandoned.'

'What was the property?'

'Something else of sentimental value. But not to me. You have a daughter, Mr Larwood, whose dark hair is at very least unusual in your family. May I tell you what I think? I think that you and your wife, denied by the Almighty issue of your own, have adopted her.'

I might have struck him. 'What of it?'

'I think you have given her a loving home she might

otherwise have lacked, and there is no shame at all in that. Heirs are adopted every day, young women taken into childless households to bear a woman company. So are you trying to protect someone else from the shame of disclosure? The natural mother?'

He was on his feet in an instant. 'How did you guess?' He motioned away his mother as she made to comfort him. She remained standing but, fearing she might faint, I rose and persuaded her to take my seat.

'The item of sentimental value was a lock of a baby's hair,' I said. 'It was not auburn, as yours is. And your daughter's is not auburn either.'

'It would ruin the woman were identity to be known. It is not my secret to betray.'

'I understand that. And believe me, when I promise you that were it not that a lady – possibly the same one – is being sought by the coroner as a witness, I would not have made this journey. Rather me than a court official or a Bow Street Runner,' I added. 'However, now I am here, I would also wish to assure myself of Miss Southey's good health. If one man is slain, and a young woman disappears, leaving behind her luggage, which is then ransacked, you will admit that there is cause for alarm.' Would my friend Dr Hansard have introduced the name at this stage? Had I been wise? But the risk might have had a result.

Without speaking, he rose and poured three glasses of wine, his hand shaking so much that a little slopped on the carpet.

'There is no need for anxiety, sir. I am a man of the cloth. You have my word that I will reveal to the court nothing that is not absolutely germane to the case.' For manners' sake, I sipped the wine, which was thin and sour. 'What I fear is that, knowing I am searching for her, Miss Southey will make the same desperate bid to escape as you and your family did, trying to elude all pursuers.'

He nodded, as if accepting the justice of that, at least.

Keeping my voice low, and, I hoped, gentle, I asked, 'Could it be that Miss Southey is your daughter's natural mother?'

'You'd best tell him, my son,' Mrs Larwood said quietly, a handkerchief to her lips. 'Then perhaps he'll go and leave us in peace.'

'If anyone finds out, we lose our daughter,' he declared, as if each word hurt his throat to utter it.

I took another risk. 'Because Mr Chamberlain does not want it known?'

He looked at me sharply. 'Indeed.'

'But he has no powers to remove her. Not unless she is his natural child,' I conceded.

'No, he is not. But he is an important man – has influence—'

Someone else had used almost the same words, had they not? I dredged my memory. At last I had it: old Mrs Powell had told me that Miss Southey had left the Hall in the company of an important man. I was tempted, however, to dismiss it as coincidence – the adjective was hardly unusual, after all.

'Sufficient influence to remove a child from a loving family? Unless he is the father indeed, I think not.'

'He is anxious to – to protect Miss Southey's good name.'

'In that case,' I reasoned, hoping that for once Dr Hansard would not have criticised my logic, 'if he is not the child's father is he the mother's?'

'Yes,' he whispered. 'But you are not here to speak of him, just of Miss Southey—'

'Am I to assume that Southey is an assumed name?'

'Possibly.'

'And is Chamberlain assumed also?'

'I do not know.' He looked me in the eyes. 'I give you my word, I do not know the true name of either party.'

Believing him, I pressed my fingers to my temples, not knowing which questions to ask next. At last I ventured, 'I think I must speak to Miss Southey herself. Do you know her whereabouts?'

'Not directly. I was told that – should the need ever arise – I must write to her care of a third party.'

'And who would that be?'

Mrs Larwood rose to her feet. 'We will have no peace from him, man of the cloth or no, until he has winkled every last secret from us.' Holding her handkerchief to her eyes, she fled the room.

'Your mother loves the child as much as you do,' I observed.

'She has brought light into our lives,' he declared. 'Mr Campion, I could not love her more dearly were she my own flesh and blood. My wife also. Can you not...must you...? Say I persuaded Miss Southey to write to this coroner of yours explaining what she saw and why she left – would not that suffice?'

'I wish with all my heart that it would. But a man has been murdered, Mr Larwood – a good man, who almost literally gave up his life so that another might live. A poor man, hoping for no reward but the good fortune of his friend. He lies even now in an unnamed grave in my own parish. Does not such a man deserve justice?'

I think I was about to persuade him, when we heard childish screams coming form outside the house.

'Dear God, that is Emma! What is happening to her?' And he dashed from the room.

CHAPTER TWENTY-TWO

It was as if the whole household, myself included, was like a flock of sheep set into a panic by the shadow of a bird. I suppose the Larwoods had already been cast into alarm by my reappearance. They must have construed everything in that light, with myself as a stage villain. So when they saw their precious child in a stranger's arms, they all thought the worst.

I at least could see that it was no vicious kidnapper who was holding Miss Emma, who was showing every sign of being charmed out of her tears. It was Jem.

'Give her back – for God's sake, man, have mercy,' Mrs Larwood implored.

Larwood looked ready to kill with his bare hands, but held back lest the vicious kidnapper harmed his daughter.

Meanwhile, I was trying – vainly, it seemed – to reassure everyone. 'She is quite safe, Mr Larwood. 'Tis my friend, Mr Yeomans – Pray, cease this noise at once. 'Tis my friend, I tell you. Enough! Jem, bring the child here, if you please.'

Not knowing what had but recently passed between us, Jem looked bemused, setting down an equally puzzled little lady, who swiftly apprehended everyone's anxiety and resolved to resume her noise. Mr Larwood darted to her and scooped her up, but she insisted even more loudly that she wanted her mama or her dear Nurse, a weary-eyed woman who now joined us.

Jem looked from one to the other. 'Miss Emma took a tumble and cut her hand. See, that is my handkerchief about the wound.' He addressed himself to the child, with his kindest smile. 'We had just decided that she would not expire on the spot, had we not, Miss Emma? And I had promised we would go and find Mama.'

'This is my friend, Mr Yeomans,' I reiterated. 'He did not wish to join me inside lest he overheard matters best kept within your family. But you may trust him with your life – and with your daughter's.'

'You said I might ride on your shoulders,' Miss Emma declared, holding out her arms to him.

Mr Larwood pressed her close, but the child was squirming so much she was likely to fall. Resigning himself to the inevitable, he set her down, and she ran straight to my friend. Nonetheless, he looked for approval from her parents before scooping her up. 'Young lady,' he said, tilting his head up so that she might hear, 'guide me to your nursery, so we can clean that hand of yours. And maybe Nurse will find you a bandage.'

Nurse Fowler smiled, however anxiously, and led the way indoors. By now Miss Emma was singing at the top of her voice – as Betty Ewers had declared, she had the sweetest voice and sang in tune, far from the monotonous yells that too often characterised our village children's music-making. The rest of us followed in stately procession, since our numbers now included the older Mrs Larwood, an indoor man, the servant who had admitted me and a sturdy and truculent-looking man whose rusty ginger hair and painful gait suggested most strongly that he might be Mr Larwood senior.

We foregathered once again in the room to which I had originally been admitted, but the ladies, both inclined to be tearful, agreed with Mr John Larwood that they should go and see how Miss Emma did. He found brandy of a far superior quality to the wine, and offered it to me and his father, with whom I exchanged a courteous bow.

'Your friend has certainly won the trust of my daughter,' the younger man conceded.

'He already has the trust and love of all who know him,' I declared. 'In fact, I ought to have asked him to speak to you in my place, for his simple eloquence would have convinced you more than my blundering words that we only seek the best for everyone. There is one thing that you should know, however,' I added. 'When I was assaulted and robbed, I sent for the Bow Street Runners, who found your address for me. The man on the case is a tenacious individual, by name of Alfred Mullins. I would not be at all surprised if he makes his way here, although I have declared the case closed.'

'Not if he is coming from London, he won't,' Mr George Larwood declared. 'I hear there's deep snow near Marlborough. Coaches jammed into the drifts, horses with broken legs – all sorts. I hate snow. We don't get much down here, thank the Lord, and if we do it doesn't lie, not like up on the moors. Just think of those poor Frenchies,' he continued, pointing to an old newspaper, 'coming all that way from Moscow in that Russian weather.'

'Nothing can make me pity them,' his son declared.

'Nay, in the general run of things, I loathe every last one. But 'tis the wicked leader of theirs, that Devil's spawn Napoleon, who I hate most. Half a million he takes to Moscow, officers and men, and 'tis said that only twenty thousand have managed to cross the Niemen. Killed not by the Russians, cleanly, in battle, but dying of hunger and cold.'

'Belike if the autumn weather had been more like autumn than winter there'd have been far more of them and all of them looking to invade us next,' his son said.

'Surely he will not make another attempt,' I said.

'That there Boney'll do anything, you mark my words. And all those Frenchies and Americans in that new prison up on Dartmoor, they'll all rise up and then where will we be?'

At least I had diverted his anxieties from his family, but it seemed that he was at peril from something far more dangerous than me. Perhaps we all were.

'What I would propose, gentlemen, is this,' I said, returning to the only matter over which I had control. 'If you furnish me with pen and ink I could write a deposition to Mr Mullins, explaining that all has been resolved and requiring him to leave you in peace. I might add a guinea under the seal to ease his conscience. But first I would ask you to trust me further. Surely you have access to Miss Southey without resort to Mr Chamberlain in case of an emergency?'

'You can have all the paper and ink you want,' Mr John Larwood declared. 'But on the last suit I cannot satisfy you. All I have is his address. I give you my word.'

'And will you trust me with that? I promise you the utmost discretion. And I will add a word to Mr Mullins to the effect that you are threatened with blackmail, and that he must give you all possible assistance should you require it.'

The men exchanged glances.

'Blackmail is what Mr Chamberlain threatens, is it not? Since you have not broken the law, you must be protected from those who do. Moreover, you are actually assisting the Warwickshire coroner, and entitled to security twice over.'

I had said something of significance, that was clear.

'Warwickshire?' Mr George Larwood repeated, but more to his son than to me. 'Is that not where—?'

'Where Mr Chamberlain lives?' I prompted. 'I beg you, let me have his address this instant.'

'We know not where he lives,' the younger man replied. 'If we ever had to contact him, we were supposed to send our letter to an inn in Warwick. The Rose and Crown. And we were not to expect a speedy response—'

'Which implies he does not collect his letters with any frequency,' I concluded. If only I had Dr Hansard beside me.

'That's what we thought. That belike he lives elsewhere, and only calls in on market day,' his father said.

Market day was a reasonable assumption if you were a countryman dependent on such things.

'Is there any reason why you might wish to write to him? Any emergency?'

Both shook their heads. 'Only *in extremis*,' the younger Mr Larwood declared. 'So that Miss Southey might attend...' He swallowed hard.

'To send such a message would be beyond all things cruel,' I said swiftly. 'I must confer with the coroner in charge of the case to see how he wishes to approach the problem. Gentlemen, in the circumstances you have been all consideration, all patience. But now I think Mr Yeomans and I must quit Devon with all speed.'

The old man nodded. 'Aye, that you should. If you don't want to be laid up at Bristol for a week with the snow.' Presumably he had the same ability to predict the weather as our villagers.

'But first your letter to Mr Mullins,' his son said, reaching a standish from a pretty escritoire, and finding passable paper in a drawer. 'Will you take some refreshment? You and Mr Yeomans? Cold meat and cheese can be had on the instant. Meanwhile I will have the gig harnessed, and a lad shall ride down to Dawlish to procure your seats on the stage. You have just two hours to pack your bags.'

'Part of it at least is easy,' Jem said.

He had flung our clothes into our valises while I paid our shot, and now we were ensconced, if not comfortably, in a coach whose only other passengers thus far were a comfortable-looking woman in her forties and a girl so young and pretty that I was surprised to see her travelling alone without a chaperon or even a servant. She was too shy to be drawn into conversation with even a clergyman such as I, and perhaps considered herself above the other woman, who spoke at length of her new situation in Cullompton. After feigning sleep the girl now genuinely slept, her rosy mouth falling slightly open. Her bonnet was sadly crushed against the squabs, as we jolted over ruts and through puddles. So far at least, as the older woman pointed out, we could be thankful that there was no snow. At each change of horses she sniffed the air, country-fashion, and declared that the worst we could expect yet was a sharp frost. As the day darkened all too swiftly into night, she was proved right, and she nodded with satisfaction as we helped her out at her destination.

'What part?' I asked Jem humbly, myself lacking the least idea of how to go forward.

'That inn in Warwick where we are to lure Mr Chamberlain. A good ostler is always required – and I am sure that you can pen a letter that will find them ready to employ me.'

'An ostler? In a public inn? Dear Jem, it is not to be thought of.'

'Nay, Toby, I am not some blushing maiden with a reputation to protect. We need someone to watch the comings and goings that a letter to Mr Chamberlain provokes. It has to be some sort of letter, I collect? Very well, I am the one to keep watch, and if necessary follow him to his home.' When I said nothing, he added anxiously, 'I believe that young Willum will tend your stable as well as I.'

'He will tend it well enough – but not as well as you, Jem. But I wonder if he – finding, as I am sure he does, that the village is sadly lacking in excitement – might not wish to join you. In such situations, two sets of eyes are better than one. And his are very sharp eyes indeed.'

'So they are. But '

'You doubt my ability to run my own stable for a week? There must be half a dozen men who will offer at this time of year. And the experience will stand them in good stead. They will not do it well, but at least you – in heaven's name, Jem, you cannot be a groom for ever. What would you like to do now?'

It was too dark to see his face, but I would have vouched for the surprise in his voice being genuine. 'Do? But I do what I am – a groom.'

'That is what you were born to. But you must know that

you have exceptional talents that would take you far in the world. If, God forbid, you were to join the army, your advancement would be swift.'

'As to that, I have often wondered whether it was my duty…But truth to tell, Toby, I like my comforts. Marching hours on end only to bivouac in the cold; camp food; intolerable tedium; and then the inconvenience, if there is a battle, of getting killed or losing a limb here or there – no, I cannot say that I wish to enlist.'

'A commission?' I knew that my mother could persuade my father to purchase one for him, if not in a cavalry regiment.

'At my age? Rubbing shoulders with all those lads straight from university? No, thank you.'

I had to agree.

'This life suits me, truth to tell,' he continued. 'Especially this jauntering around the countryside, which adds a little spice to life. What else could a man ask?'

'A man might ask for a pretty girl to welcome him home from his jaunterings.'

'Even a clergyman might. But I don't see either of us having one. That Miss Julia – she might make a man dream. Dream it would be, though – I can't see a man like Mr Twiss wanting a groom as a son-in-law.'

'Nor a village parson,' I agreed. 'But as to dreams, Jem – I have one too. You know that Lady Chase speaks of having a school for all the village children, and requiring all those on her estates to send them there till the age of eleven or twelve?'

'You did mention it.'

'Such children would need a schoolmaster. And I see you as that master.'

I heard his sharp intake of breath. But there was a long

pause before he said, very slowly, 'Nay, that is a task for a university man.'

'If it were Eton or Harrow, indeed. But do you imagine that the good women running dame schools have such an education? If they can teach their charges their letters and numbers that is all. But you! You are as well read as many of my acquaintances – nay, far better, for all they have degrees. You are patient. And you have other skills to pass on – for Lady Chase wants more than book-learning for the children. The girls are to sew and cook, the boys to grow vegetables and learn animal husbandry. Do you not see yourself –?'

But there I had to stop. Suddenly we were all thrown hither and yon. For a while it seemed as if the coach must overturn, but at last it was righted, and we continued as before. The jolts were enough to awaken the young lady, however, and she gave a screaming gasp.

'Pray to not be alarmed,' I said quickly, wondering whether I should take her hands to reassure her, but fearing that might but add to her distress, 'you are in a stage coach, ma'am. I think you may have been asleep?'

'Of course. Of course. But it is so dark, and – pray, where are we?'

'Near Taunton, ma'am, I think. And we have a long way to go yet. So why do you not try to sleep again?'

'I would be afraid – to have more such dreams,' she whispered.

I rather thought she would be afraid to fall asleep knowing that there were only two strange men. So I started a light conversation which passed the time well enough but which prevented any further talk between Jem and me. And at last I think we all slept.

CHAPTER TWENTY-THREE

'So it is decided, then,' Mr Vernon declared, sitting back expansively and tucking his thumbs into his waistcoat. Once again we were at – I almost said home. We were, in fact, in the elegant dining room at Langley Park, enjoying the Hansards' generous hospitality. 'Excellent. I will pen a missive to this Miss Southey myself, advising her that is would be to her advantage to call into my lawyer's office with all expedition. With luck she will be intrigued, not apprehensive.'

'As will the egregious Mr Chamberlain,' Dr Hansard agreed. 'Imagine, to threaten to remove a child from the only people she knows as parents. Inhuman.' He rapped down his empty port glass on the table as if defying anyone to contradict him.

Whatever we might have said to the contrary, this was no place for an argument, and in this case, I believe we all agreed with him.

The only principal in the affair not to be present was Jem, who insisted, predictably, that his place was below stairs. Certainly Mr Vernon would not have argued with him. He preferred people, especially what he regarded as the lower orders, to know their places and stick to them.

But Lady Chase and Mrs Hansard, now retiring to the drawing room where we would join them shortly, had been delighted with my suggestion that Jem was the very man to run our village school. Maria, I believe, loved Jem like a son; Lady Chase had been constantly impressed by his gentlemanlike ways in situations where others might have acted like yokels. My one reservation was that such an appointment would still not qualify him to be an equal in gatherings like this; though we all knew of occasions where the schoolmaster or mistress might be invited to large supper parties to make up the numbers at table, it was not to be imagined that they were of such social standing as to be invited to such a select group. However, I knew in my heart that though Jem was more than happy to join us on equal terms where we might be informal, and had no reservations about speaking his mind plainly as my mentor, he himself would never *put himself forward*. To my mind, that was an indication of his innate goodness and decency; moreover Mrs Tilbury, ever swift to detect a poseur, had treated him with affectionate respect.

'And Jem will seek a position as ostler at the Rose and Crown. Do you think that this young *William* of yours may be trusted to assist Jem?' Vernon asked.

'Let Jem first secure a job,' Hansard said. 'Then we can talk about Willum. Now, gentlemen, shall we join the ladies?'

Vernon might have been surprised by the precipitateness of the move from the dining table; I was not. While Dr Hansard appeared to derive enjoyment from most aspects of his life, and joy from some, he only achieved real happiness when he was in the company of his wife.

'But how will you deal without your groom?' Vernon demanded, even as we walked into the drawing room.

I caught Maria's eye. 'I will be amazed if Simon Clark, my verger, does not put himself forward as a temporary replacement. The very frequency of my visits to Langley Park would be sufficient inducement, would it not, Mrs Hansard?'

'Indeed it would. And you must admit, dear Tobias, how he has improved in appearance.' She turned to Mr Vernon with a smiling explanation. 'He is courting our cook, sir, and I believe they will make a match of it. His clothes no longer hang about him as if he were a perambulating scarecrow; his eyes have life; his hair is cut and he is properly shaved.'

'Does this mean that your cook is derelicting her duties?'

'Indeed not,' Hansard replied on her behalf. 'You saw how tonight's table groaned.'

'More than that, she is expanding her repertoire of dishes,' Maria added. 'She cooks him a version first; if he approves, and only then, does she serve it to us.'

'He must have sophisticated tastes.'

'I believe that were she to bake his boots in a pie he would eat them with gusto,' Hansard replied.

'So he would. Shall I ring for tea, gentlemen?'

Two long slow weeks passed before the second ostler at the Rose and Crown succumbed to the influenza, and Jem, who had been hanging hopefully round the inn yard chewing idly on inordinate quantities of straw, was able to offer his services.

He had not entirely wasted his days. He had learnt who were regular visitors and why, and had regularly despatched

Willum to tail them and find out where they lived. There was one embarrassing moment, he reported to me over a glass of ale at the King's Head, another Warwick hostelry, when he had almost walked into Lady Chase's steward, Furnival. We had of course prepared an explanation for Jem's continued absence from the village, but the presence of a sick aunt in Derbyshire did not explain why he should be loitering in a Warwick inn-yard. Furnival was deep in thought, however, his hat brim turned down, his collar up against a bitter wind, and Jem was swift to take evasive action. Nonetheless, he was glad at last to be taken on, and to announce that he was quitting my employ to pursue an affair of the heart. He might have sent a letter to every man and woman in the village, so fast did the shocking news travel. At each house I entered on my daily rounds, I was greeted with as much sympathy as if he had died.

Sucking my teeth and shaking my head at such apparent betrayal, I declared that I would forgive the miscreant if he came back penitent. In the meantime, Simon did his best, but as a carpenter and joiner he did not truly enjoy working with horses and found irksome my regular parish journeys through rain and snow. It would clearly be a matter of great relief all round if Jem was crossed in love and returned, his tail between his legs.

As for Willum, his disappearance must simply be the way of those London street urchins – thieves, the lot of them – and good riddance. More fool the parson for having thought he could reform him and turn him from his bad ways.

Now was the time for Mr Vernon to send his letter. All was in place. To reassure the Larwoods, now back in London, we explained what was in train, and bade them invite the redoubtable Alfred Mullins of the Bow Street Runners to protect them.

I received a missive by return. It was Mr Mullins' advice that they should take refuge deep in Kent with a cousin of his, and when they declined that, snow already falling, he had offered the services of his younger brother, but recently invalided out of the navy, as resident guard. They had accepted the offer, and Mr George Mullins would be installed by the time I received the letter. Nonetheless, though not a lover of snow, I saw that as the family's greatest protection.

Meanwhile, I recalled that I had need of a new hat and gloves for the winter, and took myself into Warwick, as if on a whim. Simon was silently resentful as he sat beside me. I had suggested that he remain at the rectory, but his sense of duty, along with what I now detected was a capacity for martyrdom, drove him to insist on accompanying me.

My horses and gig in the care of the ostler at the King's Head, I sent Simon to make the purchases that Mrs Hansard's cook desired, and applied myself to the task on which I had ostensibly set out. A country parson is soon equipped, so, having had my new apparel sent to the King's Head and having time in hand, I considered visiting Jem at the Rose and Crown. However, I realised such a move would be folly itself, and forced myself simply to stroll along the main streets. Quite by chance I found myself outside the office of Mr Vernon's lawyer. Seeing candles still burning on the premises, I acted on impulse, and called in.

Mr Knightley was a man of forty, but looked older, his teeth being much decayed and his cheeks in consequence quite sunken. He greeted me with suspicion, only giving the appearance of listening when I gave Mr Vernon's name alongside my own. To my amazement, however, he merely responded by asking how I might identify myself – just as if I had been, like Mr Mullins, a Runner.

Once again my father's hauteur came to my rescue. 'Would you prefer me to recite the baptism or the burial service?'

His face folded into what might have been an appreciative smile, and he dusted the wooden chair the opposite side of his huge and untidy desk. 'Aye, Mr Vernon told me you had a touch of the old duke about you. Welcome, my Lord—'

He bowed, but I took his hand and shook it.

'Parson Campion,' I corrected him politely but firmly.

The devil take Vernon for discovering and then revealing my secret. Should I blame the Hansards? Emphatically not. I knew they would die rather than thus betray me. 'And now we have established my credentials,' I continued, 'might I ask if anyone has yet responded to Mr Vernon's letter?'

He gestured me to the seat he had dusted. 'You might, sir. In fact, someone did this very afternoon.'

'This afternoon?' I echoed foolishly.

'Indeed, you missed him by about ten minutes. He left precipitately, I must say.'

'Why should that be?'

'Because I declined to disobey the coroner's instruction. He had insisted that only the young lady in question should receive his letter. I was therefore unable to accede to my visitor's request to entrust it to him for safe delivery.'

'And how did he respond to your refusal?'

'With great anger. I confess that I almost reached for the cudgel I keep here behind my desk. However, he seemed to think better of giving way to his passion, and left with no more than a kick at the door to vent his spleen. I pity the next person he crosses.' He permitted himself a sad shake of the head. 'May I invite you to join me in a glass of wine, sir?'

I waved away his offer, with something like impatience. 'I must pursue the gentleman, sir. What was his name?'

'Alas, that was another reason for my refusing to hand over the document: he declined to give it, or an address. As for his appearance, you will find many a gentleman about the town who looks like him in this cold wind – his beaver hat pulled down over his eyes, his collar up. He never removed his gloves.'

'He did not even remove his hat indoors?'

'A man wishful to escape recognition might well violate the laws of etiquette,' he said dryly.

'His voice?'

'That of a man of at least middle years. Perhaps it was disguised – his mouth was muffled by his scarf.'

'Would you recognise him again?'

He raised his hands. 'In the circumstances...'

'Mr Knightley, I fear my exit must be as precipitate as your unknown caller's. Even if I cannot give chase, I can at least report back to Mr Vernon what occurred this afternoon.'

This time I had no hesitation in going to the Rose and Crown, there to seek out Jem. But before I reached the inn, my eye was caught by a small crowd of citizens, gathered round something which moved and moaned. A dog? Were the people mere lads, I might surmise that they were tormenting it for pleasure. But these were decent men and women.

I ran forwards, nevertheless, spurred on by a woman's cry for a doctor. I know not what fearful premonition drew me, but even as I pushed my way to the front of the crowd I knew I would find, in that bloody mess of rags, poor Willum.

'Parson!' he moaned weakly.

'You are safe now. Jem and I will look after you.' I doubted my words, but said sharply over my shoulder, 'Fetch the new ostler from the Rose and Crown. Jem Turbeville. And bid him bring a door or gate – poor Willum's leg is badly broken.' I pointed at the jutting bone. As I spoke, I whipped off my coat and covered him gently.

My reward was a glimmer of a smile. A feeble hand sought mine and gripped it.

It seemed an hour before Jem arrived. Possibly it was less than three minutes. He was accompanied by a man I did not recognise, but who declared himself, as he pushed me aside, to be an apothecary.

I wanted no mere sawbones to treat the lad, but a rapid enquiry elicited the information that the doctor was out of town.

Together they lifted the ailing child onto a trestle table top, and swathed him with my coat.

'You've always wanted to see one of the smart bed chambers at the Rose and Crown, and now you shall, lad,' Jem said strongly. 'Come, keep those eyes open and talk to me as we go. Tell what mischief you've been getting into, eh?'

I found a likely looking boy to speed to the King's Head to summon Simon and my gig, then at a run followed the little procession – I had almost called it a cortège, so solemn was it – to the Rose and Crown.

However fast Simon rode on my breathless orders to Langley Park, however swiftly my dear friend rode back in response, I feared their journeys would be in vain. Even as I mounted the stairs, I head Willum's moans growing weaker. Pray God the sawbones had not given the child brandy. It might still be a popular nostrum, but Edmund inveighed against its hazards.

'Laudanum drops,' Jem said briefly as I took my place beside him. 'The lad's sufferings are beyond endurance. We had to cut his clothes off him to save him further agonies. You were right – the leg bone is shattered. Mr Eyams believes his skull also to have been fractured, as is his jaw, and there is damage, he says, to the internal organs. All he can do, he says, is make him comfortable until the inevitable end.'

'Why did you tell the lad to keep his eyes open? And to talk to you?' I stroked the hair from Willum's forehead, but only revealing huge bruises and contusions my touch must have pained.

'Because Edmund – Dr Hansard, I should say – believes that keeping a patient awake gives him a chance to fight. But – barring miracles, Toby – I fear the odds are against him.'

'Who did this?' I asked between ground teeth.

'Let me just find out and he will never hit so much as a fly again,' Jem declared. 'Forgiveness be damned, Toby. I want vengeance!'

CHAPTER TWENTY-FOUR

At last, as the effects of the laudanum wore off, Willum became restless. Recalling what the doctor had done when my elder brother had taken a frightful tumble on the hunting field, I applied to the burning limbs and swollen face towels soaked in cold water and wrung out. But I would not let the apothecary bleed him further, not without Dr Hansard's agreement.

Jem, still on his knees beside me as we had prayed for the child's recovery, slipped his hand under Willum's. It was by now far too swollen for him to grasp it. 'Tell me, Willum,' he said urgently, 'who did this to you?'

There was no reply. At last, through his moans, we detected a plea for water. We could not risk lifting him so that he might sip from a cup, so Jem called for a spoon; little by little he dropped water on to the dry lips. At intervals, he repeated the question insistently.

At last the words seemed to penetrate the blanket of pain enmeshing him. Willum's eyes opened as far as the swelling would allow.

''Tis all right, Willum. It's your friend Jem, and here's Parson Campion beside you.'

'No one can hurt you now,' I added.

Did he smile? The apothecary had had to remove broken teeth from his mouth so it was hard to imagine that he could.

At last a bustle in the yards announced the arrival of a horseman. Did we dare to hope that it was Edmund? And if it were, could he – with God's help – work a miracle? Had not been part of Our Lord's Ministry been to heal the sick? God grant that this night his servant Edmund might share his Master's powers.

We heard feet taking the stair two at a time. And here at last was our dear friend.

He wasted no words. 'Tobias, Maria will be following in the gig, with Simon. Jem, I have brought you your clothes from Langley Park – a fresh shirt is better than one smelling of the stables. Tobias – we will need soap and water and fresh towels, do you hear?' he added as I ran down the corridor.

He was determined to keep me occupied until Maria's arrival. First it was sheets to tear up as bandages, then the clean wooden slats he used for splints that he had strapped to his horse's side. Next I had to bespeak the Hansards a room. Then rooms for myself, for Jem, and for Simon, too. Then he was concerned about the horse itself: it was a cold night and after its exertions needed a warm stable. Each time I returned to the room a further few inches of Willum had disappeared under bandages; there was a wonderful smell not just of lavender but also of another herb or spice. It was my job to clear away bloodstained sheets and poor Willum's clothes. Edmund was working with a military precision that admitted no hindrance.

Having offered to undertake, in addition to any fetching and carrying required by Edmund, such duties as would normally fall to a second ostler, I had no idea what time it was that Simon turned Mrs Hansard's gig carefully into the inn yard. As I took the horses' heads, she was already leaping down like a woman half her age, reaching for baskets and directing Simon to collect bundles and rugs.

Only as I called did she turn from her tasks. Her hands still full, she ran to me somehow managing to embrace me without dropping anything. 'Dear Tobias, thank God you were here – but what are you doing?' She took in my shirt sleeves and dirty boots.

'It matters not. Edmund is with Willum even now, Jem assisting him.'

'Does Willum live?'

'Just.'

'Simon – pray deal with the horses. Mr Campion will carry all these things.'

Although she seemed to be asking him for a favour, there was no doubting the authority behind the request. Simon tugged his forelock and took my place.

Together she and I ran in; forgetting politeness, I led the way upstairs and to the sickroom, where only three candles now burnt. Both men were in shirtsleeves, liberally splashed with the child's blood. They knelt in attitudes of fervent prayer. Swathed from head to toe, Willum lay perfectly still.

Maria choked back a horrified wail. 'You have lost him?'

'Not yet. We may well. But the boy has good spirit. He has had beatings before. By God's Grace – and thanks to Tobias and Jem's quick thinking and actions – we may hope. Our prayers may be answered. He asked for you, Tobias. He said he had something to tell you.'

I was on my knees beside the others. 'What might that be?'

'He said – and these were his words: "Tell the parson it was the cove up at the Hall what done it."'

'Sir Marcus! Dear God! I knew him for a vain and greedy man but never thought – or perhaps I did. I know not. But such an accusation, from a lad on what might be his deathbed – it must be acted upon, must it not?'

'It must. An accusation of such seriousness must be brought before the authorities. Tomorrow we must call the constable. And I think we should summon Mr Vernon. Meanwhile, there is a more important task. Willum will sleep for a few hours, so Maria and I will take supper – I know, my love, that you will not be able to swallow a crumb but you must try. I would like your company at very least,' he said, with a tender smile.

'I will set about ordering it now,' she said tearfully, leaving the room.

'Tobias, it is now you who smell of the stables. Go and wash and change – I believe Maria has brought everything you will need from Langley Park. Jem, I leave you to watch over the lad. If there is any change at all you will call me.'

'Of course.' He nodded and sank again to his knees.

'Jem,' I said gently, 'I do believe that the Almighty will hear your prayers just as well if you sit in comfort.' I held my hand over Willum's head. 'And may He bless you and keep you and cause His light to shine upon you.' I turned in horror. 'Jem, has he ever mentioned being baptised? Let us do it now, just in case.'

'I will stand godfather,' he declared, happy to be able to do yet another act of kindness.

He fetched Edmund and Maria, and in the tiny, fear-filled room, we dedicated to his Maker anything that might be left of Willum's life.

I cannot describe the agonies, both physical and mental, for Willum and his friends over the next few days. The worst point came when Dr Hansard decided, after much prayer and in consultation with his Warwick colleague, to amputate the damaged leg. With two medical men, Mrs Hansard and Jem in attendance, I was despatched back to Moreton St Jude.

My task was to put it about the village that poor little Willum had been set about by riotous lads, full of ale and ill-humour. He had not recovered consciousness, nor was he likely to, but Dr and Mrs Hansard were caring for the dying child as best they could.

Dr Toone, once more acting in his older friend's place, augmented my story with eye-watering medical details. Everyone in the village was urged to pray – all did, I am sure, though some did not beg for his recovery but for a speedy and easy passing to a better world.

Meanwhile, Mr Vernon had also descended on the village. No one was quite sure why, except for me, and I was unlikely to betray the reason. Back in Warwick, our bedside cabal had decided that until Willum was – God forbid – no longer on this earth, or had recovered enough to be removed to Lady Chase's Shropshire estate, no enquiries must be put in train, lest Sir Marcus, afraid that the child might yet recover enough to speak, might make a further attempt upon his life. True, Willum was attended day and night, but that might make the man all the more desperate and result in other innocent people being hurt.

So the story of the drunken violence was endorsed by no less a man than the coroner himself. Our distinguished visitor stayed with me at the rectory – much to Mrs Trent's terror, since she was unused to what she called the Quality– as it was felt inappropriate for him to stay at Langley Park, his host and hostess not being in residence. In any case, he and I rubbed along well enough, Dr Toone joining us in our bachelor existence most evenings.

Lady Chase – hearing that her son was making progress – discovered that her poor nurse's ailments were troubling her again, and left Moreton Hall for Shropshire. Staying on in their hostess's absence did not seem to trouble Sir Marcus and his family, though there was talk of preparations being put in train for the family to remove to London for the young ladies' coming-out ball.

I had babies to baptise, mothers to church, and all the other pleasurable tasks incumbent on a country parson. All I lacked were daily bulletins from Warwick, though Mr Vernon, who could do so without suspicion or at least fear of interrogation, rode over regularly and brought me secret tidings of Willum's amazing, if slow, recovery from all that had befallen him. Soon he too could be taken to Shropshire, where Bess would tend him, as she had so faithfully cared for Lord Chase – with no little success, according to her ladyship's latest, but cautious, letter.

'So when,' I asked Mr Vernon, over port one evening, Dr Toone having accepted an invitation to supper with a family whose son he had delivered on a previous visit to the Hansards, 'do we beard Sir Marcus?'

'When I have been able to question *William* properly – I find the shortened version of his name, which you people seem able to accept, quite beyond me. To my mind, there is an ambiguity about his accusation. There may well be more than one "cove" at the hall. I need the exact name.'

'Surely—!'

'Oh, I doubt not that Sir Marcus is at the bottom of all this. He has a great deal to lose, after all. But I would not put it past him to employ someone else to do his dirty work. And still Mr Knightley assures me that Miss Southey has not presented herself at his office.'

'It must be, must it not, that Mr Chamberlain and "the cove at the Hall" are one and the same?' I asked, humbly aware, as always, of Hansard's opinion of my logic.

'I see no reason to doubt it. We have Mr Knightley's view that the man who left his office was fit to kill. For some reason he may have been irritated by William—'

'Willum may have been following him. Jem declares that he did not ask him to do so, and, Jem being the most honest man I know, I believe him. But Willum does not lack intelligence or initiative. If Jem was busy, and he saw something that needed investigation, I am sure he would act without reference to Jem. And thus he may have undertaken an errand far too dangerous for a small boy.'

'Or, if this Chamberlain were in a furious rage, he might simply have been the nearest thing at hand to kick.'

'Indeed. Hence all our secrecy; hence the need to remove Willum to Shropshire as soon as possible. At that point I shall invite back the man who has taken over my parish duties, and accompany them,' I added.

'Do not the villagers perceive it as strange that you are here, while the boy you used to employ is dying elsewhere?'

'You know villagers, Mr Vernon. They see no further than

their own parish boundary, and care less. Were it Farmer Lowood's son, they might consider my place to be at his side. But Willum was a "damned furriner" in their eyes, who took a job in my stables that could have gone to one of the lads from their own workhouse and saved them money. They are not bad men and women, pray believe me, but they have not yet fully grasped the parable of the Good Samaritan.'

He looked me straight in the eye. 'Yours must be a very lonely existence.'

'That is true for many of my colleagues. In their parishioners' eyes they are sad misfits, neither gentlefolk keeping themselves rightly to themselves nor men with whom you may enjoy a taproom gossip. Indeed, many are in receipt of such pittances that all they can do is rent a room with a decent family. This while our bishops amass personal fortunes and live like princes.' Unconsciously I had risen to my feet, and strode about the room, slamming my fist into my palm as I thought of the injustices I had seen. But such behaviour was unseemly. I refilled our glasses and sat down again. 'As for myself, Mr Vernon, I am blessed many times over. I enjoy the friendship of Lady Chase, the Hansards, and Jem, currently my groom. How many men can say they have as many as four true friends?'

He nodded, but each movement of the head signified doubt. 'But – forgive me if I allude to a subject you must find painful – surely if you sought reconciliation with your family you too could live like a prince. And you would enjoy the company of your social equals, not merely a country doctor whose wife was once a servant and – indeed, Tobias, your *groom*.'

'I might consort with idle gamblers, drunkards, lechers – none of whom has ever understood the concept of selflessness

and loving their neighbours as themselves. Forgive me my
plain speaking, Mr Vernon, but you must understand that to
become a clergyman was my choice. No! It was the Almighty's
choice for me. All I had to do was acquiesce. There have been
some dark moments since I accepted my calling, but believe
me, that have been more than compensated for by the joy I
encounter daily as I serve my Master.'

He took a deep draught. 'You sound like a damned
Methodist to me. But you are a good man, and keep a good
cellar, so maybe I shall forgive you.'

CHAPTER TWENTY-FIVE

Why I should ever be surprised by Mrs Hansard's talents or ingenuity defeats me. She was a lady whom only one man could ever come close to deserving, and that, of course, was Edmund.

The good doctor had left his patient for a few hours, to warn his staff at Langley Park to prepare for their mistress's return and to consult with Toone, whose opinion he valued more than I could ever do, on how his young patient might best be conveyed to Shropshire. Now, since Mrs Hansard had expressly forbidden him to journey back after dark, despite Simon's stolid presence, the four of us – for Mr Vernon seemed reluctant to quit the rectory until our problems had been resolved – were sitting late over one of Mrs Trent's excellent repasts. I fancy that Dr Hansard had also been forbidden to do anything to interfere in Simon's courtship of their cook, even if that meant the master of the house eating his mutton elsewhere.

Not that mutton had figured in Mrs Trent's extensive menu, far from it. But four happy men were considering a fine Stilton and some excellent port Hansard had procured in Warwick.

'How soon do you think I may question William?' Vernon demanded, cracking a walnut between his fingers.

'Very soon. But I would prefer it if you could travel over to Warwick to do it.'

'You still fear for his life if he were to return here?'

'I do indeed.'

'Would Sir Marcus attempt any violence in a village where he is known?' Toone demanded.

Edmund smiled enigmatically – and, I must confess, irritatingly. He took another sip of port before he replied. 'Did I say that I feared Sir Marcus?'

'Who else?'

'Let me tell you what my dearest wife has been doing.' He looked around the table; no one objected. 'Now that Willum is over the very worst of his ordeal, and beginning to recover, she is the one who mainly occupies him. At first he could be beguiled only by fairy stories and legends, of which she has an immense fund. Then she found that they might play simple games, such as a child in the nursery might enjoy. You might expect a great boy of ten to find them pitifully easy, far beneath his dignity, but you will collect that Willum has never had such a childhood as we. His mother might have inculcated him with a certain amount of low cunning, but I fear she had neither time nor aptitude for rhyming games or geographical jigsaws.'

'In that case, might not Mrs Hansard try to teach him his letters and numbers? Were he able to read, he might occupy himself some of the time,' Vernon said. 'Furthermore, a hitherto active lad the height of whose ambition has formerly been to be a tiger will need to find other means of making a living.'

'He might be naturally quick-witted, but the concussion has rendered him slow to learn certain skills. We do not wish to inflame his brain, after all. But he is able to recognise some and remember their sounds, on a good day at least.' He took another sip of port.

I sensed he enjoyed prolonging his tale – certainly none of us had the temerity to interrupt.

'Progress in all areas is slow and fitful, but he has shown, now his poor bruised and broken hands have healed, some dexterity with a pencil. But, ever in pain, his powers of concentration are weak. And when he fails at what he knows to be a simple task, he become fretful and we become anxious. At times like this, there is one story that never fails to quiet him. It is a real one, one featuring himself. It is one Jem has to tell him, however. Yes, Jem still spends a great deal of time in the sickroom – it is our great fortune that the rightful ostler has recovered from the influenza! While he is on duty, Mrs Hansard rests or walks – often in my company,' he added with a charming smile. He continued, 'It is my earnest wish, as you can imagine, that Mrs Hansard should not sacrifice *her* health for that of another, however dear. Jem tells him of the handbill that had brought his search for Bess to such a satisfactory conclusion, always stressing Willum's heroic role in the venture. He especially enjoys hearing how he had had to control Bess's desire for finery, the search for which could have taken an hour, and how he bought his own respectable outfit in a matter of minutes.'

Four men could quite understand that, and Vernon proposed a toast to male attire.

'One day,' Hansard said, resuming his narrative, 'hearing laughter from the sickroom, although she was supposed to be

resting herself, Mrs Hansard could not resist seeing the cause
of such a welcome sound. Willum's eyes rounded as she went
in, and he looked at her with new respect. "You really looked
at 'Enry's corpse and drew them pictures from the dead?"
Willum demanded. "I did indeed," she said. "And they were
so like that people could tell it was 'Enry?" It was clear he
thought this miraculous. Nothing would do but that she
should use the pencil and paper originally bought to teach *him*
to draw Jem. And then she drew Willum himself – though you
may imagine that Maria drew the old chirpy Willum, not the
thin young invalid she saw before her. Then it was you,
Tobias, and then me. Maria has arranged the sketches about
his bed so he may look at them and know himself always
surrounded by friends. Even you, Vernon, and Toone here
feature – it is known that you are going to bring the villain to
book. Which reminds me, Vernon – it was kind in you to send
that huge basket of fruit to him—'

'What are succession houses for, if not to supply sustenance
to one's friends? Besides, I like the boy's spirit.'

'How are we to bring anyone to book if we do not know
who it is?' Toone demanded.

'Because my wife is going to sketch a face, which you,
Vernon, will show him.'

'Two faces, if you please.'

'Two?' I demanded. 'When it is clear that Sir Marcus is the
villain?'

'If you show him but one portrait,' Vernon said, as if to an
imbecile, 'he will have to identify his assailant as Sir Marcus.
It is therefore necessary to produce an alternative.'

'Sir Marcus's pimply sons?'

'Away, thank goodness, at school,' Hansard said. 'What

about that cold fish, Furnival? Though at the sight of his Friday face poor Willum may have an instant relapse.'

'Meanwhile, I will pen another letter to this man Chamberlain. This time,' Vernon reflected, 'perhaps I should say that after all Knightley is prepared to convey the information designed for Miss Southey to him. But this time we will have someone – I have a handy-man suited to the task – on hand to apprehend him.'

'What if he refuses to betray this Miss Southey or whatever her name is?' Toone demanded. 'Will your man be able to persuade him?'

I had a sudden unpleasant memory of Toone's methods of *persuasion*. Perhaps he had been inspired by the Spanish Inquisition. I hoped he would not volunteer for this duty.

Vernon gave a curt nod. 'I hope so. We must do whatever we can to ensure that Justice will be done.'

There was an unwontedly sober silence. I could see Hansard's hackles rising. To prevent what might become an unseemly altercation, I raised an unwise glass. 'To Justice.'

Alas, this last bumper saw Toone sink slowly under the table. It was clear that Hansard would have been happy to leave him there, but instead we hauled him out to Hansard's gig, in the hopes that Simon would be at leisure from his courtship to help remove him at their journey's end. 'And if not, he may sleep it off in the stables,' Hansard declared.

CHAPTER TWENTY-SIX

I did not know who had provided the funds to procure a private upstairs parlour at the Hansards' disposal as long as Willum remained at the Rose and Crown. Perhaps it was Lady Chase, ever ready to dip into her purse, or the deep pockets of Mr Vernon. It might even have been the Hansards. The room, whoever its donor, had provided a welcome haven for those seeking a few hours' respite from the taxing care of the little invalid, and now, filled with all his well-wishers, from Toone to Jem, it was the scene for his first venture from the confines of his bedchamber. He had demanded a crutch, and sternly eschewed any offer to carry him. Hansard and I stationed ourselves at either side, but he waved even us away.

'I seen lots of lads worser than me in London. You know, run over by carriages, or trod on by a horse, or even burnt in a chimney. If they can do it, buggered if I can't do it too.' Pale as wax and stick thin he might be, but Willum had more pluck than I could imagine.

All the same, it was clear that even the few yards between the rooms had taxed him, and he did not argue when he was invited on to the sofa next to the fire.

'Now, Willum, we know how brave you have been throughout. We want you to do one more brave thing: to identify your assailant.'

Vernon meant well, but Willum writhed under the combination of patronage and vocabulary. He said nothing, however; none of us did.

Mrs Hansard had placed two sketches face down on a table. She had labelled on A, the other B.

Willum's eyes lit up. 'Them's your A and your B,' he declared.

'Excellent. Now, my dear, pray turn the pictures so that Willum may see them,' Hansard asked.

She obeyed. 'Willum, do you see there the man who hit you and hurt you?'

''Course I do. You aren't half a dab hand at this, Mrs Hansard.' He pointed with a skinny finger. 'There he is. There's the cove what done it.'

Before we could register the full import of what he was saying, there was a commotion in the hall below, and raised voices demanded the Law.

Toone was out of the room first, hotly pursued by Vernon, who, after all, was the Law's highest representative in the area. The rest of us followed with more dignity, leaving Jem in Maria's care.

From the top of the stairs it was hard to see who was at the centre of the mêlée. But Toone was already fighting his way through, assisted by Vernon's suddenly stentorian tones: 'Make way. Make way, in the name of the Law!' Hansard, Jem and I halted halfway down the stairs – from there we had a better viewpoint, we reasoned, than if we joined the mob.

'Over here, your honour.' This was the parish constable, whose acquaintance I had briefly made when Willum had first been assaulted. 'Me and your man have apprehended your miscreant.'

As Vernon pushed his way through, the press of men eased. Forelocks were tugged, hats removed. Someone pulled the hat from the man they had apprehended, since he was in no position to do it for himself.

'That's him.' A shrill voice rang out from the landing above us. 'That's him. That's the cove what beat me and broke my leg. I told you. It's the cove from the Hall. Mr Furnival!'

It is hard to convey the strength of the outcry. At the heart was Furnival himself, protesting his innocence, while the sight of the valiant crippled lad moved several to tears. Others would verily have strung Furnival from the nearest tree, were their threats to be believed. But our burly landlord, used to restoring calm in his patrons, demanded – and obtained – silence. With considerable presence of mind he suggested that those would had accompanied the constable might find themselves good ale in the snug; the constable and those accusing Furnival might find adequate space in his public parlour, which he would close to everyone else. Willy nilly he surged up the stairs. Used to hefting barrels, he gathered up Willum with ease, carrying him downstairs as if he were no more than a feather weight. Maria darted back for pillows and rugs, and then followed in his impressive wake.

Willum was soon ensconced on a settle, the rest of us disposing ourselves about the room. Furnival tried to outstare us, one by one, but even his eyes dropped at the sight of the lad's empty breeches leg.

'You done this, Mister, and pay you shall!' cried his diminutive accuser.

'Willum,' Vernon said quietly, but with such authority that the lad was silenced, perhaps allowing himself a smile of satisfaction that he had persuaded such a grand gentleman to use his preferred name. 'Mr Furnival, you will surely be charged formally with this offence. Let me say that it will be in your interests to confess if you are guilty. But other things interest me too. Did you cause the death of Henry Monger?'

There was no response.

'Are you Lady Chase's steward? Surely you can answer yes or no to that.'

'Yes, I am.'

'And how long have you been in her employ?'

'About six years.'

'And you have been a true and faithful servant?'

'I have.'

'And have advertised regularly for information regarding the missing Lord Chase?'

'The missing heir. Hugo. Lord Chase was still alive.'

'So now he would be the missing Lord Chase.'

There was no doubting an alert response, quickly suppressed. But he did not give himself away by any exclamation or question.

'Very well. And did you have any responses to your advertisements? Come, we know you had at least one. A man was found in a stream running through the grounds of the Hall itself, with a newspaper about his person carrying this advertisement.'

'That man who died?' Furnival's tone implied it was of little moment.

'The man who was *killed*. Think back to the inquest,' Vernon continued. 'Hard though it is to believe, someone pressed Monger's face into the mud until he expired. We have evidence to show that he was making his way to the Hall with proof of Lord Chase's existence and that someone would have found the news inconvenient.'

There was no response.

'I put it to you that only you knew of his coming, and that you, therefore, are his killer.'

There was no reply. The constable moved as if to take him away. I had seen the inside of Warwick Gaol and I did not envy him his future lodgings.

'No. Wait a while. I have further questions. Three young ladies, two of them very silly, one more sensible, discovered Monger's body. The only one who could have given proper evidence at the inquest disappeared, apparently without trace. Could you explain?'

In face of Furnival's continued silence, Hansard spoke. 'There is a witness who would testify that Miss Southey was driven from the Hall by a man of importance. We know that that man was not Sir Marcus. That man was you, Furnival, was it not? And it is logical to deduce that you had a hand in that havey-cavey business over Miss Southey's trunk, which so conveniently disappeared.'

And the attack on poor Gundy, no doubt.

Before I could put that to him, however, Furnival said, 'Take me to gaol if you will. I shall answer no more questions.'

Vernon ignored him. 'I can see that you must have killed Henry Monger, but cannot see why. Did you have a motive?'

There was no response.

'Did someone pay you to kill Monger? Are you simply acting as someone's agent?' Vernon pursued. 'Sir Marcus Bramhall's, for instance?'

'That leech!' Indeed, the thought appeared to repel him. 'Have you any idea how much of Lady Chase's fortune he has contrived to waste?'

I suddenly recalled the bad wine we had had one night. Was that after all Furnival's doing, not the butler's? Now was not the time to ask, however. There were more important questions to be asked.

'You did not want her to waste her blunt on further advertisements, did you? You have been a remarkably efficient employee, Furnival. In fact,' Hansard mused, 'you even put her interests before those of Miss Southey. You could easily have overridden Sir Marcus's fuss about the fire in her room. You could have made her altogether more comfortable. But you did manage very well to obfuscate the matter of her previous employment. Did you ever send for those references that Lady Bramhall required? I thought not.'

It seemed to me even as my colleagues pressed home question upon question that Furnival was no nearer confessing. We had no evidence, no proof. All we were doing was baiting a man clawing the last shreds of dignity about him. Perhaps Willum felt the same unease.

'What I can't make out,' he declared, having been admirably quiet hitherto, 'is why you should want to smash my leg and jump on my head. I never did nothing to you, any more than 'Enry did. And he's dead and I might have been, but for Dr Hansard and his mates wot saved me. No wonder your granddaughter's family was scared stiff of you. Was you going to kill them too? Or just your granddaughter – a taking little thing, by all accounts. Did you ever see her? Hang on, you must have. 'Cos they said they found a lock of her hair in that trunk what was nicked.'

The silence became intense. Willum had put questions none of us would have dared ask.

'I told you. Take me to gaol.'

The satisfactory apprehension but equally unsatisfactory interrogation were the subjects of most of our conversations for the rest of that day. At last Willum was forced to admit that he needed his bed, and Jem, hearing the chaos in the inn yard when several young bloods in sporting curricles all demanded service at once, felt obliged to resume his duties there.

Despite the fact that our village was left doctorless and parsonless overnight, we agreed to sup together.

'So now that it is safe to do so, will you encourage Lady Chase to return, bringing Lord Chase with her?' Mrs Hansard asked, as if keen to break the pointless repetition.

'I see no reason why not. I shall write to her before I retire for the night, but it will hardly surprise any of you if I advise her to hire armed outriders,' her husband responded. 'As far as Chase's recovery is concerned, I would have thought it would have an altogether beneficial effect, would not you, Toone?'

'Provided that he was happy at the Hall.'

'He hunted, fished and shot. He danced at balls. He did everything a young man ought.'

'Let him return, then.'

'And what of Bess?' I asked. 'She saved his life, and must be rewarded. What shall we recommend to Lady Chase?'

'There are many cases of men marrying their nurses,' Toone mused.

'But *such* a nurse?' Edmund asked. 'There is no doubting the goodness, the kindness, the self-sacrifice of the creature. But try as I may I cannot see her as a future Lady Chase.'

'Poor Bess herself hardly knows what she wants,' I pursued. 'If her ladyship gave her money, she fears she would drink it. If a regular allowance, a regular drunken spree. And each time a return to the only occupation she knows.'

'Could she ever better herself?' Mrs Hansard asked.

'No, my love, no. A thousand times no. 'Tis one thing to occupy all your spare time alleviating the problems of the village, quite another to take a stray like her into such a small household as ours. Willum, yes, because he is sharp-witted and biddable, and I do not think his lameness any impediment to becoming my apprentice, once he has learnt all his letters and been to school. If so he wishes. With Willum one never knows.'

'In any case, the poor doxy is hardly your problem, Mrs Hansard. It is the Chase family who owe her such a debt of gratitude. And from what Campion says, she is more than capable of having an opinion too.'

'She says she has never had choice before. Life has happened to her,' I recalled sadly.

Now all the drama was over, there was not one of us who did not express a wish to retire early. It was fortunate for me I did, because well before it was light the next morning I was awoken by a vigorous beating on my chamber door.

'He's hurt mortal bad, your honour, and the gaoler would have me come for you!' a young urchin announced as I opened the door a crack. 'He says he's like to die, and—'

'Who is like to die?'

'Why, yon murdering monster, of course. Mortal bad, he is. Come quick, your reverence.'

'Bid them call Dr Hansard, too,' I called, struggling into my clothes.

'Why would that be, Father?'

'Because if he is injured he needs medical care,' I declared with an asperity somewhat allayed by my various appellations.

'But he's a wicked man, and is a-deserving of the gallows. That's why they beat him up, a-hurting an innocent lad like that. His fellow-prisoners, your honour.'

And why had the gaoler not stopped them? But I did not ask. Best it would be for the man himself to die now, but if justice were to be done, he must stand trial and take his much-deserved punishment.

I picked up the little case in which I carried the sacrament – these days, with sickness in the village and Willum's precarious state, I had it about me always.

'Call Dr Hansard,' I snapped, and ran down the stairs.

They had moved the injured man into the condemned cell, not so much anticipating the verdict of a trial not yet held but, they said, to spare the other inmates the sound of his groans. As the messenger had declared, he was seriously ill, his body as bruised and battered as Willum's had been. Hitherto his appearance had been neat, even finicking. Now his sober suit was torn and covered in blood and God knew what else.

He recognised me, but turned his face to the wall.

'Mr Furnival, I am not here to seek justice, let alone vengeance. I am here as your vicar, to offer you the sacrament.

You may make a confession to me if you so desire.' Obtaining no response, I added, 'Are you a Catholic? I can send a priest to you, I am sure.'

He shook his head dully.

'Very well. But I would hope that you will unburden yourself – you would not wish to meet your Maker, as I believe you are likely to do very soon, with all your sins on your shoulders. Ask His forgiveness, at very least. And then we can share Communion.'

He blinked wearily. 'You're determined to worm everything out of me one way or another, are you not, Parson? Yes, you're as nosy of the rest of them.'

I laughed gently. 'So I may ask you if you chose the name Chamberlain for the reason I surmise: because *chamberlain* is a synonym for steward?'

'Why will you not leave me alone? But you were kind to...to Miss Southey, and I honour you for that.' He managed a painful smile.

'Anne is your daughter, is she not?' I asked gently, at last catching a shade of resemblance.

'She is. And she disgraced me! Her bastard child... I spent everything I earned on her education, Parson, sent her to the most exclusive seminaries. She was fitted to be better than a governess, by talent if not birth.'

'Indeed she was. She is a fine musician.'

'And what does she do? I find her a position at a great house and she lets a grand young man...get her with child. My granddaughter. The one who is even now afraid of me.'

'Nay, nay, she is not afraid of you. Her *parents* fear losing her to you. There is a difference. Did you once lodge with them?'

'Not I, but Anne. They were not so prosperous then. They let out rooms to respectable young women, and it was there that Anne went when she discovered that the handsome young visitor to her employers' house...that she was carrying his child. When they discovered my daughter's condition, I expected the Larwoods to throw her out, but they suggested...They had been childless for years. Perhaps they were heaven sent. I knew they were kind and honest. That is how my granddaughter comes to be in their hands. But the price was their total secrecy. Something I insisted on too.' His eyes closed, and I feared I was losing him. But he forced them open again. 'How did you find out? She changed her name...' His breath came short and shallow.

'I guessed. Your hair is snow-white now, but that often happens when it was very dark in one's youth. Like your daughter's, and your granddaughter's. She is a good and pretty child who sings like an angel. Your daughter gave her up and returned to her profession?'

He nodded.

'A new employer would ask for references. How could she provide them?'

'I wrote them. As if from my then employer, the Earl of Consett. The Bramhalls were too stupid to question them. But you will quite see that when you asked me to send for them I had to make sure they did not arrive. With these false papers she found a post with the Bramhalls. Believe me, I would never have put her name forward had I known that she would have to endure the insolence and viciousness that you have seen. And such an irony...such a vicious coincidence...that they insisted on visiting the house of the very—' He stopped, coughing blood.

'Do I infer that it was Hugo, now Lord Chase, who seduced her?' My heart wrung with compassion. 'So when you heard that he was still alive you must have wanted to everything in your power to prevent their meeting.'

'I wanted him to die in the same gutter as he left her.'

'But why kill the messenger? Henry was innocent of anything except kindness.' I regarded him closely.

He shook his head. 'You know that I am a calm man, Parson, but when I lose my temper I fear for the consequences. I could not bear the thought of such a man inheriting all I had worked for. And so...I am sorry about that lad, too,' he added. 'I was like one possessed. Parson,' he groaned, grasping my hand and looking me in the eye, 'it was I who killed that man. Can I ever hope for forgiveness?'

'Let me give you Communion, Mr Furnival, so that you may meet your Maker with your spirit refreshed. You have done wrong, and He, not your fellow men, will Judge you. But He is Merciful, and sent His Son to die upon the Cross that you may have eternal life...'

EPILOGUE

The notice sent to the *Morning Post* announced that the marriage would be a quiet one. It was indeed. The church was still almost empty as it awaited the bride. There were very few villagers standing along the path from the Hall to the church, and those that were had the air of idling away a pleasant spring morn rather than awaiting an event involving the Quality.

After a slow start, the relationship had blossomed so swiftly that I was hard put to credit it. Gossip declared that Sir Marcus wanted to get his sister off his hands before he was put to the expense of his daughters' coming-out ball, which Lady Chase had gently but firmly suggested should take place at his own London home. Although the Bramhalls had found every excuse to stay on at the Hall, by the end of the week they would at last have decamped. I understood that Mrs Hansard and Mrs Sandys had joked bleakly about counting the spoons. Mrs Sandys had been lucky to keep her post, but Lady Chase had considered that life at the Hall would be insupportable with not just a new steward having to learn her ways but a new housekeeper too. Mrs Sandys had swiftly realised that an interest in her ladyship's charitable concerns was a means of more permanently establishing future employment, and was now busily promoting a scheme distributing to villagers' cottage gardens spare seeds cadged from the Hall gardeners.

Willum had already become a firm fixture in the Hansard household, where he was reluctantly applying himself to the task of learning skills in one year what other more fortunate children acquire in five. As yet he evinced not the slightest interest in learning Edmund's medical skills, but attached himself to Matthew, daring all to laugh at the concept of a one-legged gamekeeper.

Jem too still enjoyed his work with horses, but was applying himself to extra reading. He had already taken it upon himself to visit other villages' model schools, and he too now occasionally joined Lady Chase's charitable committee, though the wedding preparations kept her ladyship away from many meetings.

The bride was late. It was her privilege, of course.

I tried to keep my thoughts from her. I fiddled with my bands, looking about my beloved church, decked for the occasion with daffodils and more exotic blooms from her ladyship's succession houses. At last I exchanged a wry smile with Dr Hansard, who had volunteered to be best man. Nonetheless, I thought of Lady Dorothea's first visit to the church, the evenings of music we had shared – even the time when she had played for our watch night service. She had greeted the returning Lord Chase coolly enough. I was, I admit, surprised. Despite the uneven growth of hair, and considerable scarring abut his neck, he was a personable enough young man. One could imagine how attractive he had been to the young governess whose life he had ruined. But Lady Dorothea had flirted more and more insistently with me, until I believed our understanding had reached the point when I should apply to Sir Marcus for permission to address his sister.

I did so after dinner one evening.

Sir Marcus was waiting for me when I quitted the drawing room.

'It gives me great pleasure to hear you and my sister perform at the fortepiano together,' he began, drawing me into the library and closing the door, 'but you must know, Campion, that I am looking for a better marriage for her than to a country parson. A lady of her looks, accomplishments and birth should be looking for a far more distinguished alliance. Do I make myself clear?'

I felt the blood rush to my face. Whether it was anger or embarrassment I could not tell. 'I assure you, sir, that any intentions—'

'I see that I did not make myself clear. You are, Mr Campion, to have no intentions. Good evening to you.' He rang the bell for the footman, who contrived not to look astonished that such a regular visitor was suddenly subject so such formality.

And within three days the engagement between Hugo, Lord Chase, and Lady Dorothea Bramhall was announced.

The following morning I sought out Bess, still the young man's nurse – and more. She seemed cheerful enough. 'He's already made a will naming this little feller.' She patted her belly. 'Oh, yes! I'm increasing, Parson. Having Lanky's brat. And he was conceived with love, not out of duty, so he'll be a happier kid than any of hers.' She jerked her head towards the Hall.

'But he is not going to marry you,' I said sadly.

'Lor' bless you, Parson, it don't bother me! Why should it? It's not what my sort are used to, and I've done better than most. He's promised me – or rather, this nipper of his – a nice little cottage on one of his estates. He ain't half rolling in lard, Parson.'

'If you are happy, he has done exactly what he ought, and I honour him for it,' I declared, though I thought I detected the hand of his compassionate mother, who had at last managed to overcome her repugnance of Bess – but only now that her son was firmly promised to another. As I turned to leave, I could not forbear to ask, 'And Lady Dorothea – what does she say?'

'Have to ask her that yourself. 'Cept I heard as how you was sweet on her, which makes is a bit awkward for you, don't it? I reckon a decent geezer like you can do better nor that. It's different for the nobs, though, ain't it? Have to marry to suit their families.'

Hardly knowing that I spoke out loud, I said, 'She is prepared to marry in those conditions?' I was aghast. 'And he...?'

'He thinks he's in love with her. But I've been talking to that nice old biddy what guards the gates, and she says she's such a cold fish...Well, I knows what I knows, Parson, and I'll say no more 'cos it's you what they've got to make their vows to, ain't it? And I reckon you'd be all squeamish if you didn't think they meant them. So all I'll say is that Lanky'll make a good husband and father. So there. And that's the last you'll get from me. Except to say you might christen my lad when he's born.'

I bowed, and found myself smiling, despite the turmoil within. 'I shall do so with the greatest pleasure, Bess. And if I were you I would ask Mother Powell to stand as his sponsor. She is as kind a woman as you'll meet.' And, what I did not add, was that if Mother Powell approved of Bess, she would not find it so hard to survive in her very unusual – and many would think deplorable – circumstances.

How could Lady Dorothea consent to the marriage, knowing that her husband's love child was not to be tucked away in an obscure corner but living openly on his land? She must know that her husband was merely infatuated with her, that this was to be a simple dynastic marriage. I sighed – a lady whom I had wanted for own my true wife, agreeing to such a match!

Mrs Hansard happened to drop by, with a recipe, she said, for Mrs Trent. In the event she tucked her arm in mine and drew me into the vegetable garden, from which the gardener had mysteriously absented himself.

'You must understand that for some families marriage is still a business, Tobias.'

'I think that they prefer to call it duty,' I said. 'However, my sisters and brothers have been fortunate enough to follow where their hearts, not their purses, lay. And I hoped that such – such *prostitution* – was a thing of the past. Maria, think of it – a woman of sense, of taste, marrying a man knowing that his heart is engaged elsewhere.'

'I gather that her fortune has diminished to the point where she had to choose marriage to him or an application for a position as companion or governess. All those fine dresses, all that expensive music, Tobias – within the month, knowing that the family were no longer her ladyship's guests, the duns would have been at the Bramhalls' door. So understand and pity her if you can.'

'I can. I do. And for Bess's sake, I am pleased. If she had a choice. For once in her life it would have been good if she could choose.'

'And you, dear Tobias – what of you and your choices?'

As the little band in the gallery struck up, I reflected that, God willing, I had made my choice. Until he called me elsewhere, I would be content with what He had so graciously bestowed upon me.

I cleared my throat.

'Dearly beloved, we are gathered here in the sight of God...'